"If you ever  **g my child fir**

"Sorry, that con

"You bet it did." She stormed off toward the Jeep.

Agreeing to come to the clinic had been a mistake. Staying would be hell. He'd promised his best friend he'd protect Lexi. Getting her out of here was the fastest way to do that.

But she was too aggravating and bullheaded to leave.

And yet she'd never mentioned the scars on his face, his limp or his missing arm. She seemed to look right past all of it. Did he want her to notice? Did he need the acknowledgment of what he'd been through? Did he abhor pity and, at the same time, want it?

He closed his eyes and exhaled. Something about her made him unsettled. But he knew one thing with certainty—the more time he spent around Lexi Galen, the more chance he'd end up dragging her through hell with him.

Dear Reader,

For every sunrise, there's a sunset. As this series comes to a close, I humbly hope that the love and adventure that readers found in it will continue to hold a special place in their hearts and minds. I know the series will live on in mine.

This final story is about Chad Corallis, whom we met as a rambunctious toddler at the beginning of the series. I immediately knew that he would follow in his father's footsteps and become a marine. However, I didn't realize just how emotional I would get while writing his future as a severely wounded marine struggling to embrace life again.

Nurse Lexi Galen has her own challenges to overcome. She's widowed, pregnant and working at a remote medical clinic in Kenya, and the only person she's willing to count on is herself. But eventually, one precious baby shows them that after darkness comes light. New beginnings, love, hope, healing and happy endings are what this book, and series, is about.

If I could make one wish, it's that this series makes a positive difference...not only for endangered wildlife, but for all of us as we face the challenges of life and love. Everything comes down to love.

My door is always open at rulasinara.com, where you can sign up for my newsletter, get information on all of my books and find links to my social media hangouts. And I'd be honored if you'd journey with me through my next series for Harlequin Heartwarming, out this spring!

Wishing you love, peace and courage in life,

Rula

HEARTWARMING

The Marine's Return

USA TODAY Bestselling Author

Rula Sinara

ISBN-13: 978-1-335-51050-1

The Marine's Return

This edition published by arrangement with Harlequin Books S.A.

For questions and comments about the quality of this book, please contact us at CustomerService@Harlequin.com.

Printed in U.S.A.

Award-winning and *USA TODAY* bestselling author **Rula Sinara** lives in rural Virginia with her family and crazy but endearing pets. She loves organic gardening, attracting wildlife to her yard, planting trees, raising backyard chickens and drinking more coffee than she'll ever admit to. Rula's writing has earned her a National Readers' Choice Award and a HOLT Medallion of Merit, among other honors. Her door is always open at www.rulasinara.com, where you can sign up for her newsletter, learn about her latest books and find links to her social media hangouts.

Books by Rula Sinara

Harlequin Heartwarming

From Kenya, with Love

The Promise of Rain
After the Silence
Through the Storm
Every Serengeti Sunrise
The Twin Test

A Heartwarming Thanksgiving
"The Sweetheart Tree"

Visit the Author Profile page
at Harlequin.com for more titles.

This book is dedicated to military men and women—active duty, veterans, wounded warriors, those who gave their lives—and to their families. Thank you for your service and sacrifice.

And a special series dedication—for it began with and has always been for...the elephants.

Acknowledgments

To Catherine Lanigan for your friendship and contagious, uplifting energy. Your heartfelt support and words of encouragement gave me the courage and confidence to keep writing when I needed it most.
Thank you for believing in me.

PROLOGUE

MARINE SERGEANT CHAD Corallis pressed his shoulder against the crumbling clay wall that ran along the outskirts of the remote village. His nostrils burned from the caustic stench of rotting food scraps and trash bags baking in the scorching sun only a few feet away. But he kept his eyes peeled on the one-story building that stood in a gated courtyard across the street. His war dog, Aries, stayed in position at his side.

Chad adjusted his helmet then held up two fingers and pointed twice in the direction of the only other nearby structure, signaling for his men to head there. Corporal Jaxon, the youngest member of their squad at eighteen, nodded and passed the order on to the three men behind him. In a flash, Chad had his M27 aimed over the wall to cover the team as they began to move.

Jaxon led them, crouched low, to their new

position—the roofless remnants of an old shop that had been stripped and beaten by years of war. A field of red poppies streaked across the landscape like an ominous river of blood flowing from the dusty, bleak village.

His men were well trained.

They'd survive this.

They had this.

The squad had captured multiple insurgents in Kandahar without a loss to the platoon. They'd endured unfathomably brutal conditions last winter at their outpost, working alongside Afghan troops to take down a Taliban stronghold. They'd even survived an ambush between Marjah and Nawa. Barely, but they were here now.

Still in Helmand Province.

Still alive.

He shifted, rising just enough to scan the street before moving to his next position. A woman draped in a burka walked briskly down the street, tugging on the hand of a little girl who'd dropped her doll. Every detail registered…the tall, lanky build of the woman, a curtain fluttering in a window across the street, a scruffy dog sniffing its way toward the trash…

Chad muttered a curse and kept firm control of Aries. He willed the other dog to stay away. One bark by either and they'd be sitting ducks.

He motioned for his men to wait. Adrenaline sizzled in his veins. He aimed his M27 and prepped for their cover to be blown.

Someone called out a name in Pashto and the dog trotted off down a narrow alley to the left. The girl grasped for her doll, as her mother held her hand tight and tried hurrying her along. Chad took two deep breaths…the kind he used to take as a kid before diving into the crisp waters of a crystal-clear pool on a swim with his sister and brothers.

He was doing this for them. For all the innocents out there…families, children, parents, loved ones. People all over the world who deserved the priceless, innate human right of peace of mind. The right to know they were safe from harm. But evil was a slippery, elusive, son of a—

A bead of sweat trailed along his throbbing temple and hit the corner of his eye. He blinked it away and focused. He was born to do this. His father was a marine. Being in the armed forces—fighting evil—was in his blood. Failing wasn't. He looked from the road to his men.

They were in position. They knew the target's coordinates. What in God's name was taking so long for the final order? He waited to hear his commander's voice come through his earpiece. He itched to move. Every cell in him was on fire.

The order came through.

Jaxon and the seven others on his team abandoned their cover and headed for the target, just as a small cart rolled down the street toward them like tumbleweed through a ghost town. The little girl pulled free from her mother's grasp, scooped up her doll and ran toward the cart. Her mother yelled and ran after her.

Something was off. The cart was rolling too slowly. It was too close to his men. Too close to the little girl. And there was no sign of its owner coming after it. Aries growled and tugged.

"Fall back! Fall back!"

Chad leaped over the wall and ran like hell toward the cart, Aries at his heels.

Jaxon's gaze jerked to Chad then to the cart. Then he looked once more at Chad, his eyes glazed with an eerie calm…and an unflinching resolve. Jaxon pushed the others out of his way and ran to intercept the cart.

"No!" Chad couldn't let him do it. Images of his younger brothers filled his head. *Family.* These men were his brothers, too.

He had to protect them. He had to protect the innocent, too.

The child stopped in her tracks, green eyes wide with fear at the sight of his men. Her mother picked her up and ran.

Chad's pulse pounded in his ears as he ran. Two more feet. He had to make it. He *would.*

The cart closed in. Jaxon lunged toward it. Chad collided with him, grabbed his arm and threw him to the left while shoving the cart as hard as he could to their right. It rolled a couple of feet before it stalled against a small rock…

And detonated.

CHAPTER ONE

6½ Months Later

LEBOO STEELED HIMSELF against the metallic stench of blood and the sight of ripped flesh. What if there was a trail of blood leading here? What if he got caught? It didn't matter at this point. He had no choice. He had to put his family first. That's what brave ones did. They were fearless. They hardened their heart if that's what it took to face danger or death. He was being tested. And he would prove himself worthy. Of being a man. A protector.

He pulled the roll of bandage wrap out of his pocket along with a handful of herbs he'd learned were good for clotting. It had to be enough until he could get his hands on something for infection. He eyed the gun that lay against the mass of mangled roots that formed the cave-like thicket camouflaged by a copse of elephant pepper trees and tall clumps of savannah grasses. He had to try. He had to stay alive. He'd do whatever he had to do...even if it meant killing.

LEXI GALEN TAPPED the syringe and slowly depressed the plunger until the last bubble of air escaped. Finally, the last vaccination for the day. She was so tired.

Maybe she shouldn't have traveled so far yesterday. They'd taken their mobile medical unit to a Luo village farther north, closer to Lake Victoria. She wasn't going to be able to endure those longer trips much longer, not now that she was well into her eighth month of pregnancy. She'd have to plan to stay closer to the rustic clinic she manned near the outskirts of the Masai Mara.

But that meant sacrificing patient care. There were children and other pregnant women in those more distant tribal villages who were counting on her. One was barely old enough to be called a woman.

She refocused on the patient at hand. "This will be over as fast as a cheetah can run," she promised.

The little Masai boy clung to his mother

and pressed his cheek against the numerous rows of orange, red and blue glass beads that adorned her chest.

"I'll need you to hold him still for a moment," Lexi said to the boy's mother. Between the few words of broken Swahili she'd learned over the past five months and many of the villagers understanding English, the clinics were running more smoothly than when she'd first moved here.

Learning Maa was proving to be a little harder, but she was determined to at least understand the native Masai language before her baby became a toddler. She wanted her child to learn it, too…just as Tony would have wanted.

Lexi planned to build a life on the Serengeti, and she wanted to embrace everything about the land, including the people, languages and culture.

She swabbed and stuck the little boy's arm. He wailed as all the others had…an aching sound that crushed her heart. Bless their hearts, she couldn't blame them. They were too young to ignore the pain…too young to understand that she wanted to help them, not hurt them.

She'd learned to tune out children crying during her nursing career, for the most part, but today it was wearing her down. Her head hurt. Her lower back and legs ached more than they had in months.

She wasn't complaining. Well, she wanted to, but she had no right to. This had been her idea. Her call. She had made the decision to drop everything, quit her position as a hospital RN in the US and move to Africa, pregnant and alone.

She glanced up and waved at the little boy as he and his mother left the clinic grounds. The child clung to his mother's hand and disappeared with her down the stone-lined dirt path and around a copse of wild fig trees.

Here she was, in the middle of this vast, mesmerizing wilderness...but not far enough away to forget. Everything back in their apartment in America had reminded her of the way Tony must have suffered. The burn scars that had rendered him unrecognizable to anyone but her had haunted her. They still did.

He'd been a dedicated military doctor. They'd met less than a year prior to getting married, though they'd tried to stay in touch as much as possible during his tours in Afghanistan. They had talked every chance they could, despite the time difference. They'd been married only three weeks before he had returned to duty. His last tour. Technology had its advantages, but it couldn't bring back the dead.

Sometimes she wondered if the fact that there had been a screen between them during much of their relationship had helped them to open up to each other more quickly. She'd never spoken as honestly about her past as she had to Tony. He'd known her parents had gone to prison on charges of fraud and embezzlement. Something no one else knew.

Her parents had been takers. Greedy in a way Lexi had sworn she'd never be. She was only nine years old when they were imprisoned. But it wasn't until almost a year later, after being shuffled from one foster home to another, that she'd realized she would never live with her parents again. There had been no other relatives to take her in. She'd never forget her tenth birthday. That night, she had gone outside long after everyone in the house was in bed, sat in the cool grass and wished desperately on a star for a permanent family. One made up of good, loving people who cared about others. *Givers.*

But instead of getting her wish, her foster mother found her curled up in the dewy grass that morning and yelled at her for unlocking the door and wandering outside after midnight. The concern hadn't been for her safety. She'd supposedly put the house at risk of getting robbed. That day had hardened her…made her a survivor. Relying on hopes, dreams and wishes wasn't enough. She had to rely on herself.

And if the other children—fosters and non-fosters—she'd spent time with during her patchwork tween and teen years hadn't been strong enough to rely on themselves, she'd taken care of them, too. That had led her to nursing school and, later, to Tony.

They'd met at the hospital during one of his short leaves in the States. He had been visiting a young woman—a medic—who'd been wounded while en route to the field hospital where he was stationed. Lexi had felt an instant connection with Tony. So immediate, it had scared her at first.

She hadn't been able to stop herself from loving him. He had been just as open with her as she had been with him. He'd been an only child, too, except he'd had good parents. He'd been raised in Kenya and had grown up with his best friend who'd been like a brother to him. A brother who hadn't been able to make it to her and Tony's wedding because of his deployment. But Tony had promised he'd introduce her to him someday.

He'd also promised she would never be alone again.

Ever.

The last time they'd been together had been the final day of his leave, only three weeks into their marriage. He'd proposed as soon as he had returned home from duty and they were married that week. In retrospect, she wondered if he'd somehow sensed he might not make it back and it had been his way of ensuring that he kept his promise in one form or another. They had married, honeymooned locally…then he'd had to return to duty. And then their life together ended. Just like that. He'd been gone less than two weeks when he was injured.

She'd rushed to be by his side but he'd been in a medically induced coma. One he never awoke from.

His death had felt like the sharp edge of a knife twisting and carving its way through her chest. She'd lost everything that day. She'd thought she had nothing left to lose… until she'd discovered she was pregnant on the day of his funeral.

Lexi's eyes burned from the memory. She blinked and sniffed to stop any tears from falling, then focused on clearing her clinic supplies. She needed to keep her head. Tony had never been comfortable around emotional outbursts or signs of weakness. She needed to stay strong for him…for his baby.

This had been Tony's dream—to complete his service as a marine medic then return to his father's native Kenya to set up a clinic and provide medical care to tribal villages that were in dire need. After he'd told her about visiting his grandmother at a Masai village, Lexi had understood his vision. She'd assured him she'd wanted to be part of it and they'd had their future here all planned out. Living in Kenya would be a fresh start for her…a way to leave the past behind and build a future with family.

They were supposed to be here, in Kenya's wild west, working side-by-side. And even though Tony had died, there was no way she could let that dream die. Being here honored him. Being here was the only way she knew how to stay strong. And for all the broken promises she'd suffered in her life, she would never break the one she'd whispered to him moments before he was gone—that she would find a way to fulfill their dream to bring medical care to the Masai and other tribes. She'd do it for him. She'd do it for the only family she'd ever had.

She picked up a small box of supplies off the table and headed for the storage room built against the side of their bungalow. They always had the exam tent on the other side of the clinic camp stocked, but there wasn't enough room there to store all their supplies.

"I finished the inventory," her assistant, Jacey, said, knotting her long dark hair at the nape of her neck. "We need more alcohol wipes and gauze bandages. Everything else is good for now. I don't know where all these supplies went, though. I could have sworn we had more, but I guess between all the clinics we held this week and yesterday's trip, we used more than anticipated. I'll restock in here first thing in the morning."

Lexi was lucky to have Jacey, who had been working as a tech assistant out here at least three to four months before Lexi signed on.

"Makes sense. Thanks for making a list. What would I do without you? I'll add them to the order this evening. I need to eat first," Lexi said.

Lexi set the box she was carrying on an empty spot and headed back to the folding table where she'd been vaccinating kids. Jacey followed her out to the central, courtyard-like clearing where they held outdoor clinics, and grabbed another box off of the table. Lexi picked up the hard, plastic, biohazard container carrying discarded needles, then returned to the storage room.

"How are you holding up?" Jacey pulled a key out from around her neck and locked the dented metal cabinet that housed their vaccine and antibiotic vials, HIV screening supplies and prescription pills for most of the conditions they encountered. Less expensive supplies, such as bandages, were kept in a separate cabinet, unlocked because it didn't come with one, but secure enough to keep dust and insects out of it. Besides, they always locked the storage room door, too. The only place some things weren't secured was in the exam tent, but they were always in and out of it and it was easily seen from the bungalow across the clearing. Lexi set the biohazard container down.

In the grand scheme of things, they had meager supplies considering the number of people they saw in a day. Inadequate supplies, really, given the conditions she was treating. The fact that they couldn't do more for some of the tribal children and their parents ate away at Lexi every night.

It roused memories of when one of her foster "sisters," a girl five years younger, had come down with a fever, yet instead of using the foster check to buy medicine or to pay for a doctor's visit or even to make soup, their foster mom had simply given her acetaminophen and told her to stay in bed. Had it not been for Lexi caring for the little girl, no one would have comforted her, given her cold cloths or gotten up at night to check on her.

But medicine itself had limits, too. Doctors and nurses hadn't been able to do more for Tony, either, and he'd had access to state-of-the-art medicine and the best care possible.

The burns and shrapnel wounds had been more than Tony's body could handle.

"I'm okay. Could use food and a nap, though," she said, as Jacey followed her back outside. "Where's Taj?"

Taj, a medical resident, came out to the clinic most weekends and was always willing to help out in any capacity. With only three of them on staff, even the most menial duties were shared. Right now, Lexi needed him to take down the temporary canopy they'd used for shade. She knew better than to try to take it down herself. At this point in her pregnancy, into her thirty-fifth week, balance and coordination were not her forte. Besides, it was more weight than she was willing to risk carrying. Her baby came first.

"Taj will be here in a sec. He's still in the exam tent, finishing up with the older fellow with the abscess on his foot. You can wash up. We're basically done," Jacey said.

"If you're sure."

"I am. Go on. We've got this. I'll help him take down the canopy, too."

Lexi squeezed Jacey's shoulder and smiled her thanks as she dragged her feet to the bungalow that served as their living quarters. She lumbered up the three steps to the bungalow's front porch, ducked inside to grab a bottle of water, then headed back out onto their narrow front porch. She collapsed onto one of the wicker chairs. There was more of a breeze out here than inside. Plus, she liked closing her eyes and listening to the sounds of Africa. The trumpeting, roars, high-pitched calls and rumbles all made her feel at home. It was a natural lullaby. It made up for the rustic and outdated living quarters.

The small plaster-and-clay bungalow they lived in had two tiny, dorm-size rooms with cots for sleeping, a kitchenette and the main sitting room—still small—where clinic records were stored in a file cabinet against the wall. Jacey and Lexi shared one room and either the clinic's founding doctor, Hope Alwanga, or Taj used the other, depending on who was covering the weekend.

As a medical resident, Taj took care of anything Lexi wasn't licensed to do at the clinic. But he had obligations back in Nairobi where he was finishing up his hospital residency. He tried to make it out to the rural clinic as much as possible because giving back to the communities where he grew up was important to him.

He was a lot like Tony in that respect. Lexi loved that about him. Both men were reminders that there were good people in the world. She took the fact that Taj's goals mirrored Tony's as a sign that she was on the right path. That she belonged here even if she was technically an outsider. Tony had been her only family, which made this land a part of her through love and marriage and a part of their child through blood. She felt more rooted to this place than she'd ever felt anywhere in her life. She felt accepted.

She took another swig of water and pushed her short hair off of her forehead.

Even Hope Alwanga had taken her under her wing, making sure that Lexi had good prenatal care. Hope used to make it out here herself more often, but she was also running a pediatric practice in Nairobi and venturing out with a separate mobile medical unit to as many rural areas as she could.

Most people out here knew "Dr. Hope." Many of them hadn't seen a doctor before Hope had established her mobile clinic program for the Masai Mara and surrounding areas decades ago. Being of Luo decent and passionate about helping children, Hope had wanted to give back, as well. It was as if Lexi had finally met kindred spirits.

Hope had told Lexi that this static clinic was only a few years old, yet the staff turnaround had been high. Living out here wasn't for the average person, but Lexi had never considered herself average. Given her past, she'd always felt a bit like a nomad, so the move from America hadn't fazed her at all.

When she'd seen the online ad for a registered nurse willing to live and work in rural Kenya, she responded immediately. The timing had been perfect. She'd still been numb from burying Tony and, to top it off, she'd discovered she was pregnant. The news had been a bittersweet gift she'd never gotten to share with him.

As far as Lexi was concerned, the job posting had been a sign. It was as if Tony had been opening a door…nudging her to pursue their dream instead of losing herself in mourning.

She'd answered the ad and Hope had responded. The two women had instantly bonded. Hope's son—also a marine—had been injured during a mission only a week before the attack on Tony's field hospital. And it was Hope that made the connection between the two men. Her son, Chad, was the friend Tony had grown up with, the one who hadn't been able to make it to the wedding.

She touched her belly. The thought of losing one's child… She shuddered. This was why she hated sitting around and resting, even if she needed to. It gave her idle time to think and her thoughts, more often than not, only reminded her of what she'd lost.

Hope was lucky her son had survived. Injured, yes, though she hadn't divulged all the details of Chad's injuries. But at least he'd survived. At least he had loving parents—a father who could understand what he'd been through and a mother who, as a doctor, could help him heal or at least make sure he was getting the care he needed.

Since coming to the clinic, Lexi had met Hope's daughter, a human rights lawyer who was well known for helping Kenya's indigenous tribes, and Hope's younger sons, currently in college, but she'd never met Chad. He'd only recently returned to Kenya and, according to Hope, he was far from healed.

Hope often lamented, with all the love and anguish of a mother, that Chad was the most stubborn, impossible patient she'd ever tried to work with. She'd been struggling to pull him out of a depression and to motivate him to resume therapy, physical and psychological, in Nairobi. But it was an uphill battle.

Lexi couldn't blame him after the trauma he'd suffered, but she also knew motivation had to come from within. A person had to *want* to survive all that life threw at them. They had to *want* to find a way to chase their goals, even if it meant taking a different path. She'd heard of individuals who, after being told they'd never walk again, had learned to not only walk but to dance. Unlike Tony, Chad still had his life ahead of him. She wouldn't feel sorry for him if he chose to waste it.

"I heard my name," Taj said, stepping out from the exam tent. He paused to say goodbye to his last patient, a thin, lanky man whose cheekbones were framed by beaded loop earrings that reached his shoulders. The man gave a toothy smile and nodded his appreciation, then adjusted a red-and-orange *shuka* that was draped over his shoulder and headed down the dirt path for home.

"You need help cleaning up in there?" Lexi asked, nodding her head at the tent, which stood about twenty meters across the clearing from the bungalow. Her legs didn't want to move so she kind of hoped he didn't.

"No, I'll get it. And this," he said, grabbing the table Lexi had used to hold her vaccine trays. He folded the legs in and leaned the table against the peeling plaster of the clinic wall. "I'll put that away in a second. Jacey can help me with the rest. Sitting there isn't enough. You need to raise your legs. You should go lie down before your feet swell to the size of an elephant's. I still think you should come back to Nairobi with me and let Dr. Hope find someone else to staff this place."

"Not happening. I'm fine here. It's good for me. Being sedentary while pregnant isn't. But I'll take you up on raising my feet. I'll be inside. Oh, and if someone can get their hands on some chocolate-chip ice cream and potato chips in the next five minutes, my hormones will love you."

"Good luck with that." Jacey chuckled as

she helped Taj pull the legs of the canopy out from the dry, red earth.

"I'll have to bring you a cooler on my next trip over so we can stock some ice cream for you," Taj said. They had a small freezer, but they needed it for ice packs and healthy foods. Not junk food. Besides, there was no room left in it.

"I would worship you if you did that," Lexi teased.

He did have that ancient godlike look to him. Tall, dark and muscular with a sincere yet dazzling smile. Jacey had most definitely noticed. The poor thing was almost too careful not to steal glances, but the way her cheeks flushed whenever she and Taj talked casually over work, gave her away.

She also got annoyed with Taj quite a bit. The blushing and bickering were a dead giveaway that the two were engaged in some sort of primal courtship ritual.

Jacey didn't like wearing her emotions on her sleeve any more than Taj did, but Lexi was convinced her two staffers liked each other. As a nurse, Lexi was well trained in how to read faces and body language. Sometimes people were too stoic for their own good…or too stubborn.

"You better share that ice cream," Jacey said. Lexi chuckled and shook her head.

"I can't make that promise. He'll have to bring you your own tub. Although sharing would save me some calories. I'm probably lucky I can't have ice cream and chips on a daily basis out here. I'd be huge." Lexi pressed her palm to her lower back. "Thanks, you two, for finishing up here. I'm going inside."

"Sure thing," Jacey said over her shoulder.

Lexi wasn't sure what was worse, the intense pregnancy cravings or the constant aches. She slipped into their mini kitchen, grabbed some cheese from their small, generator-run fridge and a banana off of the counter, then sat in a chair and propped her feet up on an empty supply box. She rubbed a hand across her belly, stopping when she felt a small kick. She lifted her T-shirt and smiled at the little bump on the left side of her belly.

"You too, huh?" she said, tracing her finger where the baby was nudging her. She had no idea if it was a boy or a girl. She still didn't want to know. As undeniably real as her pregnancy was at the time of her ultrasound, somehow the more she learned about her baby—*their* baby—the more it hit home that Tony would never share the experience with her. That she was alone in this. That he'd died not even knowing she was pregnant. God, she hadn't even realized herself. She'd assumed the light-headedness and nausea were due to being overwhelmed by all that had happened.

Her body jolted at the memory of the twenty-one-gun salute piercing the air at Tony's funeral. The baby kicked back.

"I'm sorry," she said, placing her palm against what looked like a tiny foot, until the little one calmed down. She pulled the end of her T-shirt down and dabbed her eyes, then took a deep breath. Was she being stupid? Was Taj right about getting a replacement? She had another OB-GYN appointment in Nairobi in just under two weeks. So far so good. Everyone was coaxing her to quit this job for the baby's sake but she didn't see it that way. This was home now. She needed to be here.

Man, it was hot today. She leaned her head back against the wall and pushed her side-swept, pixie-cut bangs off her forehead. She'd donated all twenty inches of her silky black locks before moving to Kenya.

She still wasn't sure what had spurred her to cut it all off. On one hand, she'd wanted to help someone else since she had been feeling so helpless herself after Tony's loss. But there had been practical reasons, too, given the rugged lifestyle she'd signed up for. And maybe subconsciously she'd been symbolically cutting ties to the past so that she could move forward to the future she and Tony had planned.

It was just her future, now. Hers and the baby's.

What had she been thinking, falling for a marine? She'd reassured herself that he was a field hospital doctor, not a special missions guy. He'd been in Afghanistan to help the wounded, not to get wounded himself. Hospitals were supposed to have some level of protection. They weren't supposed to be targets. But that hadn't stopped him from being killed.

That attack had come from out of nowhere. Her throat tightened.

The baby did something akin to a summersault then lodged itself under her rib cage and stretched. Lexi let out a yelp and contorted sideways in her chair to try to accommodate the sudden move.

"You okay?" Jacey came running in but stopped and scrunched her face when she spotted Lexi. "Ew. That looks painful."

"*Looks* painful?" Lexi gasped and held another breath. "I don't think I'm carrying a human child. I'm convinced he or she is part alien or antelope…make that giraffe." She tried nudging the little one away from her ribs. It didn't work.

"You look like an alien is about to pop out of you," Jacey said, kneeling next to her and patting Lexi's protrusion. "Like in that old horror movie."

"Thanks. That's so comforting. Especially since I avoid horror movies like the plague. Does feel like the baby is going to pop out, though. I seriously hope he or she knows that up isn't the way out."

Jacey plopped onto her bottom, laughing, and crossed her legs. The baby shifted to a more normal position and Lexi let out a breath of relief.

"See?" Jacey said. "She settles down when

I laugh. It happened last time, too. I'm already a good Auntie Jacey."

Jacey was right. Laughter seemed to calm the baby, while Lexi getting anxious and thinking about the past seemed to make the baby irritable.

"Why do you keep saying 'she'?"

"Just a gut feeling. Plus, it's easier than saying 'he or she' every time, and nicer than calling her 'it.' 'It' kind of emphasizes the creepy alien-with-human-host factor."

"Got it, *Auntie*. Promise me your bedtime stories will conjure up less freaky images in *her* mind."

"You still sure you don't want to spend the rest of your pregnancy in Nairobi before the rainy season hits? Or even head back to the US?"

"No. We've been through this. Plenty of people have raised kids out here and I'm not talking just the Masai and other tribes. You heard the story Hope told us about the vet who founded Busara. She raised her little girl out there when the camp was far, far more rustic than what we have here. And Mac and his wife have an adopted child and they live in a remote eco-camp. The point being, if others have done it, so can I."

Mac Walker was a bush pilot originally from South Africa but who had lived in Kenya's Serengeti region most of his adult life. He'd eventually become part owner of an eco-tourist camp—Camp Jamba-Walker—but still devoted flight hours to helping wildlife rescues and the Kenyan Wildlife Service with surveillance and reports of suspicious poaching activity in the area.

He was also a family friend of Dr. Hope and of Dr. Anna Bekker, the vet who'd founded the famous Busara Elephant Research and Rescue camp dedicated to rescuing baby elephants orphaned by poachers.

Mac had been instrumental in helping transport supplies to the clinic and he often flew Hope out. He'd also helped Lexi transition to the area during her initial weeks here. Even Taj hitched a ride with Mac whenever he could, to cut on commute time. Mac had a way of being everywhere and helping everyone.

"What if you end up with a complication in childbirth?" Jacey continued.

"You have a knack for putting things in

such a reassuring way." Lexi laughed. She knew Jacey meant well, though.

Lexi shifted back into a normal seated position and tugged her shirt over her belly. She was going to need something bigger very soon. Or perhaps she could get one of those giant *shuka* shawls the Masai wore and just drape it around herself. Come to think of it, maybe she should market the idea for maternity wear. "What if you stopped worrying so much? I go into Nairobi regularly for prenatal appointments and I take my vitamins. Heaven knows my diet out here with all the fruit, vegetables and whole grains is better than what I'd probably be eating if I had a grocery store around the corner. And between Hope coming out and you and Taj here, I'll be fine. If a complication develops, I'll head to the hospital. Promise."

Truth was, she felt more comfortable out here giving birth naturally than in an overcrowded, underfunded hospital. And as illogical as she knew it to be, hospitals reminded her of death…of the last way she'd seen Tony. She needed to be as far away from that as possible.

"Fine. If you say so," Jacey said, reknotting her hair at the base of her neck.

The grinding whir of a chopper broke up the chattering symphony of wildlife outside.

"Were we expecting Mac today?" Lexi asked, easing up from the chair and heading past Jacey.

Jacey stood and trotted after her. "Maybe it's just KWS flying by." The Kenyan Wildlife Service did pass over often enough, but they never sounded this close.

"Nope, it's Mac." Lexi shielded her eyes from the stab of late-afternoon sun and watched as Taj headed over to meet Mac.

Lexi and Jacey followed suit, waving as Mac got out of his chopper.

"You can only land here if you have ice cream on board," Lexi called out.

Mac grinned and adjusted his cap.

"No luck, Lex. You should have warned me. How are you doing?" he asked, meeting them halfway.

"Excellent," Lexi exaggerated. She appreciated all the concern but sometimes it got to be too much. It made her feel as if the pregnancy weakened her or made her more vulnerable. She didn't like that idea. Plus, while she knew they meant well, she'd taken care of herself for so long she wasn't comfortable with that much attention. She was self-sufficient and determined to be just fine. Why couldn't everyone just stop worrying?

Mac gave a nod then braced his hands on his hips. His forehead creased and he scratched his jaw as he looked at all three of them.

"There's word from KWS that they've had a few poaching incidents just southwest of here. They believe one of the poachers was injured before the group escaped. He might target the clinic, looking for supplies. Ben asked me to check on you and give you guys a heads-up. He couldn't make it out here himself because of his broken leg. Another three weeks with that cast, according to Hope. She must have the patience of a saint. Two stir-crazy marines under one roof."

After meeting Hope in the US and falling in love with her, Ben had moved to Nairobi with his children—Maddie, Chad and Ryan. He'd married Hope and founded a group that used ex-marines to help train KWS in security and methods for combatting poachers. Ben and Hope also had a child together,

Philip. Chad was the only one who'd followed in his father's footsteps and joined the marines, though.

"Well, Hope can always come here if she needs a break. Kick Taj out and we can make it a girls' night off the grid," Jacey said.

"Joking aside, does Ben think we're in danger?" Lexi asked.

"No one's been by here." Taj frowned at Lexi and Jacey.

Lexi shook her head in agreement. "No sign of anything unusual. I don't think the poacher would be stupid enough to come here for medical help," she said.

"Hopefully not, but desperate people do desperate things," Mac said.

Was she desperate? Was that why she'd chosen a life out here, as off the grid as possible? Desperate to cling to the future she'd planned with Tony or desperate to escape reminders of their life together back in the States? She pushed away those thoughts. Mac wasn't talking about her.

"We'll be careful, as usual," Lexi said. "If anything suspicious is noted, you'll hear about it. But I assure you, in the five months I've been here, life has been pretty routine. Not even a lion has checked out the place. Too much activity is my guess."

"And doesn't being near the Masai Mara ward the poachers off? I thought the area was protected." Jacey folded her arms as if she'd put an end to the discussion.

"Technically the area is protected, but plenty of poachers find routes through the Mara. It's true this particular group wasn't close to the clinic, but it's close enough to give you guys a heads-up. More eyes never hurt. And like I said, one of the poachers is injured and desperate. Combine that with access to a clinic… You do the math."

"I'm sure he'd be more likely to head for the Tanzanian border than here," Taj said.

Mac squinted at the sun and adjusted his cap.

"Maybe. But we can't assume. The KWS have teams scouting the area approaching the border. No sign yet. But Hope and Ben are worried. This area has always been relatively safe and well monitored by Ben, but his crew is smaller than it used to be. Plus, he's grounded with his broken leg and KWS is having to concentrate its efforts farther south. You understand he and Hope are preoccupied now with Chad, too, so Hope is considering shutting down the clinic, at least until they know it's safe enough."

Lexi's chest tightened and she felt the baby kick. Shutting down the clinic? Leaving here would mean failing Tony, his relatives and the tribes they'd both sworn to help. She didn't have the means to start a clinic on her own from scratch.

And for the first time in her life she finally felt like she was where she was meant to be. This was her life.

If she thought for a second they were truly in danger, especially her baby, she'd leave, but there was nothing in Mac's report that warranted uprooting her life again or robbing the locals of needed medical care. She braced her hands on her disappearing waist.

"Wait a minute. They can't shut this place down. We're a necessity to the people of this area. The children need medical access. There have been no reports of poaching or dangerous people around here. A shut-down of the clinic is not warranted. Besides, Ben trained us in using the tranquilizer gun. Sure, it's meant for dangerous animals bold enough to wander into our midst, but it would work just the same on a human. We're fine," Lexi said.

"I'm just letting you know it's a possibility. And, for the record, poachers *are* bold and dangerous predators. If you weren't pregnant when you first moved out here, I would have taken you to see evidence of just how ruthless they are. Your stomach wouldn't have been able to handle the stench of the rotting elephant carcasses or the sight of their faces gone in the name of ivory and their orphaned calves standing near them. These men are pure evil."

Lexi's stomach twisted at the thought of a calf witnessing its mother's murder. She swallowed hard and took a deep breath. She'd heard that elephants grieved deeply, too.

"Is this a ploy to scare me and get me to go back to the city because I'm pregnant?"

"This isn't a joke, Lex. The truth is we've all lived with the realities of poaching. That's why we have KWS and other groups constantly hunting them down and tracking evidence of their activities. We've all got homes in remote areas. I'm not saying you can't stay here. The Mara and the area just south of it is full of tourists and campers. It's usually safe enough, if you know how to handle the wildlife. But, like I said, the reason you specifically are at a higher level of risk is that this is a clinic and one of the poachers is injured. You have medicine that a wounded criminal might need badly enough to take the risk of attacking you."

"Honestly," Jacey said, "I can look out for things when Taj isn't here. It doesn't take a man, you know."

Jacey was ex-army. She was pretty fearless and could kick butt if she had to. Lexi didn't doubt she could protect them and the clinic. She'd seen the surprising amount of weight Jacey's petite body could lift.

Mac held up his hands.

"No comment," he said. "I wouldn't dare challenge you two. But I will say that you also have a baby to consider. Ben and Hope just want to ensure that anyone working here is safe. Not just because it's a liability issue, but because they care. Ben figured you'd want to stay, so he's looking into finding security personnel to be stationed here full-time until KWS locates the escaped poacher."

Lexi frowned. Full time security? Was she underestimating how dangerous things were?

"Is the situation that serious, Mac?"

"As I said, we're just being careful. One of the KWS patrols used a thermal imager to sweep the area. They didn't pick up any suspicious heat signatures in a three-kilometer radius of the clinic, so for now, you can stay put. All we're saying is keep your radar up."

Lexi was able to breathe again.

"Okay, then. He'll find someone to help keep the place secure, for everyone's peace of mind, and everything will be fine," she said, looking at both Jacey and Taj, but she really needed to hear the words to reassure herself.

"You'll know soon if they find someone. Hope told me she's planning to fly out Friday. I'll be dropping her off."

"Then I can get a ride back with you on Friday instead of driving the jeep?" Taj asked. "This news about the poacher makes me want to stay here, but the hospital will be expecting me. Maybe things will have settled by then."

"Sure, I can fly you out. The rest remains to be seen," Mac said. "I'm out of here for now. I'd like to make it to Jamba-Walker before dusk. Be on alert."

Taj folded his arms and Lexi almost missed

the subtle nod and silent exchange between him and Mac.

She had to admit, she admired their sense of honor and appreciated their desire to protect. She really did. But she'd looked out for herself her entire life. She didn't need rescuing now. Her maternal instincts only made her tougher—after all, her baby came first. But there were other children here whose lives and well-being depended on her and this clinic. She couldn't abandon them. She owed them the same care she'd want for her child. Taj glanced at her and pressed his lips together. He understood. She knew he did.

"Lexi's right," he said. "We may be in the middle of nowhere, but we have Masai *enkangs* in all directions and other tribal villages. There are eyes everywhere. The poacher won't risk it."

"Let's hope that's the case. I didn't mean to come down hard on you guys. I've just lived here a long time and I've seen things I'll never be able to unsee," Mac said, looking pointedly at Lexi.

"I get it. Thanks, Mac. For the heads-up on everything. I didn't mean to snap at you. It's just that this clinic is important," Lexi said.

"No worries. I'll let Ben know things are okay here for now. I'll be in touch." He waved and turned for his chopper.

Taj put his arm out to usher Lexi and Jacey back to the camp and a safe distance from the helicopter. They watched as Mac's chopper lifted and disappeared over a copse of fig and mango trees.

"Time to cook," Taj said, scrubbing at his jaw and scowling at the ground as he headed toward the bungalow.

But Lexi put a hand on his arm. "You can't fool me. I know that look. Do. Not. Worry. Like he said, poachers have plagued the region forever and have never bothered the clinic. These spottings are no different from ones we've heard before. Like you said, we're surrounded by Masai *enkangs* and farmland. We essentially have an army of warriors with spears around us. What more protection could you want?" Lexi said.

"You haven't been here long enough," Taj replied.

"I'm an army veteran, Taj. I can shoot better than you, I'm sure, and I've been known to take down men twice my size," Jacey reminded him. With her gorgeous features and long hair, it was easy to forget that Jacey was a highly trained fighter.

Lexi looped her arm in Jacey's.

"See, Taj? We women have ourselves covered. Think Amazon warriors," Lexi said.

Taj raised a brow at her and glanced at her very pregnant belly.

"This isn't the Amazon."

No, it wasn't. This was Africa. Kenya's Serengeti region. And even if fighting poachers was a war unto itself, at least it wasn't a military war zone in the traditional sense. This wasn't the front lines of Afghanistan or Iraq or any other war-torn country. Her child would grow up—at least during his or her younger years—without being bombarded by depressing, heart-wrenching news from television and every form of social media, including phones.

It had seemed impossible to escape from it all when she was back in the States. She didn't want her kid influenced by combat video games or pressure to serve. She needed to protect her child…to keep him or her from ending up like Tony.

He'd been counting the days until his service ended so that they could get on with their plans in Kenya. She believed in her gut that he wouldn't have wanted his child enlisting, as he had. He'd mentioned once that if they ever had kids, he'd want to make sure they were connected to both sides of their heritage. That they would understand and respect their heritage.

Lexi wanted to stay at the clinic for him… for their child. And she didn't need to draw strength from anyone else to get it done. She'd spent her entire life proving she was capable. A survivor. She laid a hand on her belly, squared her shoulders and looked pointedly at Taj.

"I'm tougher than you think I am," she said. The baby fisted her side, as if in protest. She cupped the tiny fist in her hand as if silencing any argument.

I am more than fine. You will be, too. You'll see.

But the image of the orphaned elephant standing beside its mother's remains had struck a nerve. And, for the first time in a long time, a tiny, buried part of her felt almost vulnerable…and made her wonder just how strong she really was.

CHAPTER TWO

VIOLENT PAIN SEARED Chad's right arm like a branding iron burning its way clear to the bone. Instinct had him grasping for his arm, desperate to stop the agony, but his left hand rammed against his right rib cage. He reached again, squeezing his eyes against the pain and swatting air before hitting his shoulder.

"No!" He fisted his hair and cursed a stream of words he only ever used around fellow marines on the battlefield—never in his parents' home.

He forced himself to look at his side…to remind him that a wrapped stump was all that was left of his right arm. This time, the visual didn't help to bring him under control.

He covered his face with his one hand and took deep breaths until the phantom pain subsided enough for him to stand. He walked across his old bedroom to where a half-empty glass of water sat on his wooden dresser. He took a long drink, a ritual he'd adopted to train his mind to stay grounded in the here and now. Pain like that had a way of weakening even the toughest warrior. It coaxed his mind into dark places. Sometimes it took him back to that day.

He walked over to the window, pressed his forehead against the cool glass, and looked out at the yard below. The flowering vines climbing the garden walls were more lush and dense than he remembered. Even the fig tree that flanked that far side of the grassy area had grown since he'd last been in Nairobi. A beautiful, serene and deceptively safe haven. That's what "home" was now. An illusion. A false sense of security. There was nothing safe or beautiful about the world. War and evil were insidious.

They'd left a permanent mark on him—and taken him out of the fight.

They'd neutralized him and the realization that there was nothing he could do about it drove him mad. He would never fight again and that made him feel like a man trapped behind bars, unable to do anything but watch and scream while criminals tortured helpless people. He wasn't supposed to be the helpless one.

He'd heard of injured vets, even minor amputees, getting permission to reenlist, though they were often reassigned to more "appropriate" jobs. But first they had to be cleared by a psych test to be sound of mind, free of post-traumatic stress and not suffering from debilitating phantom pain.

He failed all three of those qualifications. Six-and-a-half months since the blast and still suffering.

He turned and stood in front of the intricately carved wood mirror that hung over his dresser. Twisted, dark-pink burn scars wrapped around half of his back and up the right side of his neck. Quarter-inch-scars mottled his right cheek where surgeons had removed embedded debris. It was a miracle he still had his eyes. Though sometimes he wondered if that was its own form of torture.

Here he was at twenty-four, supposedly the prime of his life, and he was *this*. He was—had been—right-handed. He'd lost his dominance in more ways than one. But he still had his sight, just so that he could wake up every morning and be met with the monster that was left of him. Just so that he could see the looks of pity on the faces of others. Sometimes he wished he'd never woken up from the medically induced coma he'd been kept in for weeks. Everyone kept saying he was lucky that he'd recovered, for the most part, from the traumatic brain injury he'd also suffered in the blast.

"Chad?" His mother rapped at the door. He hurried to the bed and lay on top of the traditionally woven bedspread, then picked up the magazine he'd abandoned earlier because putting it down every time he had to turn a page had worn on his patience. His mother eased the door open and peered inside.

"Chad." She came in and closed the door behind her.

"Hey, what's up?" He hoped he sounded as calm and cool as possible. He didn't want his mom worrying about him anymore. As a doctor, Hope worried enough about everyone under her care, and she, along with his dad, had spent most of the past year by his side in the States. He'd given them both gray hairs and creases around their eyes these last few months. He'd taken them away from his younger brothers—even if Ryan and Philip *were* off in college—and their first grandchild.

His older sister, Maddie, and her husband, Haki, had a fifteen-month-old baby. They lived in Kenya's Serengeti where Haki ran a rural veterinary clinic that catered to the livestock needs of the tribal herdsmen. With a toddler, they definitely could have used Hope's help, but instead Chad's mother had been caring for him. He was burdening them all.

His dad, too. As an ex-marine, his dad was good at masking what was going through his head, but Chad could see past the firm "Suck it up, Marine" attitude. Still, he seemed to be emphasizing his own efforts to carry on despite the cast he was sporting. At least that was temporary. Chad's amputation wasn't.

Chad knew this wasn't how either of his parents had envisioned his future.

"Don't pretend. I heard you. If the pain is that bad, take something," Hope said.

"I'm not taking any more drugs," he said, sitting upright and swinging his legs over the side of the bed.

You still have everything from the waist down, man. Count your blessings.

"We can switch medic—"

"No." Painkillers only stole what was left of him.

"Then what? Let me do something. Let me help."

"I'm fine. Honestly, Mom. It was just a sudden shooting pain. It went away. I'm all good now. Hungry, actually."

He wasn't.

He tossed the magazine aside and stood. He motioned to the doorway.

"After you."

"You can't fool a mother, Chad. I know you think feeding you will distract me. I'll do it because, yes, it'll make *me* feel a little better, but you can't sit up here like this for hours on end."

"I don't."

"You do."

"Then let's head down and eat," he said, limping slightly ahead of her before she could say more. The deep shrapnel scars in his right hip and thigh tugged with each step. He could hear her following. "Am I smelling *chapati* and *nyama*? I thought Jamal and Dalila were with their grandkids today."

Jamal and Dalila were like grandparents.

They'd worked as driver, cook and nannies for Hope's parents, also doctors in Nairobi, since she'd been born. They'd stayed on with the family—really as part of the family—and continued to help when Hope married Ben and adopted his three children and then when the couple had their own baby, Philip.

None of them cared who was blood related and who wasn't. They'd always been a family in the tightest sense of the word.

The aroma of beef, onion, curried spices, vegetables and warm flatbread wafted up the stairwell. Chad's stomach grumbled loudly. Maybe he *was* hungry. Funny that hunger was the one pain he rarely felt.

"Yes. Dalila cooked her famous stew early this morning before leaving. For 'her Chad,' as she put it. I just warmed it all up for lunch."

Lunch? Had he really been in his room that long?

"She's a kitchen goddess," he said, quirking the corner of his mouth up. He reached for the banister and clenched his jaw when he realized he'd tried reaching with his right arm. How many more months or years was it going to take for his brain to adjust?

He made his way down the curved staircase, placing his hand against the left wall for balance when he felt a twinge in his right hip.

"I have an ironsmith coming in a few days to make a matching banister for the left side," Hope said.

"Cancel the appointment. You don't have to change anything on my account. I'll manage."

"I know we don't have to. Your father and I want to. It's not a big deal. He said he'll be back in time for lunch. He got a ride to the office. He needed to sign off on some new recruit applications. I told him someone could bring the paperwork to the house, but he was desperate to get out."

Ben's work with KWS and the Kenyan armed forces to combat ruthless poachers was just another example of how evil existed even at home. There was no escaping it…a fact that made Chad's blood curdle, especially now that there was nothing he could do about it.

His father had always been his role model… someone whose expectations he'd always tried to live up to. After Chad's biological mother was killed by a reckless drunk driver when Chad was only four, and his dad had retreated into a shell, Chad had quickly caught on to the fact that the only way for his father to notice him was to try to be just like him. He probably already *was* on some level, behavioral genetics and all.

But as soon as he was old enough to really understand how needlessly his mother had lost her life and how rampant violence and war were in the news, Chad had understood what had really driven his father to serve. And it had become Chad's mission, too.

Roosevelt, the family dog, came bounding up just as Chad cleared the last step. But rather than colliding into Chad or jumping up on him, the four-year-old mix padded around him, wagging his tail and sniffing.

"He's finally outgrowing some of that puppy energy," Hope said.

Chad's eyes stung as he reached down and scratched Roosevelt behind the ear. Losing Aries in action still gouged him in the heart.

Roosevelt licked his hand. The dog *knew.* His behavior had nothing to do with outgrowing puppyhood, if that even happened for dogs with any Golden or Lab in the mix. Nope. Chad had no doubt Roosevelt sensed something was wrong. Dogs could smell disease and injury. They mourned loss. And

Chad had lost more than his arm. When the doctors had brought him out of his induced coma, he'd discovered that Aries had died in the blast and his best friend, Tony, had been killed only a week after the blast that injured Chad.

Chad walked across the living room with the dog at his heels and opened the glass patio doors that led to their garden. He could hear his mom tinkering in the kitchen. He sat on the top step leading out onto the grass, grabbed a rubber ball and tossed it. It took a curved path into the base of a flowering bougainvillea—far from the tree he'd been aiming for. Roosevelt didn't seem to care one way or the other. His mother's vine, however, didn't look too happy.

"Here's some iced tea. Extra lemon, the way you like it," his mom said, as she stepped outside and sat next to him. She handed him a glass then took a long drink from her own.

"Sorry about your vine," Chad half muttered, setting the glass down next to him. He was screwing up even something as benign as tossing a dog a ball. It was hard to believe he'd once handled and trained military dogs. Now he couldn't even play fetch right. How long would it take to really get comfortable with using his left arm for anything other than general use? He still couldn't sign his name legibly with his left hand, let alone aim a ball with any accuracy…or a firearm, for that matter.

He'd received an honorable discharge from the marines. A medal, to boot. So why wasn't he feeling an ounce of pride at the moment?

"Are you kidding me? Any of the plants you see here survived Roosevelt's initial puppy years. They'll survive anything at this point," Hope said.

Chad hated hearing a double meaning in everything, even when it wasn't intended. He scratched his hair back and took a swig of tart tea.

"I guess."

"You know, tossing that ball is good for you. I know we're setting up additional physical therapy now that you're here—ah, don't argue about that right now—but really, there's a lot you can do on your own. Though maybe we should put up a small soccer goal, just so that you don't torture that tree when your skills sharpen," she teased.

Chad grinned. Leave it to his mom to get

a smile out of him. He actually appreciated that she didn't shy away from the facts.

"How'd you guess the tree was my target?"

"That's classified information."

"Right." A brief laugh escaped him. Roosevelt came running back with a rubber bone. "Wait a minute. I'm pretty sure I threw a ball."

"Who knows how many toys are hidden out there. I'm beginning to think your father hides them just so he can have an excuse to buy more," Hope said.

It had taken forever for Ben to give in to the "free" puppy Maddie had brought home for Philip when he was still in high school. He'd seen how devastating it could be for a marine to lose his canine—his friend had lost his dog in battle, a dog named Wolf, back when Ben had lost his wife, Zoe.

For years, Ben had refused to get a family dog, out of fear of reliving that kind of pain. But Roosevelt had been a blessing since day one and, once Philip had left for college, Ben had ended up bonding with the dog.

Chad took the bone and tried tossing it Frisbee style. This time it veered left and landed mid-yard.

"I don't want to deal with physical therapists

anymore. I worked with them long enough before coming home. It's not helping."

"You have to give it time."

"It's not doing anything."

"Chad, you have to try. You won't get better by sitting around here. You have to have physical training. I'm not just saying this as your mother. I know this as a doctor."

"Get better? Have you looked at me? I won't ever 'get better.' That implies a full recovery. That's a physical impossibility for me."

His pulse pounded at his temples and his eyes burned. He hated feeling cornered. The pressure everyone had been putting on him to get up and take action, as if he was lazy or wallowing in self-pity, was as irritating as the scars that still itched relentlessly. This wasn't about self-pity. This was about everyone thinking they knew what he was going through. But they didn't know what he needed. No one could.

His mom pressed her fingers to her eyes. Roosevelt stood with his bone in his mouth, waiting. He looked between the two of them. The dog's tail slowed to a pitiful pace. Chad stared at him but made no move to play. He couldn't tell if it was anger or frustration, but this feeling that tightened his chest and squeezed at his throat whenever anyone insisted he should make an effort to get better paralyzed him.

Roosevelt let out a short whimper then dropped the bone and settled at Chad's feet.

"Do you really want to know what I see when I look at you?"

Hope laced her fingers and tucked them in her lap. She paused and the way her dark brown eyes glistened pinched at his conscience. He didn't want to hurt her. He really didn't. Hope had always been the glue for their family. She was the voice of reason… the heart and soul of their family. She'd essentially saved them all from spiraling down and falling apart after Zoe's death.

But there wasn't anything to save now. Sure, he was alive, but she couldn't change the fact that he'd never be the same again. That the future he'd always envisioned would never happen.

All he'd ever wanted was to be a marine. To fight the bad guys and rise in the ranks. To avenge the death of everyone he'd lost in life. To try to extinguish evil so that the rest of his family could have safe, long lives. He wasn't unreasonable. He knew he couldn't stop death altogether or keep random accidents from happening. But he could pick the worst of the worst and stop them from terrorizing the world. That's why he'd joined the marines.

He'd never considered settling into civilian life, let alone trying to map out a new future without his mind and body whole.

Hope put a hand on his knee.

"I see *Chad.* I see you as the rambunctious, overactive toddler I first met. I see you as the incorrigible, confident, adrenaline-loving teen. I see the valiant, focused and proud-to-follow-in-his-father's-footsteps man you were when you joined the marines. I see *you*, Chad.

"I know you too well and love you too much to look at only the surface. I've also witnessed your inner strength and drive. The kid I raised never gave up on anything. If he had, your dad and I may have held out a few more years before getting gray hairs. These injuries? They're obstacles, yes. But they're not you."

He sucked in a sharp breath.

"That's where you're wrong, Mom. These injuries...what happened to me and the memory of it...they *are* me now. We're the sum of our experiences. Aren't we?"

She hugged her arms around her waist and glanced up at the cloudless sky. She couldn't answer because he was right. She took a deep breath and held it for a fraction of a second before letting it go.

"Have you ever considered that your mama Zoe was your guardian angel on the day of the explosion? That she's the reason you're alive? Because that would be a gift. A gift from her. Not a punishment. You're right that we're the sum of our experiences. But we hold those experiences in our minds...in our souls...not our bodies."

Chad gritted his teeth and shot up, his thigh bumping into his glass of tea. The glass tipped over and broke, causing the dog to startle and jump up onto all fours.

Hope's hand flew to her chest for a brief second before she moved to clean up the glass.

"Don't worry. I'll get this," she said, setting her own tea down on the far side of the steps.

He didn't miss the quiver in her voice. A

part of him cared; a part of him didn't. Heat washed through him and that sharp phantom pain shot through his missing arm again. He dug his nails into the back of his neck.

"Don't. Stop trying to fix things. I'm not broken glass. You can't just pick up the pieces. You know what people do with shattered glass? They sweep it up and toss it in the trash. I love you, Mom, but you don't get it. You can't come even close to understanding what it's like to be me right now. Don't you dare tell me my body doesn't matter."

With that, he stormed back in the house, trying hard to ignore the breathless sobs and clinking of glass shards he left in his wake.

CHAPTER THREE

LEBOO'S PULSE SKITTERED. *He remained frozen behind the thickest tree but no footsteps approached. They'd almost caught him this time.*

If it hadn't been for the monkey screeching, while scampering past the tent with a stolen piece of fruit and knocking over a metal pail in the process, they would have suspected a human intruder. They would have heard the noise he'd made when he bumped into the metal cabinet in the tent.

If someone found him, everything would be over. His family, especially his mother and sister, would suffer.

The evening grew dark, blessing Leboo with shadows. The voices he'd heard moments before, faded into the night.

He peered carefully around the tree. The pregnant woman gathered the bowl and what fruit was left in it, then disappeared into their home. No one else was around. This was his chance.

He secured the bandages and supplies he'd stolen in his pocket, then escaped as quietly and swiftly as he could. He was getting good at this...gifted at stealth. But a nagging feeling warned him that next time he might not be so lucky. The price for not returning with the supplies was too high to pay, yet the reward...priceless. He needed to stay focused. He needed to be prepared to defend himself at all costs.

He'd come better armed next time...

LEXI SHIELDED HER face from the sun and eyed the solitary wisp of cloud that had been lingering overhead.

"I don't think we have anything to worry about. The last rainy season practically skipped us altogether. I'm honestly more worried about what the drought is doing to the region than the clinic flooding or roads getting washed out when the rains come," she said.

She'd read about Kenya's climate and the rainy seasons back when she was making her big move. Everyone had warned her, when she'd first arrived, about the "short rains" of November and December, yet, it had not rained nearly as much as they'd described. She wasn't so sure the "long rains" of April would be that much more dramatic.

"You never know." Jacey cocked her head. "I get that climate change has done a number on everyone, but I'm a firm believer that predictable weather doesn't exist."

"Sure, it does. I predict that a minute from now it'll still be hot and sunny," Lexi said.

"Wow, pregnancy must be enhancing your intuitive abilities. It must go hand-in-hand with that mother's intuition thing." Jacey smirked at her and shook her head as she packaged up some surgical equipment for Hope to take to Nairobi to sterilize.

They had a small, autoclave for sterilizing equipment, but it had broken down a month ago. Even when it had been working, it had depended on the generator. Lexi really wished they could get one of the solar-powered autoclaves she'd read about. She wanted to talk to Dr. Hope about installing solar panels on the roof, too.

Though none of that would matter if they shut down the clinic. She'd sacrifice newer equipment to keep the clinic open. She'd boil things if she had to. Back to basics. The impact of having routine care and vaccines available to locals was so worth it. People needed this clinic.

Fingers crossed, Ben would be able to spare one of his new recruits or teammates to provide security. This clinic was important to Hope, too, so maybe he'd make the extra effort for his wife. Lexi was probably worrying for nothing.

"A little rain would be a blessing, but at least we know that no torrential storms will keep Mac from bringing Hope around today. Other than vaccinations, we can't see any more clinic patients until these supplies are sterilized. Where'd Taj go?"

"He's gathering his things so he can head out with Mac." Jacey took off her sterile gloves and disposed of them, then turned and crossed her arms. "Look, Lexi. I know we have a rule about no one staying out here alone, even without poacher threats, but I can hold down the fort until Mac brings back our equipment and more supplies. In the meantime, you should go with Taj and Mac to Nairobi. Get some proper rest. Make arrangements for when the baby comes. Go shopping."

"Absolutely not. I told you I have everything under control. I'll get what's needed when I go in for my exam. It's called efficiency. And I've already made arrangements. Hope said I can stay at her home to recover after the baby comes, if I want. I don't plan to abuse that invitation. I'll stay there a few weeks to a month, max. Then I'm coming right back here. We've organized a nurse from Hope's office to cover my clinic duties every other day. And Taj will still be around, too."

"But what about the baby?"

"What do you mean?"

"Lexi, do you have any idea how hard that would be for you? What about your child and our very basic living conditions? It's too risky."

"I've thought this through. Big houses in fancy neighborhoods aren't the only way people raise families. We keep a clean place here. Our clinic bungalow is like a small house or apartment. All this nature? Think of it as a big backyard. Jane Goodall had her toddler son at her research camp years ago. Half of Dr.

Hope's friends and family have done it. Even in America there are people who live in cabins in the woods, which are teeming with wolves and bears. And I might add that big cities and suburbs aren't without their dangers—drive-by or school shootings, for one thing.

"I'm going to build my life here doing what I was born to do. And if everyone Hope and Mac know has raised their kids out here, I can do it, too. I'd have a room and a roof over my head. I don't need any more than that. And my baby will have me. Don't worry."

"What about logistical things like dirty diapers?"

"When I first came here, Mac told me all about how he met Dr. Bekker at her elephant rescue. He said she used to take bucket showers and boil her daughter's and her friend's son's diapers then hang them on old-fashioned clotheslines. I'm sure I'll manage and get tips from everyone who has been through it. At least we don't have to take bucket showers and our well hasn't dried out. And, for the record, I don't expect anyone to diaper wash or babysit. I'll do it."

"That's not what I meant. I'd be happy to

help out." Jacey crinkled her nose. "Maybe. I'm just worried for you both."

"Don't be. I know what I'm doing. That mother's intuition thing. Right?"

"I guess." Jacey sighed.

"Any special requests other than ice cream?" Taj asked, coming out of the clinic.

"A new autoclave?" Jacey quipped.

"I wish. That's in Dr. Hope's hands," Taj said.

"Someone to secure the area so we stay open?" Lexi added.

"That's also in her hands. Or Ben's. Trust me, what Mac said is bothering me, too, and not just because I work here. Listen, we have two hours before they get here. I want to take the jeep down to the *enkang* that's just south of here by that dried riverbed and deliver—"

"Hang on. We have a patient." Lexi motioned toward a Masai man who was hurrying down the path carrying a woman in his arms.

"Oh, no."

She didn't have to say more. Taj and Jacey were already running over to help carry the woman to the exam tent. Dark bloodstains were evident on her traditional wrap dress, despite the cloth's vibrant colors. Lexi moved as fast as she could and was at her side just as they lay her on the exam cot. She was pregnant. Lexi swallowed hard. *Stay focused. This isn't you.* The young woman was bleeding out. Her eyes were barely open and her face looked pale.

"What happened? *Nini kimetokea?*" Lexi asked, hoping he spoke either English or Swahili because she couldn't recall how to ask it in Maa.

"She was grinding corn. Only that." The man stood back, his eyes intense. He draped his red-and-orange *shuka* back over his shoulder. His opposite shoulder and upper arm bore the scars of teeth marks. Lexi glanced at him. The man had stood up to a wild animal, but seeing blood from an ill family member was different. She'd seen plenty of grown men get woozy.

Jacey was pulling out clean gauze and the last sterilized set of surgical equipment. Taj had a blood pressure cuff on the woman and was setting up an IV. Lexi, already gloved, assessed the blood loss and pregnancy stage. She'd delivered several babies before, but they'd all been routine, full-term labors. This woman had to be toward the end of her first trimester or the beginning of her second. Lexi hadn't seen her at the clinic before for any prenatal care.

The man seemed to waver on his feet.

"Jacey, we don't want two patients right now." Lexi glanced up at her and Jacey immediately skirted around the bed to go walk the man outside the tent. "We'll take care of her. You were right to bring her in," Lexi told him on his way out.

Taj looked at Lexi as he hung the IV bag. They were lucky to have fluids. They had no blood on hand. Not out here. They both knew the chances of saving the pregnancy were slim to none. They couldn't stop the miscarriage at this point. She just hoped they could save the mother. A life that wouldn't have a chance if they hadn't been here to help. No, she couldn't abandon the people here. She couldn't take away medical care from all the children out here. Doing so would be akin to letting the poachers win. That wasn't happening. Not on her watch.

"ONCE A MARINE, always a marine. So, consider it an order."

Chad shook his head at his father's use of authority.

"You may be a marine, Dad, but you know an order is not going to work with me," Chad said, grabbing an apple and taking a bite. He wanted a banana and he could have peeled it using his teeth, but he didn't want to do that in front of his father. It made him feel like less of the man he'd striven to be, a man who would have made his dad proud.

Ben pulled his head out from the refrigerator and nearly lost his grip on the set of crutches he was holding out of the way.

"Listen, I'm serious. I need you to go with your mom. Scope things out at the clinic for me. I obviously can't do it. You have a trained eye. I want distances, weak spots, you name it. Including suggestions on how to secure the place. Plain fences are a joke out there and Hope doesn't want anything with barbs or voltage because of all the kids that come around. Besides, relying on their generator won't work. I don't have anyone else I can send right now. Not anyone I can trust to be thorough. Hope is furious that I said the place should be shut down until they find this escapee or even longer, given the rise in poaching activity. I need to know your mom and her staff out there are safe. Don't you want that, too?"

Chad had grown up around here. He'd heard his dad talk about poachers and some of their tactics for years: hidden snares, poisoning watering holes, guns and rifles, including automatic weapons, sawing entire faces off of elephants and rhinos just to harvest their tusks. Plus, they were swift on their feet and knew how to disappear. They even took advantage of the Masai farmers who were losing their crops and herds to the droughts, paying them for their help. Poachers took greed and ruthless murder to a whole new level, and most of the groups were backed by wealthy, ivory mafia bosses. Half of Chad's family and relatives, including Ben, worked to fight poaching. He wasn't against doing so himself. They were evil.

But he was in no shape for that kind of undertaking. Ben had to realize that. Chad couldn't help but feel like his dad was using this to get him out of the house.

"What's the point? You have plenty of guys

you train. Send one of them. Or ask Mac to do it. He can see the lay of the land from his chopper."

Ben leaned forward.

"Let's break this down Barney style. I only have a small group right now and they're all training KWS teams. One of them was actually with the KWS group that was scanning the area using thermal imaging. The rest are on fire watch closer to the Tanzanian border, to see if they can find any signs the injured poacher is hiding out there, versus having crossed over. I can't pull those men from what they're doing. They're on the front lines as it is and this isn't the only poaching case KWS has on its hands."

Chad set his half-eaten apple on the table and looked away. The back of his neck pinched.

"Chad, please. I just want to be assured the clinic area is okay." Ben hobbled over to the kitchen table and sat. "You know I'd be out there myself if I could be. I've even thought of cutting this darn cast off myself, but don't you dare tell your mother I said that. So I need you to go. Mac isn't you. He may have years of experience helping wildlife rescuers find injured animals or helping KWS with aerial spotting, but he isn't trained in combat strategy. He can't scope an area and take in a million details at once the way you can."

Chad pushed away from the table.

"Just what kind of details do you expect from me?"

"I want to know what can be done to make the clinic area safer. Mac checked on everyone there but they said the only people who'd come through were patients. No injured poachers or suspicious persons. I'm not going to assume it can't happen. You know what they say about hiding in plain sight."

Chad didn't answer. Had he been sharper that day in Afghanistan, he wouldn't have walked his men into a trap. He wouldn't be standing here right now permanently wounded. His dog would still be alive.

"You're giving me busywork I can't even do. You're the one in security. Not me. Maybe you should give up already on me following in your footsteps."

Ben banged the end of his crutches against the floor.

"Cut the bull, Chad."

"I'm just stating facts. If a poacher walks

up, what am I supposed to do? No rifle. Remember that? Kind of hard to hold a gun with one hand. Should I flick him off? 'Cause *that's* within my limits." Chad grinned and pointed a finger at his dad. "Or, no, wait. Maybe hand-to-hand combat, because you know the expression does imply only one hand is used."

"Chad," Ben warned.

"What? A one-armed man is allowed to tell one-armed jokes. It's a privilege."

Making himself the butt of jokes helped him to cope with how he was sure other people saw him. At least, that's what he told himself. The reality? The sarcastic remark had left a bitter taste in his mouth.

His dad didn't laugh. He just bore a look through Chad that made him feel small. It didn't sit well. Especially coming from his father. It didn't matter that Chad had come to terms with the fact that he was less of a man than he used to be, but seeing that judgment in his dad's eyes ate at him. He threw the rest of the apple in a compost bin by the sink and started for the living room.

Ben stood, tucked the crutches under his arms and followed him out.

"Tony's wife is there. She's the nurse manning the clinic."

Chad stilled. An icy wave spread through his chest, prickling like the cruel sting of frostbite at a winter post in Helmand Province.

"What do you mean Tony's wife is there? What are you trying to pull? Why didn't anyone tell me?"

"Because you just got here. Because we'd all agreed to limit what we said about certain things so that you could regain your strength and focus on getting better. You were devastated when we told you the news about his death, and it held back your recovery. So when Lexi applied for the job at your mom's clinic, we decided not to mess with your emotions any further. But I figure, now that you're here in Kenya, you're going to find out sooner or later. If you don't want to help protect the clinic for me or your mom, then do it for Tony."

Chad collapsed onto an armchair and gripped his forehead with his left hand before fisting his hair. Tony's wife. This couldn't be real. What was she doing there? Didn't she have family in the US?

Tony and Chad hadn't been able to talk much in the last few years, so he knew very little about Lexi other than that she was a nurse…and the love of Tony's life, according to him.

Man, if something ever happens to me, make sure she's okay. Just do that for me, would you?

Tony's words rang in Chad's ears. Tony had been like a brother to him. His best friend long before they had joined the marines. They'd met as teenagers when Tony's family decided to move to Nairobi for a few years so that their children could experience the other half of their American-Kenyan heritage. They'd bonded as expats, though Chad had already been living in Kenya awhile.

He'd showed Tony around and studied with him through high school. And though they'd gotten into different colleges in the US, they'd both decided to join the marines at the same time. He'd never met Tony's wife, though. He'd heard about her, but he and Tony hadn't been stationed together. Their leave times had differed, too, which was why Chad hadn't been able to attend their impromptu wedding.

But he had managed to call Tony to congratulate him. Those words had been the last thing Tony had said to him, and Chad had given his word. Lexi would be okay.

Chad grated his nails against his forehead. He'd asked about her after hearing about Tony's death. At least he thought he had. The pain and meds had messed with his head when he was in the hospital. He'd missed the funeral but he was sure he'd asked if Lexi was okay.

During their last conversation, he vaguely recalled Tony mentioning that he and Lexi had a plan to move back to Kenya after his tour. But Tony was gone now. What the heck was Lexi doing out in Kenya's Serengeti? Alone?

The scraping of chair legs against the floor had him straightening his back. Ben settled in an armchair across from him with his cast positioned to avoid scratching the hand-carved coffee table.

"I don't get it. Why would she move out here?"

"According to her, it was part of a plan they'd made together and she wanted to see it through," Ben said. "She's one determined woman, but she hasn't been out here long. She doesn't grasp the danger. You can help her. You *can*. You're stronger than you think you are, or you wouldn't be a marine. You still have a purpose, Chad. Mine changed when Zoe was killed. Yours can, too. You start with the small stuff that matters. For now, that means making sure it's safe for Lexi to keep running the clinic, especially in her… condition."

Chad narrowed his eyes at his dad.

"She's pregnant." Ben hoisted himself back onto his crutches and thrummed his fingers against them. "My guess is that the Chad I know is going to want to pay his respects to his best friend's wife. If you don't want to do it because it's the right thing, then do it out of a sense of duty."

Ben stalked off down the hall that led to a master bedroom suite and whistled for Roosevelt to follow him.

It took several minutes before Chad could will his legs to move. He walked over to the patio doors, stepped outside and stood there feeling lost.

Tony had never said anything about becoming a father. Given how many months it had been since his death, she had to be pretty far along...

Make sure she's okay. Just do that for me...

But Tony had made that request long before Chad's injuries. Had Tony known what condition Chad was in now, he'd never have asked so much of him, would he? Maybe Chad was overthinking all this. He wasn't responsible for his friend's widow. He simply had to check on her and pay his respects, as his father had said.

You gave Tony your word. As a friend. As a man of honor. As a marine.

A burning pain washed over his missing arm. He muttered a curse and dug his nails into his thigh until it subsided.

Danger. A threat to women and children. The image of the little girl running toward the cart flashed in his mind. Her wide eyes. The terror. The deafening noise and searing pain. A glimpse of her listless body seconds before he blacked out.

Sweat beaded and trickled down his temples. Nausea swept over him then faded. He lowered himself onto the steps overlooking the yard.

The clinic wasn't in a war zone. Or was

it? Danger was danger. Terrorism—the ultimate shape-shifter—existed in a sickening number of forms. What would it hurt to go check out the place? It'd get his parents off his back. All he had to do was to report to his father that the place wasn't safe and it would get shut down, at least temporarily. At least until the poachers were caught. Or until new ones were spotted, which essentially meant the place would be shut down for good and his duty would be done. Tony's wife and unborn kid would be forced to go live under safer, normal circumstances. Surely she had family in the States she could go back to. In any case, she'd be better off than at a rural clinic.

And his mother would be devastated. She was so passionate about providing medical care to the tribal children. They often lived too deep into Kenya's savannah and Serengeti to have access to proper care. He knew the clinic meant everything to Hope. And she'd already given up so much of her time to care for him when he'd been hospitalized in the US, taking her away from those kids. Was this how he'd repay her? Shutting down the place to fulfill a promise to a friend and get himself off the hook? Damned if he did. Damned if he didn't.

But his mother had her mobile unit, too. This was just one location. If an injured poacher was on the loose in the clinic area, then this pregnant nurse had no business running the place. Decision made. He'd go.

He scrubbed a hand over his face and squinted up at a solitary cloud making its way slowly eastward. To be up there in the clouds again…to feel the lift of a helicopter, and the surge of adrenaline he experienced before a mission… He closed his eyes briefly, noticing for a fleeting moment that he wasn't in pain. Not in that brief second, at least.

If he didn't go and something happened at the clinic, something he could have prevented, he'd never forgive himself. Ben wanted him to check out the area? Fine. He could deal with the clinic's staff gawking at him for a few hours. Maybe he'd scare the children at the clinic enough that they wouldn't notice they were getting shots. He could see it now. The looks. The finger pointing. Maybe he'd even earn the code name *Dubwana*. Monster.

He stepped back inside the house, closed the glass door and stopped at the sight of his reflection. His injuries barely showed in the faint and fuzzy image. His dark T-shirt and upper body faded against the dim backdrop of the room and all that showed of the small flecks of scars on the right side of his face was the one that pinched the skin at the end of his eyebrow.

Then his father's face appeared. Chad turned, hoping Ben would assume Chad had been looking outside and not at himself.

"Take this," Ben said, pausing expectantly then setting a black handgun case on the dining table near them.

"Like that would be of much use with my left hand."

"Your aim with your left hand is better than anyone else's best shot, marine."

Chad torqued his neck to each side, but it did nothing to relieve the strain. He let out a long, slow breath then stretched his jaw.

"Tell Mom and Mac that I'll head out with them. Just this once."

Ben nodded but his expression was otherwise unreadable. No relief. No gratitude.

"When you get back, I want you to meet some people," Ben said. "A few of my trainees.

It's important for you to talk to others who've been through what you've been through."

His trainees were military vets, some very young, who couldn't find work after they'd served. No one went into a war zone without suffering in one way or another, even if the injury was mental or emotional. But none of Ben's men had injuries as extensive as Chad's. They were whole. They had to be to do the work Ben expected of them.

"I'm sure your friends are great, but I don't want group therapy and I don't need an intervention. I'm fine. You want me to go to that Masai clinic with Mom? I said I'm on it."

"Good. One more thing, Chad. Man up. Out there, you're not anyone's patient. Hope and Lexi have enough people coming to that clinic for medical care." Ben started to leave but stopped and looked over his shoulder. "Oh, and if you make your mom cry again, you answer to me."

His father left the room. *Man up*. Chad stared after him then rubbed his hand against his shirt. Did his dad even realize what he was saying? What he was asking of him? He was supposed to man up and ignore the pain?

That's what the world expected of him? Pretend nothing happened? Blend right back in?

He pressed the pad of his thumb and forefinger to his eyes. His parents were good people. On some level, he knew that. He got that they just wanted to pull him out of this funk…that they wanted him to be okay. But no one understood. Dealing with the chronic pain, physical limitations and disfigurement was bad enough. But it was more than that. Being a marine had defined him. How in God's name was he supposed to cope and move on if now, deep down, he didn't even know who he was anymore?

LEXI HAD NEVER been so relieved to hear the whirr of Mac's chopper. After what had happened with the young Masai woman, she was anxious to talk to Hope and assure her that everything was fine out here. She couldn't imagine Hope shutting the clinic down, at least not willingly. *Please let them all be overreacting.* If anything, maybe they had found someone to help keep the place safe and secure until the poaching situation settled down.

She waited, watching the dust rise and fall

as the chopper landed safely beyond the outskirts of the clinic camp. She spotted Hope climbing out of the chopper, a bag and a box in her hands. Mac leaped out and went around to grab another box. And…there was someone else. She didn't recognize him. Blond hair. Tall. Broad shoulders and very—*very*—well built. Maybe they *had* found a guard.

He said something to Hope, took the handle of the bag she carried and turned to walk toward the clinic camp. His blue, long-sleeved T-shirt was pushed up to his elbow on one side. The other side was knotted just above the elbow, where his arm ended. *An amputee.* An ache bled through Lexi's chest. That had to be Hope's son, the injured marine. Tony's old friend.

He looked up and their eyes met. Something jolted in her stomach and she took in a grounding breath. He knew about Tony's death. No doubt Hope had told him who she was and why she was here. But how much did he know about *how* Tony had died?

She'd never gone into the details with Hope and Ben. It hadn't seemed right to bring it up when she'd first been hired. They'd still been dealing with Chad's own recovery at the time. They'd told her about how he'd saved his troop, including one guy who was only eighteen. So young. But his heroics didn't make it any easier for his parents to see him suffering. Lexi had wanted to say something to Hope and Ben that showed she understood what they were going through, but she never found the words. It wouldn't have been right to point out that her loved one didn't make it when they were still praying for their son's recovery.

Chad kept his eyes on her, his jaw set too tight for a smile. Maybe he was daring her to flinch at the sight of his injuries. Lexi wasn't one to flinch. She was a nurse. Or maybe his challenge was all in her head. His brown eyes flicked downward then up again. He narrowed his eyes at her. There was no mistaking why.

Her pregnancy.

Great. Yet one more person who looked at her as if she was vulnerable and out of place. Lexi pressed her lips together to keep from shouting out that her brains were still in her head and, protruding belly or not, she was still more than capable of doing her job. He looked right at her again and she couldn't shrug off the feeling that his eyes said too much. They saw too much. How much had Tony told him about her?

She broke eye contact with Chad to watch Taj jog up to help carry the supply box Hope had in her arms. Lexi followed suit, doubling her stride and marching over. Well, more like waddling, but she minimized the sway as much as she possibly could.

"Hi, I'm Lexi Galen. I can take that." She reached out for the bag he was carrying. He didn't let go of it.

"Chad Corallis. Hope's son. I can set it down where you need it. It's kind of heavy."

"It's no problem. I can take it in," Lexi said. She didn't wait for him to concede. She took the handle and their fingers brushed. He let go abruptly and she almost lost her grip.

She was standing too close to him. He smelled of fresh soap and shampoo, which only made her hyperaware of the fact that the day had been hot and she was sweaty. She'd barely had the chance to put on a clean shirt after their emergency patient.

Her cheeks burned. She was meeting Tony's closest friend for the first time and this was what she looked like? She swallowed and willed her face to cool down.

This was not about attraction. Yes, he was ruggedly handsome and had a sort of quiet magnetism about him, but he was also Tony's friend. She was only flustered because of her stupid pregnancy hormones. They made her sensitive to smell. And he smelled good in that manly way Tony used to. That's all it was. Hormones and embarrassment.

Get yourself together, girl. She tucked her hair behind her ear, cleared her throat and took a step back with the bag.

"Excuse me a moment," she said, rushing to catch up to Hope who'd ducked into the storage room along the side of the bungalow. Mac was already back in the air.

"Hey, Doc," Lexi said as she entered the room.

"How are you?" Hope gave her a hug and kept her arm around Lexi until she got an answer. It felt good to be held. Hope had such a soothing nature.

It reminded Lexi of how much she used to long for the kind of mother-daughter relationships her classmates had had with their mothers. The closest she'd come to that kind of bond had been with her last social worker.

"I'm doing great. But we have a patient I'd like you to check in on. Her name is Akinyi. She lost her baby and plenty of blood, but she's stable right now. Jacey's in the exam tent with her."

"I'll go check on her now. Mac will be back in a couple of hours. Tell Chad he can look around until I'm done."

"Around the clinic? Do you need me to show him something?" *Please say no.*

"No, no. Ben wants him to check the surrounding area. News of that injured poacher has him rattled. He wants Chad to report back on the security of the clinic, how easy it might be for someone to sneak up on you unannounced, that kind of thing." Hope lowered her voice and wrapped her hand around Lexi's wrist. "Between you and me, Chad is still…adjusting. He really didn't want to come out here."

"Understood." Lexi gave Hope's hand a reassuring squeeze. She knew how to deal with patients.

"I'm sure Mac also gave you a heads-up that we're considering closing the clinic. Obviously, I'd never want to disrupt providing medical care, but I can't put you, Jacey or Taj in danger. We're obligated to make sure you're safe until the injured man is either found or it's determined he escaped across the border. But even after this threat is over, we have to make the clinic more secure for the future."

"I really think we'll be fine. We've always been safe. Please don't shut down the clinic, Hope. Go check on your latest patient and you'll see why what we're doing here is so important. We have to stay open."

"Don't worry. Maybe they'll find this guy and things will be back to normal. Or perhaps Chad will convince Ben that he's overreacting. Let's see what his impressions are and take this one day at a time." Hope gave a reassuring smile, then left the storage room and disappeared into the patient tent on the far side of the clinic grounds.

That meant there was a lot riding on whatever Chad said. Between the way he'd frowned at her belly and his general I-don't-want-to-be-here demeanor, Lexi wasn't sure she could be as calm as Hope seemed to be right now.

She tightened her grip on the supply bag and started for the bungalow. But the sight of Chad and Akinyi's husband in the central clearing stopped her in her tracks. The man stood in front of Chad with his palm resting against Chad's chest.

"*Shujaa mmoja hadi mwingine.* You understand? We are one warrior to another. *Ujasiri wa moja.* You are a brave one," he said, nodding toward Chad's injury, then in the direction of his wife. "I lost a child today. A precious one." He touched the bite scars on his shoulder, no doubt inflicted in an encounter with a wild animal. "I must be brave again, too," he added. "A different kind of brave."

Lexi's nose stung and she blinked rapidly to control the tears that threatened to fall.

A different kind of brave.

That applied to her, too, didn't it? Did she have it in her? She studied Chad's reaction. Did he have any bravery left in him?

CHAD TIPPED HIS chin down and nodded to the Masai man.

"I'm sorry for your loss." He didn't know what else to say. The man's words hit home. Chad's injury hadn't fazed him. He'd called

Chad a warrior. *A wounded warrior.* Like that put them in a sort of brotherhood. Maybe it did. Only the man was carrying his injuries with pride. He wasn't worried about himself. He was worried about his wife.

Chad watched him walk over to Hope as she exited the tent. She said something to the man before he left down the dirt path.

Wife. Family. Those were the furthest things from Chad's mind. He wasn't relationship material. Not anymore.

The sense that someone was watching made him glance to his right—it was Lexi. She quickly turned her face and headed for the tiny, one-story bungalow with a corrugated tin roof that sat under the shade of a massive old fig tree at the edge of the clinic grounds. Something in her gaze made him feel even more self-conscious than he'd already been feeling.

Not that Lexi Galen's opinion of him mattered. But she was the woman who'd won Tony's heart. That had to count for something.

Chad couldn't help but imagine them meeting under different circumstances… Tony being alive and all three of them hanging out for a casual dinner. But that could never happen now.

Lexi wasn't what he'd expected. He had assumed she'd seem more fragile and maybe even shy—at least the girls Tony used to date had been that way. But that's why he'd never dated them for long. Lexi Galen was the stark opposite.

Pregnant as she was, she exuded an inner no-nonsense strength. Pretty and feminine but with a hint of tomboy. The kind of girl *he'd* always dated. Probably why his relationships had never lasted. His ex-girlfriends had accused him of being overprotective and they'd hated it when he'd tried to call the shots.

But pretty or not, Lexi was the pregnant widow of his best friend. There was nothing wrong with admiring her, but admitting that he found her attractive, or even that he was curious about her and wanted to know more, was off limits.

Besides, he'd caught the way she'd stared at him then couldn't seem to get away from him fast enough. He didn't need anyone's pity. She was a beautiful woman and he was…he was whatever was left of him. He was well aware that he made people uncomfortable. People didn't seem to know whether to console him, thank him or pity him.

He tucked his left hand in his pocket and walked toward a copse of mango trees that flanked the west side of the camp.

You're supposed to be scoping out the area.

He scanned his surroundings with a more critical eye. Wood smoke rose from several Masai *enkangs* in the far distance. Acacias and thick brush stretched to the northwest and outcroppings and boulders dappled the landscape of the grasslands to the southwest. Potential cover for a criminal, at least in those directions.

The borders of Tanzania and Uganda lay west. Tanzania was a notorious haven for poachers. Anyone headed into the Masai Mara from there would probably just slip back over to Tanzania once their gruesome business was done, unless they couldn't withstand the trip on foot. Would an injured man on the run be able to make it to the border?

If he couldn't, there were still plenty of places to hide. He shaded his eyes and squinted toward the tribal villages in the distance. The Masai were good people, but growing up here, he'd heard plenty of stories about desperate villagers aiding and harboring poachers for the sake of money when drought threatened their crops.

The sound of footsteps behind him had him spinning on his heel.

"Sorry. I didn't mean to startle you," Lexi said.

"You didn't."

She had, but he wasn't about to let on. A lot of things startled him lately.

"Okay. I, um… Dr. Hope said you needed to see the area." She held up a set of keys. "I can drive you around the perimeter so you can take in more of our setup before you leave."

Leave it to his mother to put him on the spot. It was clear from her lack of eye contact and hurried, let's-get-this-over-with attitude that Lexi was being forced to do this.

He glanced over at a dust-coated jeep parked at the side of the clinic's concrete walls. The steering wheel was located on the right side of the vehicle, since Kenyans drove on the left side of the road. That meant his right side would be facing her as she sat in the driver's seat.

He scratched at the back of his neck and

yearned to work out the stiffness. He really didn't care what she thought of his injuries, did he? Her eyes would be on the road, not him or his stump or his fleck-like facial scars. And she'd never have to set eyes on him after today anyway. It would also give him the chance to convey his condolences about Tony.

He owed it to Tony to keep Lexi safe. Which meant he also needed to find justification to close the clinic for security reasons.

"Sure. Let's go," he said.

"Hey, you two." Hope hurried over and took a second to catch her breath. "I'm worried about the patient. I think we should stay the night. Do you mind, Chad? I know Akinyi is in good hands with you, Lexi, but Taj is leaving with Mac, so you're one person short. If she takes a turn for the worse, you'll need extra hands. I told her husband he could go home and that we'd keep her here for observation, but I'm concerned she could start bleeding again."

"Of course. I'll change Taj's sheets for you, Chad. It's a small cot but it works," Lexi said.

He'd slept on plenty of cots, for God's sake. He'd slept on barren floors. Did she think he was soft? Weak?

“And we can set up the spare cot for you, Hope, in the room I share with Jacey,” she added. “Whatever you need, consider it done.”

“Chad, do you mind?” Hope asked again. “That way Mac wouldn’t have to fly back to Nairobi for no reason. He could return home and pick us up tomorrow. I’d rather not waste his time and gas.”

He gave his mom *the look* and she gave it right back to him. Fine. It *was* the right thing to do, but so much for a brief visit. Had he been set up? Were they trying to get him out of the house and around other people? He felt a phantom twinge where his arm should have been and he gritted his teeth to keep the pain from escalating.

“No problem,” he muttered. “I could even lend a hand.”

Had he really just said that? For some reason, the sound of his words left a bad taste in his mouth. Sarcasm and self-deprecating humor around his parents was one thing, but in front of Lexi and the others?

While part of him felt like he’d earned the right to lash out, he knew he was being a jerk. If his parents—and the marines—had taught him anything, it had been respect. But it was like a different soul had taken over his mind and body. One that was angry and didn't care who he offended.

Hope held up her hands in defeat and sighed. She rubbed the back of her tightly cropped hair. There was more salt-and-pepper to it than he recalled. Maybe he hadn't been paying attention the past few months. Or maybe the Serengeti sun left nothing hidden. Her cheeks were less full and the creases at the corners of her eyes had deepened. Had he done this to her?

"I'll go let Mac know," Hope said, walking off before he could muster an apology.

Lexi rolled her eyes and shook her head.

"Lend a hand? Really? You must have been a comedian in a past life. And, yes, I'm being sarcastic. Don't get me wrong, I'm sure we could use whatever help you'd like to offer, but only if you want to. Help is welcome but not needed. We all have our limits around here," she said, resting a hand on her very expanded waistline for emphasis, "but we're pretty good at working together and covering for each other when necessary. We're used to not counting on anyone but ourselves."

Was she referring to everyone or to herself as plural, since she was pregnant? He bit back an equally snarky remark.

"I'm sorry if my humor offended you."

"Me? I don't pay attention to bad jokes. They're not worth my time. But I think you hurt your mother and, the thing is, we all love Dr. Hope around here. We've all witnessed how run-down she's been since your injury, though she never complains or admits to it. She's a strong woman, and my wild, first-impression guess is that you were a handful as a kid, so she had to be."

A twisted smile spread across Chad's face. This Lexi had spunk. Now he understood why Tony had fallen for her. He'd always been one for a challenge, medical school and all. Chad figured it must have just taken him a while to figure out he liked women who could challenge him, too.

"A handful? I can't deny that," he said.

"Thought so." Lexi's eyes darkened and she scanned the expanse of savannah grasses that rolled toward a mountain range in the distance. "I—we—do appreciate that you served and all you sacrificed in doing so. You…um. You knew my husband."

Chad nodded because he had no idea

where to start. She'd said it as a statement but he knew she wanted and needed more. She'd opened the door, offering him the perfect opportunity to give his condolences, to honor Tony the way he deserved. But he couldn't seem to get the words out.

Memories he hadn't recalled in years spewed like water from a broken pipe and crashed against his temples. The time Tony broke his leg trying to save a cat when they were thirteen. Tony's first schoolboy crush… and Chad having to break the news to his friend that she wasn't into guys. And then the time he'd told Chad he'd met "the one." He'd been talking about Lexi.

She glanced up at him expectantly and then back across the dry grasslands.

There was something about her. Something that made him want to share all those times, like an unspoken circle of trust. Tony had loved and trusted her. Perhaps, subconsciously, that was making Chad assume he could, too. Or maybe it was because he knew she cared. He could see that in the way her eyes glistened and cheeks flushed as she turned away.

"We were best friends growing up. He

was an amazing guy and friend. I'm sorry for your loss," he said.

She swallowed, drawing his attention to a pair of wedding bands held against the base of her throat by a silver chain.

"Me, too. For both of us. Your parents told me you and Tony had been close. Back when I interviewed for this position, I mentioned I was a widow and Hope recognized the name," she explained.

Guilt gnawed its way down his spine. She didn't know, then, that their friendship had gotten Tony killed…that the other man had trusted him…and Chad had urged and convinced him to join the marines. He had convinced Tony that the financial benefits and experience were worth it, and that studying medicine while in the military would be far cheaper than going to a regular medical school. He had even pointed out that the training and time in the field would better prepare Tony when he pursued his dream to provide medical care off the grid in Kenya's Serengeti. If it hadn't been for Chad, Tony would have never been at that field hospital. He'd have never been killed.

She wasn't aware that Chad had as good

as sealed Tony's fate long before she'd ever married him.

But telling her would be selfish. He'd be doing it for the sake of confession, to try to lighten the weight of his own guilt. But for her, he'd be reopening a painful wound. It wasn't right to do that, let alone to a pregnant woman. He'd promised Tony he'd make sure she was okay. Upsetting her to that degree wouldn't help her. Still, guilt pounded at his temples.

Chad's right arm burned and he reached over with his left hand but caught his action in time to grip his right shoulder instead. He needed his water bottle. A bead of sweat trickled down the back of his neck and he tried shrugging away the sensation.

"Are you okay?" She started to reach her hand out but he took two steps away.

"I'm good," he snapped. "I just want to get something from my backpack over there, then take a look around," he said, taking several more steps toward his bag that was set on a wooden stool outside the bungalow.

"I can swing the jeep around."

"Not necessary. I can check things out on

my own two feet. It won't take long to find out what I need to know."

"The jeep would probably be safer and faster. Hope said to show you the area. If you're going to look around, you should do it right. I don't want you to do a cursory evaluation then tell your dad it's not safe."

"Or maybe if you drive me around fast enough, I'll miss the signs of danger and tell everyone you'll all be fine and the place stays open for business. Is that the plan?"

"Don't talk to me like I'm stupid. Maybe it's in your nature to give people a hard time, but the fact is, I loved and trusted Tony. Same goes for your mom. And they both trusted you. So, regardless of your ornery attitude and only having met you, I trust you, too… at least to do what's right and to do your job well."

She trusted him? The phantom pain reached higher and wrapped around his neck like bony fingers strangling him. Punishing him. He gritted his teeth and glanced at her sneakers. He couldn't look her in the eyes.

Tony had trusted him to make sure Lexi was safe. If his friend had known about the baby, Chad was sure he'd have included the child in that promise. Oh, yes, Chad would be thorough all right.

"My father sent me out here to do a job and I will do it. However, I trust you can understand that I prefer to work on my own. You wouldn't want me looking over your shoulder and telling you how to be a nurse, would you?"

"I have plenty to keep me busy around here. We have a critical patient I could be helping right now instead of standing here listening to you being rude. And for the record, my driving the jeep doesn't constitute trying to do your job."

"Okay, fine. But let's get something straight. Our definition of doing what's right might be a tad different. I find any sign that an escaped poacher is still around or that this clinic has serious vulnerabilities to potential, dangerous threats, you'll be closing up shop until the problem is solved. That's how I do what's right.

"And from what I've seen from just standing here, you should start packing. This place has zero security. Anyone could walk down that path at any time, or hide strategically behind those bushes and grasses. That clinic tent backs onto more trees and shrubs. A poacher could sneak up from behind it. Not to mention your lax internal security. Is everything locked up in there? Has anything gone missing?"

Lexi stared at him.

"That wasn't a hypothetical question," he said.

"No. Nothing is missing. We've been going through supplies faster than someone could steal them. There was one misplaced bottle of peroxide this morning, but it's probably in the mobile clinic van. If someone was stealing, they would grab a lot more than a single bottle of peroxide."

"Have someone check the van when we get back."

He climbed into the front left passenger seat of the jeep, trying his hardest not to fumble or misstep. Lack of coordination would make him look weak and undermine his authority. He tried to keep his eyes ahead as Lexi climbed in and adjusted the seat to accommodate her belly. Obviously, either Taj or Jacey had been the last ones to use the jeep.

She backed up. Then, avoiding the path leading to the camp, she veered left and drove straight past the mango trees and toward a small, rock-studded hill less than a quarter of a kilometer northwest of the clinic camp.

A single, lonely acacia tree graced the top of it like one of those paper umbrellas used for decorating fancy drinks. Only there was nothing fancy about this place. He hadn't seen the hill from the camp. The view would have been blocked by the trees flanking the exam tent, but he did recall seeing a hill and some outcroppings from the chopper. The rest of the area spread into farmland and savannah prairies, with the occasional tree dappling the landscape. He had to admit, Lexi was smart. She knew exactly where he'd want to go.

"A vantage point," he called out over the engine noise in acknowledgment of her plan.

"A sensible starting point. Some people get so obsessed with the details that they lose sight of the big picture." She pressed her lips together and gave him a quick side glance.

No comment.

She didn't know him well enough to make a statement like that. Not that she was necessarily directing it at him personally, but it sure felt that way. Granted he was more self-conscious and sensitive lately—two words that would never have come remotely close to describing his old self.

"I'm not sure what my mother has said about me, but I assure you, I don't need you to play psychologist. I'm sharp enough to see the details and the big picture *and* to read between the lines. So, with all due respect, save your nursing for your patients."

"My, you're a piece of work," she said, stopping at the top of the ridge and turning off the ignition. She slid out of her seat and slammed the door shut, sending a nearby flock of quail scattering into the air. "I get that you're one of those big, strong, good-looking, superhero-type guys, but that doesn't mean the world centers around your ego. I don't play games. If I think you're being narrow-sighted or pig-headed, I'll tell you so, flat-out. My intent in bringing you up here is to show you that we are fine, will be fine and shouldn't be shut down."

He got out and cocked his head at her. "Thanks for the ride. I'll take it from here."

He turned on his heel, tightening his left hamstring to keep his balance. He could feel her staring at his back as he left her standing there, judging him. He didn't care.

He scanned the almost three-hundred-sixty-degree view below. The clinic had both grasses and trees surrounding it in various places, like the grassy clearing to the east where Mac had landed his bird. He spotted the path most patients took up to the clinic, stretching many kilometers south of them. It was flanked mostly by grazing fields and farm plots with rows of grain. There were five different *enkangs* that surrounded the camp in the distance, though not in a perfect circle by any means. Far, yet within walking distance.

It was hard to miss the clusters of mud-urine-and-straw-plastered huts topped with thatched domed roofs. A thorny acacia-branch fence formed a protective thicket around each of the homestead villages. The Masai women, men and children, dressed in their famously vibrant colors, dotted the earthy hues of the drought-stricken landscape like precious gems. The stark opposite, it occurred to him, of the camouflage he'd been accustomed to in the war-ravaged regions of Afghanistan.

His sister, Maddie, who used her position as a lawyer to fight for the human rights of Kenya's indigenous tribes, had used that word. Precious. She'd said that the Masai and other tribes were precious, and the beauty of their culture and the people were in danger of being lost to the greedy. His mother had devoted her life to helping the Masai, too. As was Lexi. And here he was, ready to get in the way. Who was the enemy here? He'd grown up in this place and everything—from the people to the surroundings—was a part of him. But whose side was he on now? Protecting Lexi would mean taking critical care away from others. She was right.

He worked his jaw and walked toward a boulder-like outcropping that was blocking his view to the south. He heard the crunch of a boot against rocky soil behind him. Her gait was uneven and slow. He didn't turn but he didn't stop listening, either. How much walking was a pregnant woman supposed to do? Was there a limit?

He edged around a boulder, bracing his left hand against it for stability. All he could see beyond it were groves of trees and shrubbery splintered apart every so often by meandering, dry creek beds and rocky outcroppings. Excellent hiding places. A virtual paintball field, just like the ones he, Tony and a few other friends used to let loose on back in the States before they'd been deployed and split up.

Only here in the Serengeti, if someone—like a poacher—was using those thickets and boulders as cover, the game would be a dangerous and potentially deadly one. His mind instantly traced the path of least resistance, connecting shrub and rock like the numbered dots in one of those coloring activity books he'd used as a kid. And one particular outcropping caught his attention.

It stood like a work of art. A natural sculpture of three different boulders set against one another. Perfect cover. Something tiny glinted in the sunlight near the base of the formation. He felt a twinge in his solar plexus and squinted, but a faint wisp of a cloud passed in front of the sun. The glint was gone, but he was sure he'd seen it. He needed a closer look.

He felt his pocket and cursed himself silently for leaving his binoculars in his backpack. Lexi had distracted him. He preferred that reasoning to the possibility that he was losing his touch. He'd have never been caught unprepared prior to his injury.

Lexi's footsteps stopped suddenly. He turned and caught her wincing and touching her side. For a moment he was in Kabul, on one of his early missions, not far from the embassy. A car bomb had detonated and shots were being fired. Screams pierced the air. A woman was running down the street, trying to find shelter. He saw the bullet hit her. She grabbed her side and crumpled to the ground.

In less than five seconds he was at Lexi's side with his arm around her back, helping her to ease down onto a small boulder.

"What's wrong? Are you in labor?" He quickly dried his forehead against his shoulder.

"What? No! I'm okay. I just need to sit a minute."

"You're not fine. You looked like you were going to pass out. When was the last time you drank water?" He knelt in front of her and touched her forehead. He wasn't a doctor but he knew enough from his training. She wasn't clammy and her eyes seemed okay.

And, oddly, her cheeks went from pale to rosy as soon as he took his hand away. "I have my water in the jeep. Stay here."

She grabbed his wrist.

"I had water. I drink all the time. Trust me, the frequent bathroom trips get old fast. I promise I'm okay. Show me a pregnant woman who never feels a moment of light-headedness and I'll show you Super Woman. I'm making an entire human in here. He or she was also doing yoga stretches. I simply needed a second."

He wiped his palm across his face. He'd seen horrific amounts of blood and gore in his life and had developed a stomach of steel out of necessity, yet the image of a mini-human stretching around inside her was enough to make him queasy. He rubbed at his chest then braced his hand on his belt.

"What in God's name are you doing out here, Lexi? Do you really think Tony would have expected you to go through with this plan to live out here someday? Yes, he told me about his ten-year plan. But no way would he have wanted you doing this on your own. I knew him enough to be sure of that. He wouldn't want you in danger. He'd be furious if he suspected you were putting his child in danger."

She went from rosy to a scary shade of red.

"You have no right to tell me what my husband would have wanted, nor is it your place to instruct me in how to live my life. And how dare you accuse me of putting my child in danger." She pushed herself up and tugged her shirt down.

"There's nothing out here for you, Lexi. There could be a dangerous man on the loose and, even if there wasn't, there's wildlife and—"

"To me, *everything* is out here. But I don't owe you any explanations. It's my life and I'm not an idiot or some damsel in distress— Ah. Don't say it." She held up a finger to shut him up. "For the record. I did not faint. And you can add to that record what's *not* out here. There aren't school shootings or drugs being sold on the corner or on the playground. There aren't bullies, or peer pressures, or social media. And there aren't reckless drivers. Danger comes in many forms. I know what I'm doing. And if you ever…*ever*…accuse me of not putting my child first I'll take your—"

"Sorry. I'm sorry, that comment went too far."

"You bet it did." She stormed off toward the jeep muttering something he was probably better off not hearing.

He was getting too tied up in all this. Agreeing to come here had been a mistake. Staying here for even one night would be hell. Purgatory. A punishment he deserved, maybe, but he'd promised to protect her. Getting her out of here was the fastest way to make good on that promise. There was no way he could stick around longer than that.

She was too aggravating and stone-headed.

And she thinks you're good-looking.

Why did that matter? It didn't. It shouldn't. It was just that she'd never mentioned the scars on his face, his limp or his missing arm. She seemed to look right past all of it, and that got to him. Did he want her to notice? Did he need her to acknowledge what he'd been through and how he was suffering? He abhorred pity yet, at the same time, did he want it? Expect it?

He closed his eyes and exhaled. She wasn't like everyone else. Something about her unsettled him. Perplexed him. But he knew one thing with certainty—the more time he spent around Lexi Galen, the more chance he'd end up dragging her through hell with him.

CHAPTER FOUR

LEXI PARKED, got out and stormed over to the clinic tent without waiting on Chad to exit the jeep. Of all the aggravating people she'd ever met, Chad Corallis topped the list. She couldn't even begin to comprehend why Tony had called the man a friend. The two were nothing alike.

She understood Chad was suffering and recovering. But how could he accuse her of being a bad mother when she was so determined to be a good one...when she was making every decision with her baby in mind...when failing at motherhood was her greatest fear.

But did he have a point? Was she being selfish, like her parents had been? Putting their interests ahead of hers to the point of risking it all, ending up in jail and losing everything, including her? No. No, she couldn't be. She wasn't like them. She'd proved she could care for others throughout her years in foster care and even beyond that. She was proving it now by being here, wasn't she?

Lexi inhaled deeply then exhaled as she approached the clinic tent. She didn't want anyone reading the anguish on her face or asking her what was wrong.

"Coming in," she called out to avoid startling them inside. She opened the tent flap and slipped in. Their patient lay there, pale and limp, but her chest was rising and falling rhythmically.

"She started bleeding again, but it's under control now. She'll be okay, thanks to you all taking her in earlier," Hope said, nodding at Taj and Lexi. "She needs a lot of rest and monitoring, though."

Lexi almost missed Jacey's chin quivering. The second their eyes met, Jacey tightened her lips and lifted her chin slightly to keep it still.

"If you don't need anything else, I'll go boil up a supply of sterile water," Jacey said, leaving before she got an answer. Taj's brow furrowed as he watched her disappear, but he didn't say anything.

"Hope. Can we talk? Outside." Lexi said, not wanting to discuss things in the tent. There was no telling how much English

Akinyi actually understood. She hadn't spoken a word of it, but that didn't mean she couldn't understand it.

"Of course."

Hope disposed of her gloves and slathered her hands with disinfectant. They only had running water in the bathroom connected to their living space, so they were all in the habit of using disinfectant gel in the clinic until they could go to the main house and wash up properly. Hope stepped past Lexi into the sunshine.

Lexi gave Taj a silent head jerk to let him know she wanted him to come hear what was going on. He gave a brief nod to indicate he'd be right out.

"Where's Chad?" Hope asked, scanning the clinic camp.

"We just returned. I'm sure he's around somewhere."

"Is something wrong? You look concerned."

"I'm fine but I'm worried about the clinic. I'm not sure Chad is the best person to judge whether the place is safe."

Hope closed her eyes briefly then splayed her hands.

"Look, I know you're worried about the clinic, but Chad has a lot of training for situations like this."

"I appreciate that, but I don't think he's going to be impartial."

"Why not?" Hope asked.

Lexi glanced behind her as Taj exited the tent. It didn't feel right to complain about Chad to his mother, but this was Hope's clinic. She had a right to hear that Chad might have his own reasons for shutting it down. Taj narrowed his eyes at Lexi questioningly. Okay. She had to say something, but it was hard to phrase it without it sounding like she mattered to Chad. That would just be wrong.

"Just say whatever is bothering you, Lexi," Taj said.

She scratched the side of her belly then rested her hands on her lower back.

"I don't think he likes that I'm here. Actually, he pretty much flat-out said this isn't the place to be pregnant or raise a child. Which, by the way, is a bit chauvinistic and hypocritical considering his sister and cousins and aunt, from what you've told me, have all done it."

"I see." Hope smiled and her shoulders

relaxed. Taj chuckled. That was exactly the speculative tone Lexi had wanted to avoid.

"There's nothing to see. But the fact that he believes I shouldn't be working here because I'm pregnant makes him biased."

"Lexi, dear. I assure you, Chad is far from being a chauvinist. Yes, he can be blunt and harsh in how he puts things, but it comes from his time in the marines. Trust me, I've gotten used to the same manner from his father. They make up for it in spades, though, in how much they care. Sometimes too much. Chad's simply being protective."

"I don't need protecting." Man, that irked her. "I need to do my work without interference."

"Cut the man a break," Taj said. "I can understand being protective. I have to respect him for that."

"You're a good guy, Taj, but you never push me or Jacey around like that."

"Oh, I care and I worry. And I don't like leaving you two here by yourselves. However, I've quickly learned not to say any of those things to you," he confessed.

Lexi rolled her eyes.

"At least you know us. He doesn't."

"Don't forget he was Tony's best friend," Hope said softly.

Lexi swallowed back a lump in her throat. She had no rebuttal. Chad would always have a connection to her because of that. He'd also always be around the clinic because of his mother. They knew the same people. He'd be the closest thing to an uncle that her child would have, and if she wanted to honor Tony, she couldn't get in the way of that—if Chad ever wanted to see the baby. He didn't seem like the type to play with kids. But uncle or not, there were boundaries. No one could dictate where or how she should raise her child.

"Okay. I'll let it go for now. But keep what I said in mind when he announces that we all need to move to Nairobi. I'll pitch a tent."

"It's not going to reach that point," Taj said. He jerked his thumb at the exam tent behind him where the patient lay inside. "What would happen to her or others going through similar emergencies? I mean, I realize I have to head back to Nairobi every week, but Lexi here is as good as any doctor, and that patient needs her. Lexi and Jacey have always had things covered. The only issue is security, but there has to be a way to address that and still keep the clinic open."

"Exactly. We can't shut down, Hope. You know that. We've all been trained to use a rifle and tranquilizer gun in emergencies, and even if those weapons were meant for dangerous wildlife, Jacey has military training." She pushed her hair back with both hands. This was exasperating. *There has to be a better way.* "Why can't you just find someone to post out here as security until things settle down? I mean, they'll find this poacher sooner or later, right? Why not bring someone here instead of making us leave?"

"Trust me, I'm on your side. This clinic and what we do out here is my life. But I also don't want to put you in danger. Plus, I fund this place from what I make out of the main office. And money's tight right now. I'm not sure I can afford to hire security. If anyone would even come out here, especially on pay equivalent to volunteering.

"Taj, you know I couldn't afford you if you weren't doing this as externship experience. Besides, Ben simply asked Chad to look around to gauge if he felt things seemed safe enough. Chad's not shutting anything down. He and his father might be headstrong, but I'm the boss here," Hope said.

"He told me to start packing."

Hope covered her face then set her hands on her waist.

"I'll talk to him. Speaking of which, we should find him. Mothers worry a lot, too. I worry extra, given what he's been through." Hope gave Lexi's shoulder a reassuring squeeze and went to the bungalow.

"I don't feel good about this, Taj."

"Don't let this raise your blood pressure or you won't have a choice but to be put on bed rest."

"He's not in here," Hope said as she hurried outside. "Now I am worried."

"He's probably walking the perimeter or maybe he's with Jacey," Lexi suggested. She started for the back of the bungalow.

Taj went around the other side of the clinic and Hope double-checked the tent. Chad wasn't around.

"I took him up the hill but he didn't say anything about what he wanted to see next."

"I'll go out in the jeep to look for him. He can't be far," Taj noted.

"Thank you, Taj," Hope said.

"No problem. Don't worry. I'll have him back here in no time," Taj told them, heading for the clinic jeep parked under the shade of an acacia tree.

Lexi wasn't fooled by Taj's nonchalance. He was concerned. Despite her annoyance with Chad, she was, too. She'd noticed he walked stiffly and, of course, he had the loss of a limb to contend with.

But as a marine, he had survival skills, right? Surely he was all right out there…on foot…unarmed. Or maybe he was armed and she didn't know it. He was probably busy digging up reasons to prove the place wasn't safe enough, completely oblivious to the fact that he was making everyone anxious—in more ways than one.

She had to think positively. She'd survived hurdles in her life. This was just one more blip on her timeline. This was all going to pass. The clinic would be okay. He would be okay.

She put her palm against the small of her back and started for the clinic bungalow… just as a loud pop snapped through the air.

CHAD HEARD THE engine approaching long before the jeep appeared from around a mass of trees. He watched it cross the dry creek and come to a swerving stop in a cloud of dust. He knew the loud pop was just a blown tire, yet he still found himself backed up against a boulder, adrenaline rushing through his veins.

Get yourself together, man. A blown tire. A freaking blown tire. This isn't Afghanistan.

He swallowed hard, pushing off the boulder. Taj, the doctor he'd only met briefly, climbed out of the jeep and kicked the side.

"Got a spare?" Chad asked, limping toward the other man. The crusty red earth was mottled with small rocks and divots that jarred the muscles in his hip when he stepped on one.

Taj looked up and his shoulders sank with relief. "Always."

"Let me guess. They sent you looking for me."

"You guessed right," Taj said as he went around to the back of the jeep. He dug around and returned with a jack just as a call came through on his radio. He grabbed it as Chad reached the jeep.

"A blowout. We're fine. Over." Taj set the

radio down and picked up the jack again. "It sounded like a gunshot," he explained.

No kidding. That would have definitely given his mother a scare.

"Need help?" Chad asked, tucking his fingers into the pocket of his jeans.

Taj crouched down on one knee to set things up.

"There's a toolbox in the back. You can start unbolting the spare. And let me know if anything with four legs or no legs comes up behind me—I'm not fond of snakes."

Chad found himself glancing over his own shoulder with suspicion. He'd take on a four-legged predator any day over the legless slithery kind himself.

He rounded the back of the jeep, opened the toolbox latch with his left hand and paused.

It suddenly struck him that Taj hadn't hesitated to send Chad for the wrench. He hadn't questioned whether Chad could handle the task or not. He'd acted as if the two of them were no different than your average couple of guys working on a car in their garage over a couple of beers.

Chad held the wrench and adjusted it with

his thumb, then fitted it over the bolt that held the spare against the back of the old jeep. He held the tire in place with his knee as he worked the partly rusted bolt. He jammed his palm against the handle, trying to loosen it. It resisted.

He spotted Taj cranking the front left end of the car up with buttery ease.

Irritation pricked at him. Anger—at himself—burned the back of his neck. He hated being weak. Physical therapy had helped him build up some strength in his left arm but he still wasn't anywhere close to where he'd been prior to the bombing.

He pressed harder and the bolt loosened. He turned it as fast as he could and set it aside. Then he grabbed the tire with his left arm, nudged it off its hook with his knee, and let it bounce down to the ground. Two bounces and he had his hand on it to keep it from rolling away or falling to its side.

"Perfect. Thanks," Taj said, holding his hands out. Chad gave the tire a shove toward Taj, who leaned it near the front end then undid the bolts on the old one. He glanced over at Chad as he worked. "So, did you find what you were looking for out here?"

"I was only minutes ahead of you."

"I'm not fooled that easily. You marines have a reputation."

Chad grinned and scratched the stubble along his jaw.

"You're obviously pretty sharp yourself. Okay, yes. There's a cluster of three boulders over there I wanted to check out. There are enough natural formations—like these boulders and outcroppings, trees and shrubs—to give anyone an opportunity to hide or sneak up on the clinic. You guys have virtually nothing protecting you out here. I'm not sure what my dad was thinking, letting my mother set this place up to begin with."

The trumpeting of elephants vibrated the air and was met by the deeper rumble of lions. This place was as wild and off the grid as a clinic could get.

"You underestimate you mother."

"I know she's as wise and determined as they come, but my dad would give his life to keep her safe. *That*, I guarantee. She means everything to him."

"Like father, like son, I take it?"

"Meaning?"

He caught Taj's glance at the knot in his

right sleeve. Chad still had his life, but he hadn't known that would be the case when he'd thrown himself in the way of that bomb-rigged wagon. It had been instinct. Or had it been something more…love for his brothers, his country and his fellow man? At least Jaxon and the others had made it out okay. That's all that mattered.

He thought of his parents and the way they looked at each other, or the tender way they held hands. Ben's earlier threat regarding Chad never making his mother cry again echoed in his ears. What had made Chad so willing to sacrifice himself had been a completely different kind of love. He'd never experienced the kind his parents shared and likely never would. He didn't expect it. He didn't want it. That kind of love made a person vulnerable. It set a person up for failure, loss and emotional pain.

Lexi's soulful eyes flashed in his mind. She'd loved and lost on his account.

"This was about duty," Chad said, tipping his chin toward his knotted right sleeve.

Taj put what was left of the blown tire in the back of the jeep and slammed the door to get it to latch shut. Monkeys screeched in a nearby tree and rattled the branches as they scampered to a safe distance from the intruders. Even they knew to keep their guard up.

"I understand duty. Doctors and nurses have a duty, too—to save lives and heal. That goes for most of us here. But we feel compassion for people, too," Taj said. "I think Ben understands that, which is why he supports Hope in all she does out here. But he also trained her in self-defense and taught her how to shoot. You didn't expect less of him, did you? As for the rest of us, I believe that's why he sent you out here. Not to jump the gun—so to speak—and shut down the place, but to give your expertise on keeping it safe. He knows that you care about people or you wouldn't have given your right arm for them. There are always options."

"There's also a pregnant woman back there. Some risks aren't worth taking," Chad said. He realized he wasn't being half as honest as Taj when it came to his motivation, but he was justified, wasn't he?

"Would you abandon a fellow human in need? I guarantee she won't."

The answer was no, of course. He wouldn't. He picked up a small, rough stone and chucked it a good seven meters into a mass of elephant grass. Something snorted and scurried off, detectable only by the grass dancing in its wake.

"What about that other woman at the clinic? The one with long black hair."

"Jacey?" Something shifted in Taj's face and he shrugged. "She's as independent as they come. She can take care of herself."

Chad had never specialized in interrogations, but he knew enough about body language and expressions to note that he'd hit a nerve. Taj was holding back where Jacey was concerned.

"So, when you're not here, it doesn't bother you that Jacey and Lexi are alone?" Chad asked.

Taj grimaced and got behind the wheel.

"It does, but I'd never say that to them. Jacey would have my neck. Tough as nails and doesn't want anyone looking out for her. She came out to Kenya to join Ben's program for vets when she couldn't find employment after her service was done. Why do you think he got her to work out here? Besides, and keep this to yourself, I've had a word with some of the Masai around here to keep an eye on the clinic, too. I treat their children and they keep an eye out."

Interesting. Chad liked the guy more every minute.

"Let's go before the women think we've been eaten by lions." He started the ignition and waited for Chad to climb in.

"I'd like to go check out those rocks first. That smaller kopje with the three main boulders. There's something about them I can't shrug off."

"Fine. I'll drive you over."

Chad settled in and kept his eyes on the granite outcropping and surrounding area.

"It's good that you've enlisted the help of the Masai, but the villagers may have their own agenda. My sister is a human rights lawyer, and she lives with her husband, a veterinarian, just west of here," Chad said over the engine noise. "She had a case where a Masai tribe was colluding with the enemy. Poachers. A drought like this one had destroyed crops and drove them to help the enemy in exchange for money. How do you know one of the village *enkang*s around here isn't harboring this fugitive and just not telling you?"

"I know these people. I highly doubt that.

Sure, it happens, but not with these particular families," Taj said, driving through brush in the direction Chad had indicated.

Chad didn't trust so easily. He'd encountered too many terrorists who'd used the innocent as shields. And poachers were a type of terrorist. Criminals.

They neared the kopje and Taj parked the jeep to one side. This grouping wasn't like the flatter granite outcroppings in the area. It was large enough to form narrow, cave-like cervices between each formation.

He recalled learning, when he was still in school in Nairobi, about the Serengeti ecosystem and how the kopjes were like mini ecosystems, teeming with life. They stood out like small, stony hills, complete with vegetation and micro habitats. Whether that also included a hideout for a human remained to be seen.

Chad eased onto his feet, his hip muscle catching briefly. All the standing and walking on uneven ground he'd done today had been taxing on his weak muscles.

He reached into his pocket and pulled out his switchblade. No gun, but this was better than nothing if someone was biding their time here. The man would have heard them approach, but if he was a practiced poacher, he would know better than to jump out and run with no cover and a speeding vehicle on his tail. No, he'd wait, still as prey, hoping to go undetected. Predator and prey. Funny how quickly the table could be turned.

Chad's veins thrummed with energy…a drive…control he hadn't experienced since his last mission.

He almost felt whole.

"Do you plan to fill me in?" Taj kept his voice low and scowled at the blade.

"Just following a hunch. Stay in the jeep."

Taj stepped around the jeep. Instead of getting in, he unlocked a metal chest in the back, pulled out a rifle and had it loaded fast enough to be impressive—for a civilian.

"I don't take orders," Taj said.

A silent agreement passed between them. Chad walked on with Taj only steps away. The dusty, red earth crunched beneath his boots as he made his way around the right side of the rocks, jerking his head to signal Taj to go around left.

There were no footprints other than the paw prints of an animal, most likely a hyena.

No broken branches. Not a sound but their own steps and the protests of wildlife scurrying away. A pair of monkeys hissed and screeched at the intruders then climbed higher into the canopy of a young, solitary acacia growing on the mound.

He and Taj's paths crossed on the other side of the tree and Chad signaled for Taj to wait. They were at the opening between the boulders. Something caught the sunlight like a mirror near his boot. A good-size piece of pyrite jetted out from the earth. Fool's gold.

Who was the fool here? Had he brought them on a wild-goose chase? Next thing he knew, he'd be accused of paranoia or PTSD. But his gut still twisted and screamed that someone had been here.

He jerked his head at the opening. He hardened his resolve and entered, blade ready and Taj covering his back with the rifle.

The place was empty but for the wasted bones of a rodent and the shed skin of a snake. Taj lowered his rifle.

"Were you expecting to find the missing poacher that easily? If this is where he's been hiding, KWS or one of the locals would have found him or seen signs of him. He couldn't have stayed here for long. There's no fresh water. Not even dirty water. He'd be lying here dead with vultures circling overhead," Taj said.

Chad pocketed his knife and sat on his heels, chin down.

"Maybe so."

He should have known he wasn't cut out for this anymore. He gripped the rock to keep his balance as he stood. He stopped halfway up. There, along the crevice wall, was a dark red smear.

"Take a look," he said, moving back so that Taj could peer in. "Dried blood," Chad said, as if it needed explaining.

"That doesn't mean it's human. This isn't the city, Chad," Taj said, waving his hand at their surroundings. "Any large animal like a wild dog or lion could have dragged its kill here. And, no, before you ask, I don't have a way of sampling a stain right now, especially without ample evidence. Those bones tell me this was likely nothing more than a predator's dining spot."

"You don't know that for sure."

"Nor do you. And even if the blood was from a human, he's long gone from here by now. We should get back," Taj said, leaving the small cave.

Chad looked around once more then followed him out. Something caught the sunlight a couple of meters to his right, just outside the opening near the base of a clump of wild grass. He went over for a closer look.

A shard of glass. He picked it up.

"The broken end of a bottle. What's that doing out here? You want to tell me this isn't a sign someone was here?"

Taj frowned.

"I'll give you that. It's possible. But it's also possible that some curious monkeys stole a drink from one of the homesteads and thought it would make a good toy. Or perhaps one of the Masai kids got their hands on a soda and didn't want their parents knowing they'd squandered money on sugar water. I want the clinic as safe as you do, Chad, but this simply isn't proof of anything. It's mere conjecture. You can't let your imagination create something from a stain and piece of glass when there are infinite other possible explanations."

Chad tightened his lips. His head pounded and the tension in his neck crept down his shoulders.

"Okay then. Let's head back to camp," he said. He wasn't getting into an argument with Taj. He'd never ignored his instincts before. They'd always led him to something. He couldn't say that they'd always kept him safe. Had that been the case, he wouldn't be a wounded warrior.

He got in the jeep and waited for Taj to lock up his weapon.

Neither said much on the road. For someone who'd never cared what anyone thought of him—save for his father—Chad couldn't help but wonder what was running through Taj's mind at the moment. Relief that Chad had no concrete justification to shut the clinic down? Pity after witnessing a medaled veteran fail at something he'd once excelled at?

There was a time when Chad wouldn't have stopped hunting down the terrorists. He and Aries would have stayed on their trail until the mission was complete. Not anymore. This whole setup—having Chad scope the area—was a load of—

"May I ask, when was the last time you shot a weapon? Automatic or even a pistol?" Taj asked.

"Not since the explosion. I won't ever be a sharpshooter, if that's what you're asking."

They hit a rut in the road that made Chad wonder if there were any shock absorbers left on the jeep.

"If you're only going to be armed with a knife, perhaps you shouldn't go off alone. We have a policy about that, for safety."

"I can take care of myself just fine. At the same time, I have no problem with anyone tagging along, so long as they don't get in my way." He paused. "I appreciate you covering me back there."

It had made him feel like part of a unit again. Like old times, everyone with a common goal: neutralize the enemy. Neutralize evil.

His pulse kicked up a notch. Maybe he still had it in him.

It's what you do, man. You get out there and snuff out the bad guys.

Yeah, his mind knew that. He craved it. But his body wasn't the same anymore.

Improvise, adapt and overcome. He closed his eyes and let the unofficial motto he'd learned as a marine echo in his head. He was part of an elite group. A smaller, less funded, powerful group, but still unsurpassed. He was a marine and always would be. *Do more with less.* The words his fellow marines had lived by charged him.

Suddenly, Tony's voice filled his head. *Make sure she's okay.*

He pressed his finger and thumb pads against his eyes then opened them. That was the only mission he needed to concentrate on here. To make sure Lexi was safe. The easiest way to do that, he reminded himself, was to get her to return to Nairobi with him.

"No problem," Taj said, breaking his train of thought. "But next time give me some warning. Special ops is not exactly my line of work."

Chad gave him a lopsided grin.

"Could have fooled me."

The clinic came into view and Taj slowed the vehicle, pulling up under the acacia that flanked the central clearing. He cut the engine and the discordant symphony of predator and prey filled the air again. Jacey came rushing out from behind the bungalow. She pressed a hand to her chest, but quickly tucked her hands in her pockets and trudged over to Taj.

"What took you so long? I— Hope has been worried. It doesn't take that long to change a tire." She stopped her tirade only for a second to call out to Hope, who was apparently with the patient in the clinic tent, to let her know they'd returned.

Lexi appeared in the bungalow's doorway and stood there with a fiery look in her eyes.

Chad walked over, much too conscious about minimizing his limp, and climbed the three steps onto the narrow porch.

"So, did you think he shot me out there to keep me silent? To keep this place open?" Chad taunted.

Lexi tightened her lips. "You're really not funny. You do realize that, don't you?"

"Guess not. So, tell me, why are you standing there glaring at me? Planning to ask me something? Argue about my potential findings? Or maybe I scared you."

"Scared me? Why would you think that?"

"You know, the blown tire. It can sound like a gunshot. It worried you, didn't it? You thought maybe I'd gone nuts and Taj got wounded or killed. Or maybe…you were worried about *me*."

He wasn't flirting. Was he? Nah. He was

trying to irritate her. It helped to keep his guard up. He was also avoiding having to explain where they'd gone on his false hunch.

Her cheeks flushed to a shade he'd only ever seen at sunset on a Serengeti campout when he was a kid. Disconcertingly beautiful.

"I was *not* worried about you," she said, turning and disappearing through the doorway.

But she had been. He could tell. Her reaction felt strange. A bit scary. He didn't want anyone caring or worrying about him, especially not Tony's widow. Especially not when he had to keep tamping down those same feelings for her.

He'd come out here because he'd had a duty to his friend, but meeting her had somehow made it more personal. He raked his hair back. Personal? What was he thinking? He wasn't any more concerned for Lexi Galen than he'd be for any pregnant woman living in this situation. Getting her back to Nairobi was the right thing to do. Sure, she was attractive and he felt an immediate draw to her, but it was only because they'd both known and cared about Tony. They were connected through him. A shared history, in a sense. That's all it was.

At least that's what he needed to keep telling himself. Because if there was ever a rule he wouldn't break, it was that a marine never betrayed a fellow marine…or a best friend.

CHAPTER FIVE

THEY HAD ALMOST caught him this time. The cut on his arm stung from where the acacia thorn had ripped his skin. He pressed the crushed leaves of the yellow flowering plant against it as he caught his breath. The makeshift bandage would slow the bleed and help the wound heal, but he'd probably have to sew it up soon.

He needed to think. There had to be a way to get the medical supplies he needed. The only place they didn't lock up was that tent, but they were keeping a patient in there under close watch. Too many people went in and out of the tent for him to slip in unnoticed. And there was a new man around he had not seen before. He would have remembered him. He bore the scars of a fighter. A survivor...like him. It was clear from his movements and his eyes that this one could feel his presence. This one wasn't like the others at the medicine camp.

He was a hunter, not a healer.
And he was going to be in the way.

LEXI STEPPED OUT into the moonlight and settled down on the wooden bench outside the door. She couldn't sleep. Too many bizarre dreams, none of which she could recall upon wakening. Pregnancy was beginning to take its toll on her. This inability to sleep through the night, whether from dreams or discomfort, had to be nature's way of training her to wake up every few hours for a crying baby.

She leaned her head back and took in the night air. Was she going to be able to do this by herself? She could, right? She had it in her. The baby rolled gently and settled in a new position.

A lantern light flickered in the patient tent then went out again. Hope had insisted that she keep watch over Akinyi so others could rest. They didn't typically have overnight patients, so it usually wasn't necessary to have someone man the tent. But nothing seemed usual since Chad had arrived.

Dinner had been mundane. Everyone seemed cautious about topics of conversation, trying to keep from offending or starting an argument. No one spoke of politics or poachers or injuries. Jacey thought she'd heard thunder in the distance, but apparently even the weather was a divisive topic because everyone had disagreed with her. Judging from how bright the moon was right now, they still had a while before the drought broke. But sooner or later the clouds would roll in and the rainy season would begin. Or so she'd been told.

Lexi drew a thin shawl over her shoulders and hugged it over her belly. Thoughts of Chad were eating away at her. She tried to imagine what he might have been like prior to the accident. A little less sarcastic and ornery perhaps? Or less cocky?

She couldn't believe he'd come right out and accused her of worrying about him. And he'd put her on the spot. She *had* been worried, and she was even more mad that he'd *made* her worry. Being protective was simply something that came with being a mother-to-be. It was instinctual. Blame it on the hormones. She'd witnessed how much more protective and defensive animals, from wild geese to rhinos, got when it came to their young.

So, yes, she had been worried, but not because she was in any way attracted to him. They'd only just met, for crying out loud. She blamed her curiosity about him on his connection to her husband and Hope. She had worried because she was pregnant and because she was as a nurse. She worried because of all he'd been through.

Had he been diagnosed with post-traumatic stress? Chances were good that he suffered from some level of it, given the nature of his injury.

She had heard a sharp sound crack through the savannah air before. Usually it was a blown tire, a common occurrence with the terrain, or an actual gunshot—the sickening evidence of an illegal hunter after a trophy. But this time, knowing that Chad had just stalked off on his own, her mind had gone in crazy directions. He was right. For a second, she had wondered if Taj was the one shot, but that didn't seem as likely as Chad being the one injured. What if he'd shot himself? What if he was more depressed over his injury than anyone had assumed and he'd come out here to end his suffering?

Her gut rose, fell and cramped up against her lungs. The emotions that had wreaked havoc on her when she'd heard the news of Tony's death threatened to flood through her again. Loss. Death.

Could Tony see all that had happened since his death? Did he know what his friend was going through? Did he know Lexi was pregnant? Had he somehow brought them together so that Lexi could help his friend?

Help me understand what's happening, Tony. Give me a sign.

A shadow stretched out from the clinic tent. The crunch of footsteps joined the rhythmic song of crickets calling to their destined mates. She jolted and almost called out a warning to wake everyone, but Chad, with his unmistakable, strong jawline and broad shoulders, stepped out of the shadows. His eyes met hers. How long had he been watching her?

She released a breath but her pulse still skittered. His mouth settled in a firm line and she wasn't quite sure if he was offering a faint smile or if he was disappointed that he wasn't alone. That he'd been caught doing something noble like guarding the place.

She knew he'd stayed out here because his mother and a patient were in that tent. Maybe he wasn't a healer like Tony had been…or like her…and perhaps he was even struggling to heal himself, but Hope was right. He was clearly a protector. He had his mom's back. He had them all covered.

Lexi licked her lips and looked down at her hands. As rough as he was on the surface, Chad Corallis was a man of honor.

Honor, trust, caring. All things Tony had valued and embodied. All things she valued, too. That had to be why she couldn't get Chad out of her mind.

You're attracted to him. Admit it.

No. Absolutely not. The sting of guilt spread through her chest like the venom of a wasp. *He's the enemy. He wants to shut the place down and make you leave. Remember that.*

She could hear his footsteps getting closer.

But you just admitted he was a man of honor...a protector. What if he guarded the place every night?

She took a deep breath and looked over at him again. Chad as their guard? That wouldn't work. Being around him all day, every day? She couldn't handle it. They'd either both be miserable or…she'd keep feeling this…this…she didn't know what it was but she didn't like it. It made her feel out of control, ungrounded.

It's okay to be attracted to him. You're human. Besides, nothing would happen between you two. A guy like him wouldn't find you attractive.

What was it the old married ER receptionist at the hospital she'd worked in used to say whenever the hunky EMTs wheeled a patient in? "Look all you want as long as looking is all you do." The older woman used to wink at them, too. Lexi did not wink. Ever.

Chad reached the bench but studied the stars for a moment before speaking.

Goose bumps trailed down her arms and she hugged her hands to her sides.

Forgive me, Tony.

"Mind if I sit?"

She shrugged and scooted over on the bench. He settled next to her, making an effort to keep at least several inches between them.

"Have you slept at all?" she asked.

"Have you?" He kept his voice as hushed as hers. It was deep and it hummed with warmth.

"Answering a question with a question?" She raised a brow at him.

He grinned and tapped a finger against his jeans. "I might have gotten two hours of light sleep. Good enough," he said.

"That's *so* not good enough, but I can't judge you, seeing that I'm up, too. I don't think I've slept more than three hours straight in the past month, not without at least a bathroom break." She cringed inside. Too much information.

"I don't have as good an excuse as a baby."

"What's your excuse then?" She almost asked if pain kept him awake, but she stopped herself. Judging from how he'd acted earlier that day, he threw walls up pretty readily. And she kind of wanted him to sit for a few minutes. Maybe she was lonelier than she thought.

He paused and looked up at the stars. Soft grunts and wildlife chatter filled the night like restaurant background music on an awkward blind date. She shifted, about to get up, make her excuses and get back to bed, but she couldn't seem to draw herself away from him.

"You saw me walking the grounds. You

can guess why. I don't like the idea of my mother—anyone—alone in a tent with an incapacitated patient. Humans aren't the only ones who could invade the camp. I know my mother told me overnight care isn't typical, but still, it's not okay."

The expected answer and one that, if he relayed it to Ben, would only make both men more paranoid about the safety of the clinic.

"You're right. Which is why we don't usually use the tent at night. Your mom is saving a life, though. Sometimes we have to weigh the risks." She started to push herself up again.

"My sleep was messed up because of you, too. You were in my dream," he said.

Oh, heaven. She looked over at him, but there was nothing flirtatious about the expression on his face. He frowned and worked his jaw.

"Nightmare?" she hedged.

"You were standing with Tony. Strange, since I've never seen you two together. Meeting you probably brought him to the front of my mind. Not that I don't think about him often. I do. It's just… I don't know. I should have said this earlier, but I'll say it now. You were his world. I mean, I'm sure you know that, and he told you, but it's different when a guy says that to another guy when he doesn't even have to. Shows how true his feelings are. How much he cares. He did. You were it for him. I thought you should hear how he spoke of you the few times we had a chance to talk."

Lexi's eyes stung and she blinked to try to stop the tears. She didn't want to make Chad uncomfortable but hearing his words ripped open a wound she'd carefully stitched. She quickly wiped her cheeks dry and cleared her throat.

"Thank you for telling me. You were important to him, too. He cherished your friendship above all others. And I'm not just saying that. He mentioned it to me more than once. He wanted you to be his best man. It wasn't your fault, but he hated that you couldn't be there. In my mind, I couldn't quite understand how the guy Tony described as always being there for him his entire life, like a brother, was never around during the time that I was in Tony's life. No introductions. Not there for our vows. Not there for his funeral."

She wasn't being fair. She wished she could take back the words, but it had been eating at her ever since her marriage. At the time, she'd blamed the "friend" who was never there for her own apprehension and pre-wedding jitters. The anxiety that came from questioning her life and how no one had ever made her a priority. How all the people in her life had put themselves first. Everyone always seemed to have a bigger dream or goal to chase. She was never enough.

People had a tendency to disappear from her life, including Tony. The one person she'd finally trusted to always be there for her. Yes, he hadn't intended to desert her, but the fact that he had only proved that she was simply meant to be alone. At least she was good at it. She'd had plenty of practice. She was comfortable with it.

Chad rubbed his palm against his jeans.

"I visited his grave before I returned to Africa. I made sure of it. In fact, I had to insist on going because no one thought I was strong enough to handle it. I reacted...badly... when I found out Tony had been killed. Lexi, I had been in a coma and then recovery. I didn't learn about Tony's death until after I woke up several weeks later."

She placed her hand on his.

"I know. I shouldn't have said it that way. I didn't mean for it to sound like I was blaming you."

He turned his palm and held her hand firmly.

"I'm sorry I missed the wedding. I'm sorry he'll miss the birth of his child and all the milestones ahead. I'm sorry for everything. More than you'll ever know. But I'm here now because he asked me to be. I have to make sure you'll be okay. I owe him that."

"Did he somehow sense he'd never return? Were things getting bad over there? Did he suffer?" Her voice cracked and she covered her mouth.

"All service men and women are well aware that there's risk involved."

"Then why? I mean, I know there are reasons people join the military. And I know we wouldn't have our freedom without those men and women...people like you, Ben, Jacey and Tony. But why did he have to choose that route? What if he'd never joined? Why did you want to serve?"

He let go of her hand and rubbed the back of his neck.

"I joined because I was sick and tired of bad things happening in the world. My father was in the military when I was very young, but I understood he wasn't around because he was making sure life was safe for me and our family. Then, when I was four, I lost my mother and he ended up staying home to be with my siblings and me. I remember wondering if he wasn't out on a mission, keeping us safe, then who was? And what if they stayed home, too? Would more bad things happen, like my mother getting killed by a drunk driver? I couldn't separate the different evils at the time. Bad was bad, all around."

She nodded, her heart aching for the grief he must have suffered at such a young age.

"But as I got older, I saw more deaths, more bullying, more news on TV. And after you witness firsthand what bad people like terrorists or dictators do in real time, you can't turn your back on any of it."

"I'm sorry about your mom."

"Thank you. It was long ago, and Hope's been the best mother anyone could have. Our family is strong because of her."

Family. Strength.

"Hope is amazing. She makes life look easy—motherhood, work...all of it."

"I'm sure you'll be a great mother, too. Tony believed in you enough to marry you. I think that says it all. That guy always did want kids. He'd be happy right now. He *was* happy. Know that."

A sob did escape that time. She tried to get up but her muscles suddenly felt weak and tired. She swallowed hard against the lump forming in her throat. She missed Tony. She needed him desperately. She had to get inside before her tears broke loose.

Chad stood. He probably wanted to escape her shaky emotional state, too. She couldn't blame him.

She put her hand on the arm of the bench for leverage but Chad reached out and took it in his. His fingers were warm and callused around hers. He helped pull her up and immediately let go.

"Thank you," she said, but it came out as a gasp then a sob. She covered her face and was about to apologize, but he put his arm around her and held her to his chest.

"I'm sorry. I didn't mean to upset you. He

meant a lot to me, too." His chest rose and fell with each gravelly word. He didn't let go until a hiccup escaped her and she placed a hand against his chest to regain control and nudge some distance between them. He released her and took a step back.

"Don't be sorry," she said. "It happens. The tears, I mean. I cry more easily now—hormones—but the memories do that to me, too. I still cherish them and always will."

"Did he know?" He glanced at her belly. She shook her head and something shifted in his face.

"I'm going to go back to bed. Try to get some sleep, Chad."

He didn't nod or move. He just stood there as she closed the door behind her. She doubted he'd get any sleep.

She knew she wouldn't.

CHAD DOWNED ANOTHER cup of coffee, set the mug on the ground next to him and dug his spoon into the bowl of *ugali* Lexi offered him. She stirred the pot and spooned some out for the others, as well. The traditional corn grits tasted like home to Chad.

"This stuff always reminds me of when

we first moved to Kenya when I was a child, back when it took a lot to coax me to try new foods," Chad said.

Hope laughed as she joined the group with her bowl. They all sat on the front porch as the rising sun backlit the trees.

"You should have seen the look on his face the first time he tried *ugali*," Hope said. "He thought we'd forgotten the sugar. And let me tell you, this little boy did not need sugar in his system."

He'd expected the porridge-like dish to taste similar to the instant packs of sweetened oatmeal he'd eaten in the States. Boy had he been wrong. But looking back, he could totally understand why his parents had been eager to get him to eat less sugary foods.

"No kids need sugar. You are what you eat. That's how I plan to be able to handle at least six kids. Any sugar will be doled out wisely. It'll give me bribery power when needed. I'll be in control," Taj said.

"Sounds dictatorial," Jacey said. "Is that why some people have so many kids? To create their own population to control? Minions?"

"It's not a dictatorship. It's parenthood.

Rules for the greater good." Taj shook his head at her.

"Ah. Socialist then." Jacey smirked.

"Goodness, you're both going to scare me off having kids and it's a little late for that," Lexi said. "I agree with Taj. Minimal sugar. But I won't be a dictator. I want this child to *like* me."

"My children will like me," Taj insisted. "Besides, there will be a balance of power because I'll have such a big family. Only one of me against all of them."

"Or you could not have any kids and lead an autonomous, uncomplicated life," Jacey said.

"Complications make life interesting," Taj said.

Chad didn't comment on that and he noticed Lexi didn't, either. They'd both suffered "complications" and neither would call what they were going through "interesting."

"I say, before you populate this place any further, let's see if we can handle Lexi's little one." Jacey got up at the sound of the satellite phone ringing. She hurried inside to where she'd left it.

Chad scraped the last bite out of his bowl

then reached for a hard-boiled egg. He wasn't sure if someone had peeled all the eggs in the bowl because of him, or if they always did it that way. He refrained from asking and took a bite out of the "natural protein bar," as his physical therapist had once called it. She'd been encouraging him to eat right and rebuild muscle. He'd been too stubborn to listen most of the time. Just like he hadn't listened to Lexi about getting some sleep last night.

Staying up and watching the place had made him feel like he was back on duty in the field at a marine post. The lack of sleep felt oddly natural. He'd been fired up, though a part of him wondered if it had been the company that had kept his mind running at full speed.

He took another bite of the egg and avoided looking over at Lexi. He tried to forget how comforted he had felt while trying to console her.

"Mac just called in," Jacey said, returning. "He said that he'll be by in the early afternoon and wanted to know who all was heading back."

Time for the elephant dung to hit the fan.

Chad brushed his fingertips against his jeans and picked up his mug for a swig of coffee.

"What does that mean?" Lexi stopped rolling her piece of cheese in a round of *chapati* and shot Chad a look. He simply grabbed a piece of the flatbread and took a bite.

Jacey grabbed a fresh fig and started peeling it.

"Don't look at me. I assumed he only had room for Dr. H, Chad and Taj, but Mac seemed to be under the impression that he might have to make two trips. Almost sounded like an evacuation plan," Jacey said. She glared over her shoulder at Chad and he glanced into his empty bowl.

Nah. She wouldn't poison the traitor. Would she?

"Did you radio your father already? Before we could talk?" Hope gave Chad a stern look. Funny how that could also make him feel at home. He really had been a handful as a kid. But at least he'd learned to direct all that energy constructively, for a while at least. Up until his honorable discharge. He popped the last bite of egg into his mouth.

"Nope."

His mother's shoulders—and Lexi's—relaxed visibly.

"*He* radioed *me* when you went to wash up," Chad added. Everyone stopped eating. His mom had left him outside the patient tent so she could go use the restroom and wash her face an hour ago. She'd missed hearing the call.

"And you didn't tell me? What did you go and do, Chad?" Hope set her plate down and tightened the bright scarf she had tied around her head.

"Nothing more than what he asked me to do. He asked if I thought leaving a couple of women here alone was safe in light of recent events, and I answered him. Honestly, I might add."

They all stared at him. Chad raised his brow. As if his answer to Ben wasn't obvious enough. Did he have to spell it out?

"You can't do this," Lexi said. "You know we have a patient. I thought you were…" She didn't finish.

He could guess what she was going to say. That he'd seemed like a nice person last night. A guy with a heart. Not a threat.

He dug the heel of his boot into the dirt and finished off his coffee.

He cared more than she knew. He was doing this for all of them, especially for her and Tony and their unborn kid. The blood on the boulder yesterday and the broken glass bottle…not being able to prove they were left by a human also meant there wasn't proof that they weren't.

"I hear your patient will be allowed to go home today, so that's a non-issue," he said.

Lexi put a hand to her forehead and began pacing.

"I'm *not* leaving. We have twenty children to vaccinate tomorrow. The supplies are already here."

"She's right," Hope added. "I want everyone safe, too, of course, but those children's lives may depend on those vaccinations. There are many kinds of *safe*, Chad. I'm used to your father going overboard. I honestly didn't think it would come to this."

"Dad said KWS sent out word this morning that there has been another poaching incident only fifteen kilometers south of here. One dead elephant, ivory gone. Busara took in the orphaned elephant calf they found hiding nearby. They have reason to believe it's the same group of poachers. And they think this group has an insider. Someone's helping them. Someone from this area. You want to argue that you're safe now?"

"I have to admit, I don't like the sound of that," Taj said. "I'd stay longer to keep an eye out, but I'm expected for hospital rounds later today. Maybe we don't have a choice. This clinic has always been a safe haven, but my gut is saying we should listen to Chad," Taj said, scratching his jaw.

"Why can't you all trust me to handle things?" Jacey yelled. "It's really ticking me off. Just because I'm a woman, I can't keep the place secure?" Jacey shoved the wooden cooking spoon into the pot and didn't bother with the bowl she'd filled for herself.

"Maybe because you're army." Chad smirked. He couldn't resist the gibe. Marines—particularly Special Forces—had an untouchable reputation. Well, there were also those Navy SEALs, but he was backing his bros on this.

"Don't you give me that marines-are-better-than-everyone-else crap." Jacey stalked over to him. Was she really going to challenge him on that?

"Hey, Jace." Taj put his hands on her arms and urged her to sit on a tree-stump stool. "I know you're capable. It's not about your sex. It's just that you're already multitasking around here. There's only one of you, and you only have two eyes. You can't help with patients and keep watch. Your military background would be enough under normal circumstances. But we haven't dealt with a situation as dangerous as this before."

"My background and experience are more than just enough. The only thing I don't have is a gun on me at all times, but that can be arranged. Even without it, I'm probably more fit than you are, judging by the fact that you have yet to beat me at arm wrestling."

Taj raised his palms.

"You can wrestle me anytime, but—" Taj froze when he noticed the ruby flush on Jacey's neck and the smiles on Hope and Lexi's faces. A chuckle escaped Chad. Was there something going on between those two? Taj scrubbed his hand across the stubble on his jawline. "That's not what I meant. You can *arm* wrestle me all you want, but that's not the same as handling an armed intruder."

"Exactly right," Chad cut in. "You know full well that in any kind of military division or even law enforcement, you always have a partner. You always have your back covered. The two of you alone is not enough. If you're busy vaccinating or whatever you do out here, no one's got your backs," Chad said. He put his mug in his bowl, picked the stack up and stood, then turned to Hope. "Call Ben yourself if you'd like."

Hope frowned and looked off in the distance. She rubbed her hand the way she always did when her mind was churning.

"We just need someone who can stay here and provide security until these criminals are caught. I'll talk to him. He said he'd try to find someone. If not, we'll have to send word out that the clinic will be closing until further notice," Hope said.

"He can't spare any of his guys. His words," Chad said. He started for the kitchen area.

"*You* could stay."

Chad turned slowly at the firm tone of Lexi's voice. Had she lost her mind?

"I don't think so."

"Why not?"

"Because, if you haven't noticed, I'm a little incapacitated right now."

"Your injuries haven't stopped you from making a decision about this place. They didn't keep you from going off on your own yesterday," she said.

"I agree with her on this one, Chad. You were functioning quite well yesterday," Taj said.

Lexi pressed her lips together and glanced at Hope. His mom crossed her arms and walked over to him.

"Technically, you've refused PT appointments, so although I still want you to get on a schedule so you can get more used to using your left hand, it would take at least a couple of weeks to get you in. And that's if you stop resisting. So, in the interim, your schedule is free. I think it's a great idea. It would at least buy us a little time," Hope said.

His back prickled. The first twinge of phantom pain threatened to take hold. He raked his hair back. He hadn't had any full-blown phantom pain attacks since he'd gotten here, which was unusual given how frequently he'd had them back in Nairobi. He'd managed to get the last one that almost hit yesterday quickly under control. Why was he having one now? He dug his fingers into his left palm. How could his mother put him on the spot like this?

You loved following your hunch yesterday and heading out on a mission to that boulder, even if all you found was blood. You can't quit. Shut down the place and you'll lose the chance to go after this poacher yourself. You know you're dying to.

He gritted his teeth.

"Not interested. Security isn't my thing. I've kinda been thinking of going into modeling or maybe even neurosurgery."

"Don't, Chad." Lexi stomped over to him and stood as in-his-face as her belly would let her. "Don't start with the bad jokes. We're being serious. If you're not interested or capable, then why were you out here last night? *All* night." She looked back at everyone. "You heard right. He stayed up most of the night guarding the grounds because Hope and our patient were in the tent."

"And you helped me with that tire, so I'm not buying into your 'I'm not capable' argument. Even injured, you're probably more capable and sharper than most people on their good days," Taj added.

"I'm not doing it."

"Do it for Tony," Lexi said softly.

Now that was low. He curled his lip and sucked in a breath.

"I *am* doing this for Tony. I promised I'd make sure his wife was safe if anything ever happened to him, and that's exactly what I'm going to do. Safe means out of here."

Her mouth opened but no retort came.

No one spoke.

He didn't appreciate feeling like a wild animal backed into a corner. He hated the hurt smearing Lexi's face and stinging her eyes. How was he supposed to look out for her without hurting her?

Lexi cleared her throat.

"Give me a week, Chad. By then, maybe a replacement can be found or maybe the situation will be under control. A week. That's not asking much. Please, Chad. Living out here and serving the Masai villages was Tony's dream. Our dream. Everything he did was with the goal of giving back. I want to raise his child out here, just like we'd planned. I want to help all those other children and people, just like your mother does. Just as Tony had planned to do. I need to. I've already lost him. Don't take this away from me, too."

She might as well have punched him in the gut with everything she had, then beat him to the ground. Maybe he'd said too much last night.

He looked away and held his breath, willing the hammering pain in his right shoulder to ease. All eyes were on him. He couldn't let them see his pain. He didn't want to be perceived as weak. But then why did he joke about himself? Why did he lay his limitations out on the table? To control everyone's thoughts and opinions of him? To put words in their mouths before they could come up with their own? He swallowed hard and stared her down. Somehow, focusing on every fleck of gold in her brown eyes lessened the pain. Something touched his hand.

"Here," Hope said, handing him a canteen of potable water. He took it but walked off before taking a long drink.

Don't take this away from me, too.

He squeezed his eyes shut. He had nothing to give himself, let alone others. How was he supposed to be worth anything here? A tiny, infinitesimal part of him was drawn to the idea of staying. Something about the place—the desiccated land, the wilderness and lurking danger…*her*—made him feel like he'd never been injured. Like he could travel back in time. Like he could get out there and fight the bad guys again. He could fight evil again…evil that took lives.

Don't let Tony down. You already did that once. Consider this a way to avenge his death and a way to make amends for not being there for him.

God, he wished he could change things, make things right…so that Tony would be standing here alive, with his wife. And Chad would still be at the front lines instead.

Lexi wanted a week. A week away from his parents would keep them from prodding him about his health. A week was nothing compared to the months he'd spent at desolate, cold outposts. A week might be enough to ease his conscience. He looked back at Lexi then at the others.

"Seven days. Not one day more."

CHAPTER SIX

TWO DAYS LATER, Lexi wiped her face after splashing it with cool water and tried changing her sweaty shirt, only to find the next one didn't fit. That meant the only two left that fit needed to be laundered. She'd been wearing the other earlier, when she cleaned up the exam tent after discharging their miscarriage patient, who'd stabilized sooner than expected.

She was getting frustrated and impatient, with her body and with the clinic situation. Taj and Hope were back in Nairobi today, and Ben had said they hadn't been able to hire a more permanent guard, yet.

Chad stalking the clinic's outskirts was both a relief and a curse. On the one hand, his being there bought them time—assuming Hope and Ben were doing everything possible to find a replacement—but on the other hand, he, too, seemed frustrated by how difficult the area was to secure.

The clinic wasn't a house or business in the suburbs or city where all that was required was a call to a company to hook up an alarm system or remote-control gates. And it wasn't just about cost. They couldn't cut down shrubs or trees or, in good conscience, obstruct the natural habitat.

When they'd erected the clinic structures, they hadn't disturbed so much as a weed. Even stringing tin cans or booby traps like in old children's adventure stories wasn't practical. The vervet monkeys would turn it all into a noisy playground or worse, some animal would get tangled or caught in their web. They were here to help, not endanger. With children amongst patients coming through, they had to be conscious of that. And they couldn't afford the latest security technology. Plus, any power they had came from an old, sometimes unreliable, generator.

But his frustrations weren't the only thing getting under her skin. There was also the fact that he kept glancing over at her and watching her work.

She laid out the supplies she'd need for

today's clinic on the table under the shade canopy they'd erected and got ready for the families to arrive.

She'd set up extra clinics prior to the wet season, per Hope and Taj's advice. The rain was critical to the villagers, yet the muddy pools and wet conditions also meant a rise in the mosquito population and hence, malaria cases. Other infections like river blindness were also of particular concern during the rainy season.

There was no vaccine for many of these diseases, so the best she could do was to pass out bars of soap. Each kid who got vaccinated would also get a lesson on keeping their faces washed. At some clinics, they would hand out colorful toothbrushes to the kids and go over dental hygiene. Some of the most important preventative measures were so basic. Things that so many people took for granted.

Their parents taught them to do so at home, but just like with anything, kids often listened better to someone other than their parents.

If followed, basic hygiene did wonders for disease prevention, but what Lexi really hoped was that the kids would be excited about getting something and want to come back to be vaccinated again.

"Here's the last bag of soap. I found it under the cabinet. No idea how it got there unless it fell without me realizing it." Jacey opened the bag and set it at the end of a second table.

"Good. I'll do the shots and you do the wash-up lesson. I hope we have enough vaccine. I'd hate to turn anyone away. Did you find any more vitamins?"

"None. Taj and Hope both said they were going to try to get more samples or pharmaceutical donations, though."

Malnutrition was one of the most serious concerns for the children, especially when so many of the village crops were dying. No wonder Tony had been so passionate about medical care out here. No wonder his grandmother had encouraged him to pursue medicine so that he could help others. His grandmother had told Tony that education and knowledge were useless if they weren't shared.

She understood what his grandmother had meant. Lexi, herself, had worked hard to earn every scholarship she could to be able to afford going to college. Her hard work had meant something. Being here was sharing it.

Chad walked over, eyed the table.

"I'm taking the jeep out."

"Wait a minute. You're going to drive? Alone?" Lexi glanced down the path. The first group of villagers was starting to arrive. Had he waited to bring this up when he knew she'd be busy and distracted?

"The driver's side is on the right, so I can change gears with my left hand."

"But the steering wheel and—"

"It's called using your *knees*. There aren't any red lights and speed limits. I'm good. And I wasn't asking permission. I wanted you both to know I'd be within a half-kilometer radius. Jacey, keep your eyes out and call me on the radio if I need to rush back."

"Lexi's right. You shouldn't go out alone," Jacey said. "You agreed to that with your mom and Taj. Why don't you wait until we're done here and I'll go with you?"

"That would leave Lexi alone after all the patients have gone. You're both safer with all the folks who'll be here. I can't see or do much from camp. I prefer taking action to waiting. Preemptive strikes are better than being a sitting duck. I'm planning to drive by the *enkangs* where these families are from. With some of the women and children away and the men out of the village trying to find a place to graze their herds, I have a short window to check things out."

"You're planning to sneak around a Masai homestead? You've got to be kidding me," Lexi said.

"Not sneaking, just observing. If someone is hiding out in one of the *enkangs*, they'll slip up sooner or later. Or if he's hiding in the bush, I might catch him taking food from an otherwise empty *inkajijik*." He glared past her at the small crowd forming. "You have patients to tend to. I'm out of here."

He left for the jeep, shaking the keys in the air and turning his face to hide a smile.

"How'd he get those?"

"I swear I didn't leave them in the jeep. Did you?" Taj asked.

Lexi slapped her forehead. "I've heard stories about pregnant women putting their keys in the refrigerator and milk in the cabinet. I didn't think it would happen to me."

"Leaving keys in a vehicle isn't quite as mindless, but...well, there he goes," Jacey said.

Chad took off with a sharp veer.

"I don't even know if he ever drove in Kenya before heading to college. So now he's behind the wheel on the wrong side of the vehicle for an American driver, using one hand...and restless." Lexi sighed and picked up her radio.

"Calling in reinforcements?"

"I'm letting Mac know, just in case."

"You should be happy Chad's going off looking for the guy or, at least, clues. Isn't that what you want? For the poacher to get caught?"

Lexi took advantage of a Masai woman approaching with a toddler and young girl in tow to avoid answering. Jacey was right. Wasn't Chad doing exactly what she wanted him to do? Why was she worried about him leaving the camp? Was it only out of fear for him or was there more to it?

The little girl coughed then gripped her mother's skirt.

"Has she been coughing a lot?" Lexi asked. She remembered the little girl—Malia. She'd been to the clinic about a month ago, but she had been in pretty good health then. Lexi knew her mother spoke good English.

"Only a little. It is so dusty and she was playing with her brother near the goat pens. You told me to bring them back for a second shot."

"Yes. I'll get their boosters ready. Jacey, would you mind pulling out her file?" They kept all their records the old-fashioned way—with paper and file folders. Computers and the generator to charge them were too unpredictable. They had a laptop, but when it came to patients, she had to be able to access their records no matter what. Jacey handed her a mini-file and began triaging the next family.

Lexi took her stethoscope and listened to Malia's chest and back.

"Cough for me, sweetie."

Malia obeyed.

"Well, she sounds clear right now," Lexi said to Malia's mother, as she draped the stethoscope around her neck again. "But promise me you'll let me know if that cough gets any worse, or if she makes whistling noises when breathing or if she develops a fever."

"I will."

Lexi gave the kids their requisite boosters and sent them to Jacey for the rest, while she took over the second family. The path to the clinic had now filled with people, and the sound of their voices, traditional greetings and small talk, and even the cries and laughter of children, warmed up the clinic. These people, she realized, made Kenya and this tiny camp feel like home. It wouldn't be without them.

Her decision to put down roots here didn't necessarily make it home. It was the people. And disconcerting as it was, something about having Chad around the past few days had made it seem more complete, somehow. A little more secure, like she could let her guard down just enough to sleep more soundly.

She bit her lip as she disposed of a needle in the designated red safety container. It angered her that she felt that way. She didn't need anyone else to make her life complete. She'd gotten this far and survived. She didn't need Chad or any other man to make her feel secure. All she wanted from Chad was his presence so that they could keep the clinic open and functioning.

CHAD SLOWED DOWN as he approached the second *enkang*. The first had showed no signs of unusual activity. His outing so far had been uneventful. So uneventful that he had radioed in to check on the clinic enough times for Jacey to yell at him and order him to stop mothering them.

Him? Mothering? He'd never live it down if another marine overheard that one.

He'd called out of guilt for leaving them for a few hours, but he couldn't take sitting around the clinic anymore. If he was going to spend a week out in the Serengeti because of a poacher, he was darn well going to find him…even if it meant attempting to drive.

Only days ago, he had convinced himself he was as good as bedridden and now here he was, driving—badly, but driving.

He stopped near the open gateway to the homestead's thorny enclosure. He'd chosen this village because it had no nearby trees or boulders to hide behind. One of the herdsmen, clothed in orange and blues, had even waved to him from a distance.

He took a drink of water before getting out. An older fellow with loop earrings that stretched his earlobes to his shoulders and a staff of twisted olive wood nodded in greeting.

"*Sopa. Kasserian engeri?* The children are well?" the man said to him.

"*Asante*. Thank you, yes, they're good." It was a customary greeting of the Masai. It didn't matter that he didn't have children. He had his second cousins and Maddie's little one…and Lexi and Tony's unborn kid. "Has everything been okay here? Your family?"

"Yes, yes. Everything is good. May the rains come and make everything better." He tapped his staff against the earth and shook his head at the horizon. "There will be rain soon."

Chad followed his gaze. The sky was a crystalline blue without as much as a smidgen of cloud. Except…he squinted thirty degrees south and saw black smoke rising in swirls and billowing outward like a bomb.

"You see that?" he asked. The elder turned and looked. The deep, leathery creases that had framed his smiling eyes and high cheekbones tightened.

"*Hatari*. Danger. Fire like that is from burning ivory and a dead animal. It means the KWS rangers found a kill. Dead elephant. KWS was here yesterday and looked through our homes. We are peaceful. Raising our children, like you."

Like you.

"I'm sorry you were put through that. I'm staying at the clinic camp just east of here. You know it?"

"Yes. Dr. Hope's clinic. She helps many. And Nurse Galen, she stitched my son's leg after he was bitten."

Of course. Everyone relied on the clinic. On Lexi.

"If you see anything, any sign of poachers, send someone for me."

"Okay. *Asante*. Thank you."

Chad hurried back to his jeep. The pyre was kilometers away, nowhere near the clinic. A lone wolf couldn't have made a kill alone. This had to be a different group. Still evil was evil, and if any of these guys had gotten away, he was going to keep them from crossing the border, if KWS had not already. He grabbed the radio and called the one guy who could get him to the site quickly.

Mac.

LEXI AND JACEY dropped everything and ran down the path toward the group approaching them. Jacey was well ahead of her, but the rush of adrenaline allowed Lexi to move faster than she usually could lately due to her pregnancy.

She took in the patient. The wire biting into flesh. The swollen, blue skin around the snare. The child's pale face.

He couldn't have been more than nine years old.

"*Kekidim ateretoki!* Help me!" The boy's father and another man, possibly an older brother, held the boy as they ran toward Lexi and Jacey.

"Get him to the tent." Lexi lifted the boy's leg and the branches still attached to the end of the snare. The men had broken the branches to free the boy and to get him there, but the wire choking his ankle was a different challenge.

Jacey took the boy in her arms and rushed him the rest of the way to the tent. They had him on the bed in seconds.

Lexi couldn't think of the other villagers watching from the courtyard in horror or about all their expensive vaccines that she'd left out—a thought that wouldn't have crossed her mind but for Chad's questioning about missing supplies. All that mattered now was saving this child's foot.

"His pulse is weak and BP is dropping," Jacey said.

"He's having a vasovagal reaction. He's not bleeding much. We need wire cutters." She cursed. Wire cutters weren't part of their primary care and first-aid setup. At least not the kind used on the twist-ply, thick wire of a snare. Damn poachers.

"Toolbox. I'll be right back." Jacey disappeared.

The boy cried out when Lexi forced the flat end of a pair of forceps under the wire and used it to wedge enough space to slip the closed tip of a pair of curved, blunt-end scissors into the space to hold it. The snare would only tighten the more she touched it, but she wanted a gap so she could insert the cutter.

Jacey rushed in, poured a splash of alcohol on the cutters and handed them over.

"Hold these. Tip the forceps a little. I'm so sorry, baby. I know it hurts." Lexi snapped off the wire and immediately grabbed the gauze and sterile saline Jacey handed her. "Can you run out and get the Tdap vial?" The kid needed the tetanus vaccine for sure. She had no idea if he'd ever had one, but he'd get it now regardless.

They stabilized his blood pressure, but his foot was still a deathly shade of blue. "We should call a medic chopper. Let me talk to his father. The boy needs to get checked at a hospital for nerve and tissue damage."

"Go ask. I'll keep an eye on him," Jacey said.

Lexi stepped into the sunlight and sucked in a deep breath before calling the father over to see his son.

Father and son. Childhood dangers.

Maybe Chad was right. Was she putting her and her child at risk by choosing to live out here?

CHAPTER SEVEN

CHAD SURVEYED the landscape as Mac circled the chopper once before landing safely just beyond the group of Kenyan Wildlife Service vehicles. The acrid smoke and rotting stench assaulted Chad's sinuses the minute he opened the chopper door. It took him back to more than one battle scene, but Chad refused to let memories cloud his judgment. He was in control. He wanted to be here, where the action was.

Flames engulfed the tusks that KWS had secured, both from this kill and from stashes they'd found earlier that day, just south of here, while the faceless body of an elephant cow lay motionless nearby. Chad let Mac introduce him to one of the officers, who shook his hand and asked him how Ben was doing. Everyone seemed to know his father. Everyone commented on how he looked so much like him. Only he'd never be just like him. He had already failed at that.

The officer cleared him to examine the area. KWS rangers were experts at what they did, tracking poachers night and day, but a spare set of eyes never hurt.

"Fresh kill. The men are all in custody. They've been interrogated and aren't from the same team the fugitive was a part of," Mac said, as he walked over from talking to the KWS team leader.

"I figured they must have got here in time, considering no one made it off with the tusks."

"The poachers had the tusks buried over there…under that tree. They do that. Bury the ivory, make their escape then return when it's safe enough to collect their winnings." Mac adjusted his cap. "You satisfied? Want to head back?"

"No. Look over there." Chad headed for a broken branch a few feet to the right of a wide path of broken and flattened brush the elephant had trampled in an attempt to escape.

"She came through here," Mac said.

"Not the mother. Over here to the right.

See that branch pushed aside?" This path was smaller, narrower, much less obvious. Too narrow for an adult elephant. "Are they positive they arrested everyone?" Chad asked in a lowered voice.

"I'm not so sure anymore. But something—call it experience—tells me a poacher didn't go through here. The team catches and arrests first, then they scout the area for other fatalities or casualties. They've started at that end and you can see them working their way around the perimeter," Mac said.

Chad followed the trail a good ten meters and stopped in his tracks. It ended by the massive, gnarly trunk of a boab tree. Standing frozen and terrified at its side was a baby elephant. Chad wiped a hand across his face.

An orphan like the ones his aunt Anna saved and raised down at Busara. An orphan like Tony had once told him Lexi had been.

"I think we just found what KWS is looking for."

Mac took off his cap and swore.

"I'll never get used to it. In all my years finding orphaned calves, it still infuriates me every time," Mac said, approaching the baby slowly. It backed up nervously. Mac stopped moving toward it. "Keep track of her. I'll go let them know," he said, heading down the trail in the direction they'd come.

Chad whispered softly under his breath and held his palm out, the way he did when gaining the trust of the war dogs he'd handled. Not just the service dogs, but the local abandoned ones he couldn't leave behind. He'd helped to rescue as many as he could, finding shelter and food near the military compounds.

The baby touched his palm with its trunk, then proceeded to wrap its trunk around his wrist. *Trust me.* He took another step and was at its side.

A child whose mother was killed, just like his had been. It was almost as if this baby knew he understood.

"You'll be okay."

This. This was why he couldn't sit back and wait for things to happen. This was why he needed to do more to stop corruption and atrocities…to stop violence and sociopaths who stole good people's peace of mind.

The problem was that needing and wanting to do something weren't the same as being able to.

LEXI SAT BACK and kicked up her feet.

"Was this the longest day we've had in months?"

"It's not over yet," Jacey pointed out as she took a long drink.

They still had to put things away, but they needed a breather. At least they'd taken care of all the kids, and the little boy had been flown to the hospital in Nairobi where experts would make sure he got the treatment he required. She'd actually called in the case to both Hope and Taj so that they could do what they could, in terms of professional connections, to get him good care.

In the meantime, they had reported the location of the snare and the authorities had sent a team to scour and clear the area near the boy's homestead. It was about eight kilometers away. She still wasn't quite used to thinking in metric.

Chad wasn't going to like it when…if… she relayed the information. Though the way word traveled around here, he'd probably already heard.

"I'm sure Chad's okay," Jacey said, reading her mind.

"I'm not worried."

"Yes, you are. It's all over your face, and if you don't stop chewing your lip we're going to have another bleeder on our hands."

"Mac called in and said he met up with Chad near the Ngotori *enkang*. Besides, I'm not thinking about Chad any more than you're thinking about Taj."

Jacey's eyes widened and the tip of her nose turned red.

"That's so far off base it makes Kilimanjaro look like it's only meters away."

"Jace. We've known each other for five months, working together day in and day out with hardly anyone else around. Truth be told, I'm closer to you than I've been to any other woman in a long time. I know, that says a lot about me. But it's the truth. I mean, Hope has been wonderful, too, but she doesn't live out here. You don't have to trust me, but you can. Just saying."

"I plead the fifth. For now. I'll give you that he's more than cute, but that's all there is. Don't make assumptions."

"Fine. If you say so. Same goes for Chad. He's not on my mind, other than in a professional capacity. Don't read into anything."

"If you say so." Jacey chuckled as she got

up and started putting supplies away. Lexi rose to help.

"You know, if Chad brings up the snare and starts arguing that he can't keep us safe, I want to be able to point out that nothing is missing from our supplies. All this stuff we had to abandon while we helped the boy and not even a bar of soap is out of place. That proves we're surrounded by good people who care…who help watch the area. I never doubted it, but I think he has seen too much evil in the world to realize that most people are good. The evil-doers just stand out more. They make the news."

"If that injured poacher tried swiping anything with that boy's father and all the mothers around, he'd have been in for one wicked surprise," Jacey said.

They exchanged glances at the sound of the jeep approaching.

"We were fine. Got it?"

"We did totally fine on our own," Jacey said. "Don't worry. I'm not going to add any evidence to his case."

Chad parked but just sat staring at the wheel for a moment before getting out.

"That's strange. I'm going to see what's

up." Lexi set down the bag of soap and met him halfway. "What's wrong?"

Chad cranked his neck.

"I met up with Mac out there. He flew me over to an ivory burn. We had to call Busara for help with an orphan."

"Oh, no."

He walked past her and straight for the copse of trees on the side of camp. She frowned at Jacey and followed him.

"I'm sorry for what you witnessed. Are you okay?"

"Are you? No problems out here?"

"Just medical cases, as expected."

"You expected a snare case?" He raised a brow at her. "Mac heard the medical call over the chopper radio and told me."

She tipped her chin up.

"Good. I'm glad he did. Now you know that we can handle just about anything here."

He closed the gap between them, resting his hand against a tree trunk.

"Lex. Have you ever seen in person what these poachers can do? They are bad men with absolutely no compassion or respect for life in this world. I just saw more evidence of that today."

She sucked in a deep breath.

"I'm not as ignorant as you assume. Why do you think I'm out here trying to do good? Maybe you could give me the benefit of the doubt for once instead of assuming I'm in over my head."

"Maybe you should trust my judgment for once," Chad quipped.

Lexi glared at him, then turned and stalked back toward the bungalow.

EARLY THAT EVENING, Chad rested his forehead against the creviced bark of a tree that faced the western horizon. The trunk was rough and coarse but it didn't relieve the itching and tingling along the upper right of his back. Still, he didn't dare scratch. He knew the rules. The doctors and nurses had warned him numerous times not to scrub at any of his scars, especially where he'd suffered burns. His skin had healed for the most part, but the itching that would sometimes flame to life like a disturbed mound of fire ants was beyond irritating.

No, it didn't compare to the soul-changing pain he'd suffered during his hospital recovery, but still, it shook him. It made him feel weak and vulnerable, bitter and angry, restless and agitated. And there wasn't anything phantom about the itching, though he'd been told the same relaxation and meditation techniques that were supposed to help the pain in his missing arm would help ease the itching of his scars.

Yeah, right. Staring at the sunset just now hadn't done a drop of good in the name of comfort. But what he really hated was the fact that, prior to the explosion, a crawling feeling on his neck or back would have been a sign…his intuition warning him of danger or that something just wasn't right.

Now the blasted, godforsaken prickling was nothing more than a reminder that he'd never be the same again. That he'd never be capable of the same military duty again. That he simply was…less. He was nothing but a walking, talking example of how war stripped a man or woman of their soul…

Not that the world would ever heed the reminder. There were too many sociopaths, fanatics and fundamentalists out there—enough to keep perpetuating the cycle. Crazy, self-righteous people unable to fathom that their way wasn't the only way. Greed had driven conquerors for millennia. Poaching had many masks. Evil was nowhere close to being eradicated. And he couldn't really do anything about it anymore. He'd been sidelined.

Life goes on. War goes on.

He pushed away from the tree, spared the bloody sunset one last glance, and stalked off toward the bungalow, making an extra effort to ignore Lexi and Jacey.

He should try lying down. The pressure against his back might help ease the itching. What he really needed was to sooth the tight skin with some lotion or oil, but he couldn't reach that area on his own.

"Hey, Chad. Could you give me a hand?" Lexi called out. She was taking down the tables they'd used for the outdoor clinic they'd held earlier in the day.

So much for avoiding her. Maybe she'd calmed down from their earlier argument. Maybe he should apologize, though for what, he wasn't quite sure.

Chad squeezed his lids briefly and let out a breath. He straightened his shoulders the best that he could and went to her, hoping she couldn't see through him. For some reason he couldn't quite define, Lexi was the last person he wanted perceiving him as weak. The fact that she was a nurse scared him a little in that sense. Nurses were trained to pick up on a patient masking pain.

But he couldn't ignore her. Jacey had hitched a ride with Mac to deliver some feminine hygiene products and soap to a neighboring village and Lexi wouldn't be able to put away the tables on her own.

He quirked the corner of his mouth up in as casual—albeit annoyed—smile as he could muster and walked toward her as she stood by a folding table near the medical tent.

"What can I do for you?" he asked, even if it was obvious what she wanted him to do.

"This has to be collapsed and stored. I can tip it over and fold the legs, but I don't want to lift it. I figured you—" She hesitated and sucked in her lower lip.

Was she as nervous as he was? There was something about them both being out here alone that—as expansive as their wild surroundings were—felt intimate and personal.

"We don't like leaving the table outside—bird droppings and such," she explained. Enough said. "I could wait for Jacey to get back, but I figured if I helped guide it, you could—"

"I can get it," he said, sparing her from pointing out that she'd assist him because he only had one arm. "Keep it from falling over and I'll get the rest."

He grabbed the edge with his left hand, tipped it gently and folded the legs in, as she held the top in place on its side. Then he gripped the center of the long edge as tight as his could and carried it into the medical tent before she could try to assist.

He frowned as he set the table against the tent pillar she'd motioned toward and released his grip seconds before the table would have slipped from his fingers. The task had almost been beyond him. He should have let her help him. Why had he been so determined to prove to her he could do it himself?

"Anything else?" he asked, dabbing at the bead of sweat that trailed down his cheek. The brief distraction had given him some relief from the itching in his back, but the gnawing discomfort was returning.

Lexi wiped her palms against the sides of her shirt. Her cheeks were rosier than usual and she seemed to be avoiding looking right at him.

He could guess what was going through her mind. Since the explosion, he'd encountered three types of people: those who stared, those who avoided the sight of his injuries and the few—typically medical personnel and his family—who looked but made a concerted effort not to acknowledge the limitations of his injuries, as if doing so would rob him of hope and keep him from trying to heal.

Lexi wasn't family and, even as a nurse, she avoided eye contact with him. That said enough. He gave her a terse nod to let her know he got the message that she didn't need anything else and he started to leave. Job done.

"Wait." Lexi stepped between him and the tent exit. It was a tight entrance, putting them very close. Close enough for him to pick up the lingering scent of her shampoo. Close enough that it wouldn't take much for him to reach out and touch her and let her cheek warm his hand. Close enough to feel an undeniable energy between them.

No. This had to be a one-way thing. How

could he not be drawn to her serene, unassuming beauty…to her healing heart…to her stubborn, determined inner strength? She resembled some sort of earth goddess in an oil painting. No sign of weakness. Lexi was in control. She didn't want anyone complicating her life, least of all him.

"Is there something else for me to help clean up?"

"No. But I'd like to help you."

Real nice. She could keep her pity. He shook his head and tried to walk past her, but she held his arm.

"Chad, please listen. I saw you earlier, standing out there alone. If you're in any pain, you have to let me know. I have some pain medication for you in the cabinet here. Your mom left it, just in case."

"I'm fine."

"She also warned me you'd say that."

"The last thing I want is the two of you hovering over me or worrying about me."

"I'm not worried. I'm concerned. They're slightly different things. I know you can take care of yourself."

"Good. We're on the same page then. I realize it's in your nature to care for patients, but you have plenty of them around here. I'm not one of them."

Her eyes glistened and he couldn't help but notice the movement in her smooth neck as she swallowed. Part of him wanted to rest his face there, breathe her in…kiss her. He pinched the bridge of his nose and rubbed his eyes.

You can't think of her that way. She's off limits. You're just trying to forget the pain… the past.

"I'm not offering help to a patient," she said. "I'm trying to offer it to…to a friend. I know you haven't been here that long, but you know Tony. I'd like to think that makes you a friend of the family."

She rested her hand on the top of her belly and, this time, didn't take her eyes off his. She wasn't staring at him with disgust. There was an intensity in the way she gazed at him…warmth, caring…sincerity.

Chad's chest cramped and he took a deep breath. Who was supposed to be looking out for whom here?

"I'm not taking any drugs. The pain isn't that bad. Besides it's not my arm. I have some scars on my back that sometimes itch badly, that's all. I can handle it."

"Are you putting anything on them? You're still less than a year out from your injuries. Aren't you applying a lotion to help with scarring and healing? Dryness alone can make the itching worse."

"Mostly. But like I said, I'm fine."

"Mostly? For goodness' sake, Chad. If you can't reach all the areas, I can rub it on for you." Her face flushed and he could feel the heat rise in his neck. "I'm a nurse. It's what I do," she quickly clarified.

"I don't need—"

"—my help. I get that. I'm not one to ask for help, either, yet I've accepted your assistance with the table, so we can call it even. Come sit down."

She motioned toward the exam tent behind her and gave him a firm look. She'd gone from hesitant and almost shy to professional nurse mode in an instant.

Fine. He'd let her examine his shrapnel and burn scars. She'd seen the ones on his face, and if that wasn't enough to extinguish the chemistry between them, a close-up view of his chest and back would. It wouldn't change how he saw her, but it would certainly change how she saw him.

And that was a good thing. He needed to keep his distance. And he definitely had to keep himself from acting on whatever attraction was building between them. He stepped into the tent and waited for her to close the flap, then pulled his shirt off, all the while keeping his eyes on her. He wanted to watch her reaction…to see the truth.

She didn't so much as flinch.

Instead she stood in front of him as he sat on the edge of the exam table. Then she touched the tips of her fingers to the pinkish, pale burn scar that extended from his right shoulder around to his spine, then across a similar scar that spread from the side of his waist to his lower back. Her eyes swept over him, inspecting every scar, including the wrapped shoulder stump that was all that was left of his arm.

"What's bothering you the most at the moment? This scar here?" She touched the area of his back that was the hardest to reach. He nodded.

"They actually look like they're healing well. Surprisingly well, in fact. I've seen worse scars." She put her hand on his knee. "I don't mean to make less of what you suffered. I didn't mean it that way at all."

"They used some of the latest techniques in burn treatment. I was in an induced coma for most of the initial treatment, but I was told afterward that they used the latest methods to speed up the healing of the burns and to keep inflammation around the amputation down. I was lucky. My combat uniform offered some protection, or it would have been worse. So I'm told."

She took a bottle from one of the cabinets and went around to stand behind him.

"Tell me if anything I do hurts. This is just mineral oil. Basic, but it'll help moisturize the skin and maybe stop some of the itch. If you have a different lotion you want me to fetch, I can."

"This'll work," he said, clearing his throat to get the words out.

She placed her hands on his back and began working the oil into his skin. Her touch was soft and gentle and caring. His eyes closed and even the roughest of the scars seemed to smooth out under the silky glide of her palms. Her hands worked magic, soothing all his pain and discomfort…massaging away the tension that had been festering deep in his bones…clearing out the memories of that day in battle, if only for now.

Neither spoke, but her touch and the sound of her steady breathing seemed to wash over him, drowning out the chatter of the world outside the tent and lulling him into an almost meditative calm. A depth of quiet he couldn't recall ever experiencing before.

Peace.

There were no battles within. No images of war in his mind.

Lexi was giving him something no one else had been able to. A moment of unadulterated peace.

Even with his eyes still closed, tears stung the rims of his eyelids. He swallowed them back and willed them to stop.

Hope had always told him that the strongest of men were the ones who were brave enough to show their emotions…that crying wasn't a weakness but a strength. Yet his father—a fellow marine—had never cried around others. In fact, the only time Chad recalled him breaking down was when Chad's mother, Zoe, had died.

Even then, with Chad too young to fully understand but old enough to remember, Ben had only cried in private. Chad used to hear him from behind his closed bedroom door. Chad had understood then and there that if he wanted to grow up to be just like his dad, he'd have to channel his tears into taking action. Instead of showing weakness, he'd have to be strong and fight all that was wrong in the world.

But right now, he wasn't sure what he was feeling. Everything seemed to blur in his mind. Strength, weakness, peace…love. No. Not love. Gratitude. It had to be the latter. Or maybe, as she'd called it, friendship.

His muscles relaxed as Lexi rubbed circles over his shoulder blade, adding oil as needed. Then her hands reached around his waist, as she tended to the old wounds along his torso. He heard her step around the table to stand in front of him. Her extended belly inadvertently brushed against his knee as she spread oil along the side of his waist.

He didn't dare open his eyes, not because he feared what he'd see in hers, but because he wanted to hold her…rest his forehead against hers…kiss her. And if he opened his eyes, a tear might escape.

Whatever this feeling was—gratitude, relief, whatever—he didn't trust himself around her. He had to remind himself that she was merely administering care as she'd do to any patient. He couldn't breach that boundary, friendship or not.

"All done," she said softly.

He forced his eyes open as if waking from a dream. He blinked at the brightness from the evening sun streaming in through the window. "I didn't want to startle you."

"I, um, I'm good. Thank you. That actually helped. With the pain, I mean. And the itching. Thanks."

Why was he bumbling like an idiot? He flexed his fingers and rolled his shoulders.

"Good. I'm glad. Studies show that massage can help. Any relaxing exercise, such as meditation, can give you relief, actually. Don't hesitate to let me know if the scars are bothering you again. We should do this daily. While you're here, at least."

He stood without answering and slipped his shirt on. He was relieved that she didn't try to assist him with the shirt.

She turned toward the sound of Mac's helicopter approaching. "Jacey is back," she said.

They stepped outside just as Mac took off, after Jacey safely cleared his landing area and was headed toward them. She was yelling into a satellite phone as she trudged over.

"Who's she talking to?"

"Must be Taj. He calls from the hospital sometimes, though all they ever seem to do is argue."

"They do seem to annoy each other. I don't understand why he doesn't go help out at another clinic if she drives him so crazy," Chad said.

Lexi turned and frowned at him. "You're kidding, right?"

"No. Why would I be?"

"Chad Corallis. For all your observation skills, you're missing the most obvious signs."

"Of what?"

"Of when two people really like each other."

THE END of the week approached and Lexi was worried. Chad seemed to prowl around the camp day and night. He never seemed satisfied by what he saw, and often disappeared into the brush, searching. Yet he was friendly with the villagers who came in for medical care, and his expression seemed to soften whenever he watched her tend to a patient.

Still, Chad was a man of action and she knew he was forming a strategy. But to do what? Shut them down?

On Thursday morning he approached her as she was setting up for the day.

"I have a plan, but I can't exactly do it myself. As soon as Taj returns for the weekend, I'm going to head out to my sister Maddie's place. I'm hoping with her connections to human rights groups, she can help us out."

"With what exactly?"

"This place needs some sort of barrier around it. It's easier to keep an eye out for trouble when there's only one way in and out. Like with an *enkang*. Sometimes you don't have to look far for a solution—the Masai had it figured out long ago. Build an organic, natural thorny fence out of acacia branches. Better than barbed wire. Only it would take forever for us to build a fence like that. So, I'm hoping Maddie might be able to help facilitate some food donations to the nearest homesteads in exchange for their expertise with building one of these fences. They'd get needed food for the kids, the medical facility would stay open longer, assuming this works, and you'll be safer."

"Are you planning on staying to oversee this construction?" She tried not to get her hopes up.

He tensed.

"For a bit. I may have...other things going on. I can't stay long."

Of course he couldn't. She hoped he meant that he was finally ready to resume therapy sessions.

"I'm confused. I know I asked you to stay to buy us time, but I thought you wanted to shut us down. After that poaching a couple of days ago, I assumed you'd order us back to Nairobi, but now you're offering to stay longer?"

"Let's just say too many people out there have a high regard for you."

She studied his face. That was too easy. There was something he wasn't saying.

"And once this fence is done? Then what? We get your seal of approval?"

"We'll take it from there. You'll still need a guard around here, after I'm gone."

After he's gone. So he would go, after all. She knew he wouldn't stay. Why did hearing it feel like a stab wound?

"When are you going to Haki and Maddie's place?"

"Mac said he'd fly me over after tomorrow, when he drops Taj off. Um… Maddie said if you want to come, she has maternity clothes you can try on and borrow if you like. Plus a few newborn items you could use instead of buying new ones in Nairobi. It's about forty minutes by air to her place. Her baby is fifteen months old and has outgrown a few things."

His sister wanted to share with her? A warm feeling swirled in her chest and balled up at the base of her throat. That was something a friend or family member would do.

"I… I don't know. I probably do need a few things, but we've been so busy here."

"I discussed that with my mom. She suggested Taj bring one of his fellow interns, just for the day. It would free you up, and maybe convince the intern to work at one of my mom's other locations part-time, like Taj does."

"That is a good solution for me, but aren't you still worried about the safety of the camp if you'll be away?"

"I've already talked to an elder at one of the *enkang* homesteads about the fence. He offered to send a few family members to at least get started on one for the clinic. Mac also mentioned that he heard KWS was going to be out this way to make sure there aren't any more snares endangering anyone. There'll be plenty of people around. So, of all days, the clinic will be safe without me. If you want to go, that is."

He had just emphasized that he'd be leaving. So why did he sound like he was asking her out on a date?

Because you're tired and have a wild imagination.

Or maybe it was because he was building her an acacia fence and offering to give her items that would make her and the baby more comfortable.

And then he'll leave. What's the point of getting close to Chad and his family if they'll only desert you?

She placed her hands on top of her belly. "Okay. I'll go."

It was a risk, but only if she let her guard down around Chad or Maddie. If she kept her heart protected, it couldn't get broken.

CHAPTER EIGHT

HAKI AND MADDIE had built their home on a rise overlooking a river valley and grasslands below. The view was absolutely breathtaking. The hot wind rippled the grass, and gunmetal-gray boulders dappled the slope leading up to the plateau. The view across the valley was spectacular. A herd of zebras grazed along the side of the dried creek bed that meandered farther than the eye could see. Hawks flew overhead, their shadows sweeping over the herds. An elephant trumpeted in the distance and Lexi saw several emerge from behind a copse of trees. This was artistry at its best. Their home embraced the African architecture used in some of the tourist lodges, incorporating timber poles and thatching. Yet the house was humble and every detail had been made to fit into the scenery, as though it were part of every boulder, blade of grass and sprawling acacia tree.

Very Frank Lloyd Wright in that respect. And it all stood against a sky streaked with wispy, white clouds like a piece of blue lace agate.

Mac led Chad and Lexi up the wide stone steps, embedded naturally along the rise and fashioned from the same granite that was native to the area.

Chad held out his arm to her.

"Take my hand or hold on to my arm. These steps are a little steep. I don't want you to fall." He stuck his elbow out as if she was his date at a formal event. Only he wasn't in his Marine uniform and his T-shirt meant their arms would touch. Skin to skin. And she was definitely not his date.

Lexi hesitated then took his arm.

"Thanks. I have to admit, my center of gravity is a little off these days."

The stairs opened onto a wide front yard and a breezeway-style porch gracing the house.

Off to the right lay a small building, similar to their clinic bungalow but flanked by pole-fashioned animal pens. Haki was a veterinarian and he seemed to have quite a few patients at the moment. Masai homesteads dotted the landscape in the distance.

Haki had told Chad many times of his dream to open a clinic to serve the farmers and their livestock. His father was also a vet who'd helped his aunt Anna start Busara, an elephant research facility and orphan rescue.

But Busara mainly served rescued elephants, and Haki had seen a need for animal care among tribal farmers whose herds, including farm dogs, often suffered death due to untreated yet preventable and curable diseases. He believed if he helped the people, he would relieve suffering and desperation, which would in turn help prevent some individuals from falling prey to bribes offered by poachers.

Maddie, as a humanitarian lawyer, embraced his dream, too. She often commuted to her practice in Nairobi and stayed at her parents' if she had to spend lengthy hours in court. But she also did pro bono work and took on cases for humanitarian groups like Native Watch Global.

He hoped his sister would be able to help him out with respect to their mom's clinic and Lexi's work, but it wasn't the only reason he was there.

"Have you seen this place before?" Lexi

looked over at Chad, then must have realized she was still hanging on to him. She slipped her hand away and a breeze stole the lingering warmth of her touch. He was tempted to reach out and weave his fingers through hers.

"No, but I've seen similar places. I lived in Kenya for many years, so we used to go on safari road trips to visit my aunts, uncles and cousins who live off the grid. I didn't realize Maddie and Haki had finished building their house. Maddie only told me about it when she came out to our parents' place the day I returned."

"You're here!" Maddie came bounding outside. Haki stepped out from the glass door behind her and waved. He had a toddler propped on one hip. Maddie wrapped Chad in a big-sister hug. "You took long enough to get out here and visit."

"I'm here now."

"You look good, too," she said, placing her palms on his cheeks. Leave it to a sister to embarrass him. He gently guided her hands away and looked toward Lexi.

"Maddie, this is Lexi. Or have you two actually met?" he asked.

"Only once, briefly," Lexi responded.

"I had just flown into Nairobi but I hadn't moved to the clinic yet. I'm sorry, I think I was a bit distracted and flustered at the time."

Maddie gave her a hug.

"No worries. It was a big, stressful move. It's good to see you again. I'm so glad you could make it."

Haki came over and shook Lexi's hand as Maddie scooped their daughter from his arms.

"It's good to have you here. Welcome." He turned to Chad and grinned. Haki had grown up alongside Chad's cousin, Pippa. He had been like family even before he'd married Maddie. "It has been a long time, man."

"Too long. Sorry I missed the wedding." Chad noticed Lexi glancing at him from the corner of his eye. He'd missed a lot of weddings and family events. His brothers' graduations… Pippa's wedding to some seismologist—he thinks the name was Dax—who came complete with twin, ten-year-old girls…his parents' twentieth anniversary.

Haki did their old handshake—left-handed—then pulled him into a man hug. He slapped his back.

"Good to have you here," Haki said.

Chad nodded his appreciation.

"This little one is Zoe. Named after our first mom," Maddie explained to Lexi.

"A beautiful name and a sweetie pie." Lexi let Zoe curl her hand around her finger.

Chad couldn't help but stare. It was the first time he'd met little Zoe. Maddie hadn't brought her daughter along when she'd visited him in Nairobi. She was a beautiful child. He could see bits of Maddie and Haki in her face, but there was something of his mother in there, too.

And something about the way Lexi lit up as she spoke to little Zoe gave him a warm feeling in his chest. This wasn't her being a nurse, as kind and personable as she was with patients. This was her in mommy mode. Relaxed. Happy.

"Why don't you come inside?" Haki said.

"Yes, come along," Maddie put her arm around Lexi and walked her in as if they were old girlfriends. Then she turned back to Chad and mouthed *I like her.* Chad shook his head at her. This was not an introduce-his-new-girlfriend-to-the-family sort of visit. Maddie was well aware of that. He'd made it clear. At least he'd tried to. Knowing her, she'd probably claim the satellite phone reception had been bad.

He loved his sister. She'd overcome a lot after their mother had died. But struggling with selective mutism after that tragedy wasn't the same as him losing his limb and career. She had been a kid. Kids were adaptable. Weren't they? For the first time since his return, he was realizing just how much he missed being around her and his younger brothers, Ryan and Philip.

He followed everyone inside, not wanting to be the center of attention, and let Maddie lead Lexi in.

"Surprise!"

Lexi yelped and jumped back, slapping a hand to her chest. She started to step aside, and he realized she must have assumed this was a welcome-home party for him. But the coffee table was covered in gifts wrapped in various unisex baby designs.

He noticed the flush on her cheeks when she realized the party was for her. She covered her mouth and looked back at him.

"You knew?"

He shrugged and smiled at her and, for

some reason, felt very proud of the fact he'd managed to surprise her.

"I can't believe this," she said. "Thank you, all. I don't know what to say." A tear escaped and she sniffed and wiped it away. Maddie gave her a hug. "Thank you so much. I didn't expect to get a baby shower at all."

"Mom was the one who first mentioned it, but we couldn't have done it without Chad getting you to come along," Maddie said.

"Thank you, Hope. And, Chad. You," she said, shaking a finger at him, "are dangerously smooth. I never suspected a thing."

"Skills."

That earned him a laugh.

"And Jacey! How did you get here? We left you behind and Mac was with us."

"Magic." Jacey grinned and came to give her a hug.

"Lexi, you haven't met Pippa." Hope pointed out a sparkly eyed young woman with auburn, corkscrew-curly hair. She waved excitedly then put her arm around two identical girls.

"It's so great to finally meet you, Lexi. Hi, Chad. These are my daughters, Ivy and Fern, and that's my husband, Dax, by the kitchen,"

Pippa said. Dax waved as he joined them and offered Lexi a glass of water.

Anna and her best friend Niara had raised both Pippa and Haki under rustic, rural conditions. She'd probably been putting ideas into Lexi's head about raising a child off the grid.

"Nice to meet you, girls," said Chad. "Pippa and Dax, I'm sorry I missed the wedding last year."

"We totally understood. You're here with us now and that's all that matters."

"Well, I'm glad you're happy."

"Thanks," Dax said, extending his hand and shaking Chad's. "I'm honored to finally meet you."

Pippa's mother and Niara approached, along with Mac, his wife, Tessa, and their five-year-old son. The women gave him a hug then turned to Lexi. "Hi, Lexi. I'm Anna, Pippa's mother, and this is Niara, Haki's mom."

Mac slipped behind his wife and put his hands on her shoulders. "And this here is my wife, Tessa, and our son, Tai."

Lexi exchanged hellos.

"It's so good to meet you all," she said. "I've heard so much about all of you that I feel like I know you already. I'm just blown away by all of this."

"Well, from what you do at the clinic, you deserve this and more. Today, my dear, you get to sit and be pampered," Hope said, giving her a kiss on the cheek and a hug. "Come sit."

Hope led her away from Chad and the group to a comfortable-looking armchair. Tai ran to her and began showing her his toy helicopter. The twins hurried to the kitchen island and began frosting a cake. Jacey stood off to the side, watching the kids from afar as Tessa stood talking to her.

Without Lexi beside him, Chad suddenly felt alone and he wasn't sure what to do with himself.

"Chad, I was about to show Mac the vet clinic and pens. Want to come?" Haki asked.

Chad glanced at Lexi. She smiled and he couldn't help but smile back.

"Don't worry, we won't be long. Maddie said the food's almost ready."

Chad gave Lexi one last look, though he couldn't have said why. Shaking off the pull to go to her, he followed the other men out the door.

"BREATHE, MAN. She'll be okay in there," Mac said with a laugh.

"I never said she wouldn't be," Chad said, scowling at him.

"Dare I say you looked like an expectant father in there?" Haki held up his palms to ward off an attack.

"Enough. Way off base, guys."

If the guys were noticing something happening between Lexi and him, he seriously needed to step back and make sure he wasn't leading her on.

"Okay, okay. We won't mess with you," Mac said.

"Speak for yourself." Haki grinned. "Come on. I'll show you around. I ended up hiring a couple of assistants, Ali and Johnathan. Huru and Noah used to come out to help at first, but now they're off at college like Ryan and Philip."

Noah was Pippa's younger brother and Huru was Haki's.

A dog, basking by the pens, jumped up and ran to Haki.

"Hey, boy. Down. This here is Kashi. She lets us know if a predator is nearby. That fence helps somewhat, but it's not foolproof."

The fence was mostly posts and wire and only surrounded the area around the tin-roofed, one-story facility and pens, which wasn't very large. Kind of like a small corral.

"You're lucky the area here is clear. I thought about using wire fencing around the clinic to help secure it, but there are too many rocks and trees. We'd be tearing up habitat. I'm hoping acacia branch fencing like the Masai use around their homes will work. I wanted to talk to Maddie, to see if any of her connections can help me fund it by donating some food in exchange for labor."

"She might be able to help."

"You're not worried about poachers out here?" Chad asked.

"There aren't as many incidences this far from the border," Mac said.

"He's right. But just in case I always have someone around here when I'm out in the field, which is often, since the farmers can't bring their entire herds here. We also have solid doors with good locks on the house, just in case," Haki explained.

"You've done well for yourself," Chad said.

"The way I see it, if you dedicate your life to helping others and follow your heart in the process, you can't go wrong. Everything will fall into place," Haki said.

The guy was smart. He'd always been way ahead of the rest, even as a kid. Maddie had been the only one able to challenge him, academically, in reading or even in a game of chess. The two had definitely been meant for each other from the start. Hard to believe Haki had almost married Pippa instead.

Helping others and following your heart. That's what Chad had been doing as a marine and it had almost gotten him killed. But it had also led him to the clinic and to pursuing his hunch earlier in the week.

Maybe...just maybe. No. Was it even possible?

He was functioning better now than he had been during months of therapy in the States. He was driving. Maybe he could even learn to shoot again. Not as accurately as a sniper, but well enough to qualify for some level of duty. He'd never be Special Forces again, not with one arm and his limp, but maybe...just maybe...they'd let him serve again in some capacity. He'd heard of other vets, even injured, who were able to reenlist.

Maybe if he was lucky, they'd take him back.

It would be better for everyone, especially Lexi. And if he couldn't find the injured poacher or secure the clinic before leaving, then she could always work at Hope's office in Nairobi. She would understand…eventually.

THERE WAS BARELY enough room for all of the gifts in the bungalow. Four days later and gifts from the shower were still piled up in bags.

But Lexi felt like a million sparklers at a New Year's or Independence Day celebration. The party had been amazing. Everyone had been so accepting, so warm toward her. Like she was part of a family. The family she'd never had but had always wanted.

She had to keep reminding herself that Chad's family wasn't hers to keep. But that didn't mean she couldn't enjoy their friendship.

She stacked some of the baby things. Yellow and green outfits, cloth diapers, a small basin carved out of teak—nothing like the plastic baby bathing tubs in chain stores or online. Oh, and several lovely and comfortable outfit basics that Maddie said she'd worn during her final month. Lexi finally had a shirt that didn't feel or look stretched to the max over her belly.

And this kid was growing. She knew because there was movement, but not in the contorted, painful way. He or she didn't have enough room to stretch that much anymore.

There was a tap at the door and Chad peered in.

"Here's the last bag. Jacey told me to bring it in. By the way, is everything okay with Jacey?"

"Why do you ask?" Lexi took the bag and set it near the rest.

"I don't know. Taj came up and started asking how things went and then all of a sudden Jacey handed me this bag and walked off."

"I'll talk to her. Between you and me, sooner or later she and Taj are going to have to admit they like each other."

Chad shook his head.

"I still don't see it."

"It's called being stubborn. I can't believe they haven't figured it out yet."

Which couple was she really talking about?

"Whatever you say. I'm staying out of it." Chad started to leave.

"Wait. Chad, I wanted to thank you." She

stepped up to him and kissed his cheek. His stubble scraped her lips and made her forget why she'd come so close…why she'd dared to kiss him. She moved away, but the warm sensation of his skin against hers lingered. "Um, so…thank you."

"I didn't really do anything." He touched his cheek, then tucked his hand in the pocket of his jeans.

"That's not true. You helped with the baby shower surprise, and it meant a lot to me. I didn't even have a bridal shower. Not even a fancy wedding…just a small restaurant reception with colleagues. One of the nurses at work took pity on me, I think, and invited me out to dinner across the street from the hospital."

"I can't imagine you not having friends."

"I tended to focus on work. And people in the hospital tended to come and go—acting like best friends one minute and as if they barely knew you the following week. I didn't have time for that. But things have been different with you. You're still here. You just introduced me to some of the nicest people I've ever met in my life. I realize we started out rough, Chad, but I consider you a friend.

I hope you know that. If you ever need anything, I hope you'll trust me enough to come to me."

Something changed in his face and his eyes darkened.

"As a friend or a nurse?"

"Either, I suppose."

"Is that what this is about? Your need to do your job? To fix people? To show the scarred amputee that he can still have friends? I don't want anyone's pity, Lexi."

She couldn't move. Her throat tightened and any joy she'd been feeling fizzled away like a sparkler dunked in a bucket of water. She'd opened up to him and that's the way he responded?

"You think I pity you? That's what you see on my face right now? Pity?" Tears dampened her cheeks and she wiped them with the back of her hand. "This isn't pity. This is gratitude. Beyond what you've done for me and this clinic, I also have profound respect for what you gave to save another soldier's life. There's a young man out there who is still alive because of you. Someone as brave as you might have—"

"Saved your husband, too? No, Lexi.

I'm not the hero you're making me out to be. Tony is dead because of me. You were right about one thing. Being a rural doctor in Kenya was his dream. *Not* joining the marines. He'd planned on taking the normal route to becoming a doctor—medical school, dedicating a few years to nonprofits to help pay for tuition.

"Me? I was born to be a marine. I can't remember a time when I didn't imagine my life as one. I urged him to join with me. I hammered the idea into him throughout high school. I didn't let up because, to me, it was the plan that made sense. I didn't stop to consider that maybe he'd agreed to my plan because he was that kind of friend. Not because it was in his heart and soul the way it was in mine. He was being loyal. He had my back and look what he got from me in return."

"No." Lexi shook her head slowly.

"Don't you understand, Lex? He wouldn't have been at that field hospital if not for me. He wouldn't have had to spend months away from you. He would be here right now. I killed him. I told him to join the marines and it got him killed. I was reckless, fearless, invincible. I had no sense of mortality, not the way he did, until I finally spent time on the front lines and on special ops. By then, it was too late. Tony was already stationed. He was going to finish his tour soon anyway. I convinced myself he'd be fine. I faced more danger than he did at a field hospital. It was supposed to be a safe haven…just as you'd called this clinic."

She dried her face with the hem of her shirt but the tears kept coming.

"You can't blame yourself, Chad. You can't reason your way into being guilty of Tony's death. He was a loyal friend and husband, but he was a smart man, too. He had a mind of his own. What do you think drove him to study medicine? He had his mind set on living and practicing out here. On having his children grow up with a connection to their ancestors. He used to say the world was changing too fast. That not only were species like rhinos and elephants being driven to extinction, but that beautiful, unique cultures were, too, and that the only way to save them was to teach the next generations to appreciate them. To give back.

"Maybe you inspired him to join the marines, but he could have changed his mind if he'd wanted to. And even if he didn't, he could have been discharged from the military alive and well. You couldn't have predicted that attack any more than your father could have predicted a freak accident would kill your birth mother. You must know that. Tony had a goal, and he chose the path he felt was right to get there."

"I pushed him down that path."

She took his hand in both of hers and hugged it to the side of her belly as the baby gave a big kick.

"Everything happens for a reason and sometimes it's beyond our comprehension. I truly believe that. I'd go crazy if I didn't. I'd get stuck in the past. What good would it do if I sat around wondering why I conceived when I did? How could it possibly help me or my baby if I felt sorry for us? Or if I dwelled on the fact that I didn't get to tell Tony we were going to be parents? I've chosen to be positive and proactive for my child. I know I'm lucky that I'll still get to see a part of him every day of my baby's life…that I'll get to share memories of him with his child…with others who loved him, like you. Maybe, as awful as it is, this clinic was put in danger to draw us together so that Tony's kid would get to know his Uncle Chad. I'm pretty sure Tony would want that."

CHAD SWALLOWED hard and tried blinking away the sting in his eyes. An uncle to Tony's kid. The chance to be a part of his or her life. A chance to keep the child safe and give him or her guidance. Not the narrow-minded advice of a young adult, but the wisdom of a grown man. The kind of advice a father would—no. Uncle, not father.

Chad wasn't father material. It was too much responsibility to take on, now or in the future, especially with his track record for dangerous choices. He didn't trust himself.

The baby nudged his hand again, then settled against it, as if he or she trusted him. He slipped his hand out from under Lexi's.

"Tony hated guns. A marine who hated weapons. Show us one of those psychological picture tests with a blade and he'd probably see a scalpel while I'd see a dagger. Saving others, quality of life and family were always his priorities. I'd probably be the last person on earth he'd want influencing his child."

"You're wrong. He respected you. There's

more than one way to save people and ensure they have good, peaceful lives. It takes a rare, selfless person and an incredible amount of inner strength to sacrifice their own comforts and life for the sake of others. You may have seen a dagger but not for the sake of violence. You're a protector. I lo—like that about you. I respect and appreciate it."

He looked at her. Her spunky short hair. Her rosy cheeks…her full lips. They had felt soft and tender against his cheek. She glowed the way he'd heard mothers-to-be often did. He'd never witnessed it himself, though. He'd seen plenty of pregnant women, but none had ever been as beautiful as Lexi. Not even close.

He wanted to hold her. Kiss her. Protect her and the baby. But he wasn't right for her. Beauty and the beast…

Only she didn't see him that way, did she? A fact that was making him fall for her even more.

It takes a rare, selfless person and an incredible amount of inner strength to sacrifice their own comforts and life for the sake of others.

She was describing herself, too, yet she

was too humble to realize it. Too humble to see how amazing she was.

He loved that about her. Guilt swarmed through his chest at that word. He meant that he admired her for her humility. He admired her. Nothing more. It couldn't be. She was too good for him. The fact that he could even consider her as more than a friend proved it. He was disloyal. A traitor. As forgiving as Tony had been, falling for his wife would be crossing the line.

"Thank you. For not walking away after what I just confessed," Chad said.

"Chad, I would never walk away."

If only he could promise the same.

CHAPTER NINE

LEXI HELD HER arm out to Malia's mother, who was carrying the little girl toward the exam tent.

"I promised to bring her to you if the coughing got worse. Her head is warm. The *laibon* gave me herbs for a tea, and it helped the fever a little, but she won't drink it anymore."

Lexi took Malia's temperature. It was high. She listened to the girl's lungs again. They didn't sound so good. A *laibon* was a village elder and a sort of experienced medicine man. She, herself, preferred to do things naturally if possible, and she'd even referred a few patients to holistic or naturopathic doctors when she was in the US. But sometimes it wasn't enough. Serious infections required a more aggressive approach. She believed it all depended on the situation and there was a place for all approaches.

"Okay, let's get you up on the bed, Malia. Thank you for bringing her back," Lexi said to the girl's mother.

The woman nodded, her hands clenched together.

"You can make her better?"

"She might require different medicine than I have here, and I'd also like to X-ray her chest. Dr. Hope has one on her mobile unit, but we'd have to wait for her to drive it down here, which could be a few hours. Any blood when she coughs?"

"No."

"Has she been eating?"

"Not well. That's why I said she also didn't want to drink the tea."

"We'll need to get her hydrated." By IV if necessary, but she wasn't going to mention needles out loud and upset Malia. The girl cried uncomfortably. "How is your son and the others at home?"

"All good. No one else is coughing."

"Okay. Can you stay? I'd like her to rest here until we can do an X-ray. I'll give her something for the fever right now. I believe she has pneumonia, but I'd like to confirm and run some tests to see what triggered it so we can treat her better. She'll get past this," Lexi said reassuringly.

Pneumonia, yes. But which type? It could be bacterial, fungal or viral, and they were all treated with different medication. Malia's mother had said the girl had been playing around the animal pens and a lot of dust. Lexi was most suspicious of bacterial or fungal at the moment, even if fungal was much less common.

She left Malia and her mom inside the tent and went to put a satellite call through to Hope and to find Jacey. She found Jacey first at the back side of the bungalow, on the roof of all places, trying to fix the small satellite dish that helped give them access to the internet…when it was working.

"We have an in-house patient. Malia. That little girl with the cough. Is that thing working? I was going to call Dr. Hope's mobile unit on the satellite phone."

"Just about. Something had been chewing on the wire. I stripped it and it's almost ready."

"I told you to wait on Taj. Never climb on the roof like that without someone at least steadying the ladder for you."

"He hasn't returned from the village yet and I wasn't waiting on him."

"I'll hold it then, so you can get down."

Someone called out from around the front. Another patient?

"Don't do anything dangerous. Let me go see who is calling. I'll be right back."

She hurried out front. It was Malia's mom.

"Please, come. Her head is getting hotter."

Lexi ducked into the tent to check the girl's temperature. It had gone from one hundred and two to one hundred and three point five in the short while she'd been outside.

"I'm going to go ahead and start her on antibiotics. If the tests show we need to change treatment, we will, but I'll start her on one that covers most strains. Okay?"

"Yes. Please, make her well."

She wasn't one to jump to antibiotics, but with the girl's fever spiking so fast, it was warranted. High, rapidly raising fevers were often bacterial in nature.

"I'll do all I can. Here's a bottle of water. See if she'll sip some, even when I'm not in here."

Lexi went to the cabinet and took out a bag of saline, an alcohol swab and a butterfly needle. "Honey," she said, returning to the girl's bedside, "this is going to feel like a quick prick, but be brave and hold still for me. Can you hold her hand so she doesn't move?" Malia's mother held her gently and Lexi got the IV set up and started the drip. "This should help a lot."

Lexi could hear a jeep screech to a stop outside and, within seconds, Taj was screaming Jacey's name.

"I'll be right back. Stay here with her."

Lexi rushed out just as Taj came around the bungalow carrying Jacey in his arms. She was wincing and had her face pressed to his shoulder.

"She fell. What in the world were you doing up there?" he yelled, directing his concern at Jacey.

"Fixing things. You can make the call now, Lexi," Jacey said.

"Are you okay? I told you to wait," Lexi said. "You'll have to take her into the bungalow. The tent is full. I'll get the ice pack out of the freezer."

Taj carried her inside and set her down gently on the bed, then began removing her boot. Jacey reached down.

"I can do that. I'm fine. Sort of."

"Sit back, would you? For once, let me take care of you," Taj said.

Jacey obeyed, but her face turned bright pink as she glanced at Lexi.

"I'll be in the kitchen, making the call to Hope. Let him take care of your foot, Jacey," Lexi said.

She left them alone and took a moment to close her eyes. Was it a full moon tonight or something? She grabbed a cup of water and took a drink. She needed to take care of herself, too, for the sake of the baby, and it was starting to feel a little muggy.

She could hear Taj scolding Jacey, going on about how she could have broken her neck. The panic in his voice was unmistakable, which was unusual, since he'd always been ultra calm in emergencies. He was trained to be. But then things quieted and his voice softened.

Lexi peered into the other room as she waited for the satellite phone signal to go through. Taj set Jacey's wrapped foot on a stool, then sat next to her. Without a word, he took her hand and laced his fingers through hers. Jacey held on for a moment, but then slipped her hand away.

Why did it take an injury or tragedy for some people to stop and let someone else care for them? And who was Lexi to preach?

CHAPTER TEN

"I WARNED YOU," the poacher hissed.

His Swahili was different, yet Leboo could understand him, except for the one or two slang words he muttered. The man grabbed the gun and cocked it, his hand shaking ever so slightly. Sweat dripped down his temple and his eyes darkened. He'd refused to give his name, but it didn't matter. There was only one name for evil.

"I swear I tell the truth. There were too many people today. And they stayed outside last night, by the fire," Leboo said. "But I brought chapati and stew. It will give you strength."

It wouldn't fix the shattered bone in his leg or the flesh wound, but it would appease him. If it weren't for that gun...

The poacher glared at him before uncocking the gun and taking the food.

"Did they say anything about patrols or dogs?"

"No." Leboo wished he had a dog. Or that a lion would find the man's hideout and have a good meal. Thinking like that was evil. Wasn't it? Either way, the man was protected by the thorny branches he'd ordered Leboo to place around his hideout, just like the mass of acacia branches that fenced his family's village.

"You're thinking of lying to me, aren't you? I see it in your eyes. You will warn me if you hear of patrol dogs or anyone coming near, yes? You know the consequences if you don't."

"I speak the truth."

The man shoved a bite of stew into his mouth, not bothering to wipe where it dribbled down his chin.

"I need the medicine," he said, ripping at the bread with stained, crooked teeth. He set down the wooden bowl and spread a clump of tall grass to his right, just enough to see through it. He glanced at Leboo, making sure he got the point. The reminder that the man had a clear view...a clear shot...to the area outside Leboo's homestead wasn't necessary.

"I see them. I watch them. My aim is good. You understand?"

Acid burned in Leboo's chest. He nodded.

"Good. You are a brave warrior. One that understands the value of a life and a reward. I'm sure you'll figure out how to bring me the medicine." He aimed the barrel of the gun through the brush and right at Leboo's sister, who was gathering sticks for firewood. "By tomorrow. Or else."

THE RAINS were coming.

Lexi watched as the first cloud she'd seen in months wafted across the brown savannah, as if inspecting the damage done in its absence. The decaying skeletons of parched animals who'd collapsed at the edge of dry watering holes they'd depended on. The failed grain crops of disheartened farmers.

The power held in a single drop of water. The power to control the ebb and flow of life...and to take it away. She'd read once that water symbolized emotion. She now understood why.

She rubbed the small of her back. She had work to do. She loaded the box of glass vials into the truck. There was a special padded holder to keep the more fragile items. Then she went back into the tent to see what antibiotics and anthelmintics they had on hand.

Malia's X-ray had been clear and she'd been responding to treatment, but Lexi had kept her for observation for a few days.

Then Lexi had gotten word that there was a little boy at one of the nearby *enkangs* suffering from stomachaches and diarrhea. She was heading to that village anyway to administer a final round of vaccines before the rainy season, and she planned to examine the boy.

She wanted everything she might need on hand, including something to kill parasites, a highly suspect diagnosis given he helped care for his father's livestock. Loss of fluids wasn't a good sign. She grabbed a few packets of electrolyte powder and headed back out.

"I wish you weren't going alone," Jacey said, hobbling over on crutches. "They'll make it back soon, I'm sure. Can't you wait?"

Both Chad and Taj had gone to pick up the promised food supplies to deliver to everyone who had helped work on the acacia fence. It was only half done, but they were getting there. Chad and Taj had left early that morning, in the camp's mobile unit, and were supposed to be back by now, but delays out here were pretty common. In fact, nothing ran on time. One had to account for flat tires, someone else being late or even wild animal crossings. Sometimes there was just no way around a herd of elephants or wildebeests.

With Mac's schedule full the past few days, Chad had asked Ben to have his friends at KWS fly over the area a few extra times to make sure they didn't see any suspicious activity. Nothing had been noted or reported. The unofficial consensus was that the injured poacher must have made it over the border or died by now. They figured someone badly injured wouldn't have survived hiding out in the wilderness this long.

So Lexi felt quite safe making the trip to the village on her own. Less than ten kilometers one way was quite doable, especially for the sake of that child.

"This can't wait, and you can't drive, or I'd switch places and watch over Malia. I want to get the vaccines done before the rains come and wash out the road. But more importantly, that little boy with the stomach issues can't wait. I need to make sure he's treated and staying hydrated, or he could die. If Taj and Chad show up, one of them can drive out to the *enkang* and help if they want, but I really don't think it's necessary. I'll probably get back before they do."

"I know this is an emergency, but I'm just worried about you. What if you go into labor?"

"There are plenty of women around here who've given birth before. I'm sure I'll be fine and have plenty of help if I'm at an *enkang*. Trust me, you'll get word if I go into labor. I've worked with hospital staff who stayed on the job until their contractions hit. I wouldn't be the first."

"They were at a hospital, though. Kind of convenient, I would say."

"Jacey, stop worrying." Lexi grinned. "Imagine me giving birth at a Masai homestead. Tony would get a kick out of that."

"You laugh now. Just wait until the contractions hit." Jacey shuddered at her own words.

"Ever the comforter. You must have been a labor coach in another life. Today isn't the day. Okay? I think I'd sense it. And when Hope was out here with the mobile unit, she checked me out, to save me a trip to Nairobi. My cervix didn't show any signs of softening. The baby hadn't dropped, either."

"Ugh, I don't need the visual, thanks! The whole thing freaks me out." Jacey scrunched her face.

"Trust me, if I could avoid labor, I would, but I think it's a little late to consider that option. One of these days you'll be in my shoes and the idea of holding your baby in your arms will mask the labor anticipation anxiety. Just a little."

Jacey nibbled at her lip and adjusted her crutches.

"Guess it's a good thing I won't have to worry about it then," she said with a weak smile.

Lexi abandoned the supplies and turned to give Jacey her full attention. What was she saying? That she couldn't have children?

"Jacey, how long have you known?"

"Years."

"Years?" No wonder Chad had noticed her mood shift after the baby shower and whenever Taj mentioned kids. "Why didn't you say anything before?"

"It's not something I like to bring up, especially when one friend is expecting and the other is always talking about having a big family."

"Oh, Jacey. Never feel like you have to hold back with me. May I ask, as a nurse and a friend, what happened?"

Jacey put her crutches in one hand and leaned against the tree. She stared at her wrapped ankle for a minute before deciding to share.

"I was in severe pain as a teenager. While other girls bragged about starting their periods, I dreaded mine. I'd gotten it early, along with the fibroids and endometriosis that ran in my family. I was miserable, depressed from it all, and fed up. By the time I was nineteen, I had too much scar tissue.

"I searched and didn't stop until I found a doctor who was willing to do a complete hysterectomy. Given how young I was, they kept telling me I'd regret it. That I should hang in there and try more 'clean-up' surgeries. I had no money for that, or to freeze my eggs. Besides, my uterus was too scarred to safely carry a baby to term without high risk of rupturing. I made a choice. It may not have been the right one for other women, but it was the right one for me."

Lexi closed the gap between them and gave her a hug.

"I always knew you were a strong woman, but you're even stronger than I realized. You had every right to make that decision for yourself. Everyone is different, and no one could know how much you were suffering except for you. I'm sorry if I ever said anything that came off as insensitive, since I had no idea. I hope my pregnancy didn't make you uncomfortable."

"Oh, gosh, no. I am so genuinely happy for you. I'm still grossed out by the details, but truly happy for you. I have no regrets. Well… maybe just one," she said, sparing a quick glance at the clinic. "But it's not important in the grand scheme of things."

Lexi took a deep breath. She'd been right about Jacey having feelings for Taj, though she'd underestimated the issues between them.

It all came together. The way Jacey would blush one minute around him and fall on petty arguments to distance herself from him the next. The way she'd overreact about what a burden and pain kids were, every time Taj mentioned that he wanted a huge family someday. Yet she'd seen how wonderful and patient Jacey was whenever they were treating crowds of children. Was this part of the reason why she'd agreed to work here?

Lexi sighed and watched the light gray cloud pass beyond a canopy of acacia trees and out of sight.

"Jacey. I don't want to butt my head in your business and I know you'll order me to shut up if you want me to, and that's fine. But just talk to him. Tell him."

"I don't know what you're talking about."

"Yes, you do. Don't think I haven't seen how you two look at each other. I knew something was happening between you."

Jacey avoided eye contact.

"Taj isn't attracted to me like that. Tough ex-army girl isn't his style. He wants someone feminine and delicate who'll give him a million kids."

"First, that hyperbole just made my cervix ache. Second, he totally looks at you like he's lovesick. Third, you're gorgeous and the best kind of feminine—strong and caring all at once. And last, he thinks you don't really like him, yet he *still* cares and worries about you. You should let him know how you feel. Tell him the truth and let him decide. You can't make that call for him any more than you'd want someone else making it for you."

"Lexi. I understand you're trying to help, but I won't do that to him. I can't and won't put him on the spot. Even if he said it didn't matter that I can't have kids, I'd know it did to him. I'm not going to start a relationship that's bound to be filled with regrets. Don't you dare say anything to him."

"I won't. It's not my place. I just wish you would. No relationship has guarantees. I've experienced that firsthand. And after all I've been through, I have to admit that sometimes taking risks is worth it."

She gave Jacey another hug, then climbed awkwardly into the driver's seat.

"Be careful. Radio me when you arrive and before you head back so I know if I need to send a posse out," Jacey said.

"It's not that far, but okay."

The sound of an engine nearing had them both shading their eyes and gazing toward the plume of dust billowing down the road.

"Just in the nick of time," Jacey said, exhaling in relief. "He's not going to be happy when he sees that you were about to drive off."

They stood waiting as the guys approached the far edge of the clinic grounds. They parked and both men got out and began lifting a large bin out of the back of the van. The sight of Chad working like he had the strength of ten men sent Lexi's heart into a skydiving free fall.

"Why is it that men in labor is so much more attractive than women in labor?" she half whispered.

Jacey sighed her appreciation. "So long as we're talking about two different types of labor, I totally agree. Until they say something stupid, like we women can't protect ourselves."

"Oh, I don't know. It's kind of nice to hear that someone cares enough to worry and help, even if we *can* take care of ourselves," Lexi said, realizing that there was a time she'd never have admitted to that.

Chad glanced up and narrowed his eyes at her.

"Uh-oh. I think he noticed you were heading out alone. He seems ready to throw you over his shoulder like a Viking warrior and plop you down in a hut for safe keeping."

Lexi's face heated. "Where do you come up with that stuff?"

"Books. What do you think I do in my downtime?"

"Well, he knows he can't tell me what to do."

Chad tugged his belt loop up and started over.

"Uh-huh. Then I guess it's that invisible cosmic thread between you that's drawing him over here right now."

"God, don't say that. There's nothing but friendship between us. He was Tony's best friend. It's an entirely different situation than what's going on between you and Taj."

"Right. Even a blind man could sense the energy between you two. I think Nurse Lexi should practice what she preaches and take a risk." Jacey smiled at Chad as he approached. "Miss us?"

Lexi jabbed her with her elbow.

"Jacey, don't you have a patient to check on?" Lexi grabbed the crutches and shoved them into Jacey's hands.

Jacey chuckled, took them and hobbled away.

Chad scrunched his forehead.

"Where do you think you're headed?" he asked.

"To the Mingati Homestead."

"Alone? You're killing me."

"Lighten up. You guys were late. There's a sick child and I needed to leave so I could get back before dark. Besides, I know what I'm doing. I told Jacey to ask one of you to follow me to the village as soon as you got here."

He glanced over his shoulder at Taj and gave him a signal.

"Don't go anywhere. Give me a minute. I'm coming with you."

Lexi crossed her arms and leaned back against the jeep.

"Hurry it up, then," she said, acting just slightly annoyed. But the fact of the matter was, she was glad he was coming. She wanted his company, so why not enjoy it?

CHAD STOOD OUTSIDE the *inkajijik* as Lexi treated the little boy. His crying and whimpering were getting to Chad, not because of irritation, but because it hit him. Raising a child was petrifying…and he'd faced some darned scary situations before. What if this kid didn't make it? How would his parents cope? What if something happened to Tony's kid, too? How would Lexi handle that on her own?

He scrubbed the back of his neck. He needed to stop thinking like that. He was getting too involved. All he'd ever intended was to make sure she was okay. That was it. But somehow that had turned into a daily ritual. It was dragging him into the future. He needed to let it go. This was her life, not his. Coming here had helped him heal, but leaving was the only way he'd reach his potential again.

He scanned the circular boundaries of the *enkang*. Anxious children were being ushered out of the individual *inkajijiks*, clinging to the vibrant wraps their mothers wore. One toddler grabbed the beads that adorned his mother's neck and tried gnawing at them. Those kids seemed to know they were getting shots. Amazing how kids everywhere were the same.

There weren't many men around, only the elderly *laibon* sitting beneath a copse of trees just outside the homestead's protective fence. The old medicine man was handing a woman a cluster of herbs and presumably telling her how to use them.

Traditional versus modern medicine. He believed in both. He had grown up around enough family members who knew both the old traditional ways and the new ones. They each had their benefits. Maybe that's what he'd been missing in his care. Balance. Maybe that's why he'd been feeling better and recovering faster ever since he'd agreed to guard the clinic…because out here he was one with the sunshine, wind and earth.

There was a distant rumble and a cloud passed over the sun. He squinted toward the west and noticed the *laibon* had, as well. Thunder. He knew most of the men were either in warrior training or off in the fields grazing their herds of goats and cattle. They would be thrilled that the rains would finally turn the golden grasses into shades of bold malachite and jade. He, however, needed to get Lexi back home before the sky broke loose. Droughts had a way of ending with a bang.

Another rumble shook the air. Lexi hadn't even started the vaccinations yet.

He headed for their jeep and started lay-ing out what she needed for the vaccinations, then grabbed the water container she used for washing when gloves weren't enough. He needed to do whatever he could to help speed things up. He started to walk back to the entrance of the *enkang* and almost stopped. *Almost.* He knew enough not to draw attention. He slowed just enough to get a good look.

Every cell in him went on alert.

A single footprint.

Not the stamp of bare feet or the flat soles of the sandals many Masai wore, which were made from tire rubber. This was the partially eroded print of a sneaker. It wasn't fresh. But not that old, either. A day or two at most. Hiking or military ration, but all that mattered was that it wasn't Masai, and there weren't enough prints for it have been left by a KWS team member. And as far as he knew, the KWS hadn't been out this way in the past week. The flyby he'd requested had been for the clinic area. Besides, boot and sneaker prints weren't the same. He picked up his pace and reached the hut Lexi and the sick boy were in just as more thunder rumbled.

"Did you hear that?"

"Yes," she called out from inside the mud

and thatched hut. “Almost under control here. We still need to get the vaccines done, though.”

That footprint isn’t right. You have to warn her.

He didn’t want to say anything within earshot of anyone. He didn’t want to raise an alarm or to clue whoever was hiding out here that he was on to them.

A ribbon of dark clouds lined the horizon.

“We don’t have a lot of time, Lexi.”

“I put patients before time. That poor child. He’ll be okay, but he’s lost a lot of weight,” she said, stepping out of the hut. She took off her sterile gloves, disposed of them in a biohazard safety bin she’d brought and held her hands out. Chad grabbed their jug of water and poured a gentle stream as she washed up and then used alcohol to further clean her hands.

A girl who looked to be in her teens hovered next to her. Too close for Chad to say anything.

“I want to be a nurse, too, someday,” she said.

“That’s a wonderful goal. If you ever want to talk about it, let me know. Why don’t you come watch us give the shots, since you already had yours?" Lexi smiled warmly and dried her hands.

"Thank you. I will. I am going to go to a different school soon to study science. I have been going to Miss Pippa's school since I was younger, and she always told me I can be anything I want to be."

Pippa was passionate about teaching children from the rural homesteads to read—kids who typically didn't have access to education. She used to travel long distances to teach, and had been particularly concerned with young girls in the Masai tribes having the opportunity to pursue careers rather than get married at a young age.

Pippa'd made a name for herself and now had a small, rural school built in an area where children from multiple tribes could gather to learn. She still drove out to some villages, though, and, from what the girls themselves had relayed at the party, her step daughters often helped her.

His mom had told him that Pippa's husband was a wonderful man, and that he'd helped stop a fracking project and illegal dumping that had contaminated well water in the region and caused many children to get sick. Chad bit at his cheek. He'd missed a lot while in service and during his recovery. He'd almost forgotten what it was like to be home again. To just *be*.

He kept his eyes peeled at every shadow and movement around and between the domed huts. The feel of his gun pressing against his left calf was only slightly reassuring. It wasn't the most efficient place to keep it, considering reaction time, but it was the only place he could carry it without anyone noticing. He didn't want to use it—not with all the children around—but if there was a poacher hiding out here—

"Chad, are you not listening?" Lexi asked.

"Sorry. What did you say?"

"I asked if you could pass me those alcohol wipes." She settled onto a stool and began sweet-talking the first child, a toddler that squirmed so effectively he nearly fell out of his mother's arms.

Chad set the box of wipes within reach, along with disposable syringes and vaccine vials. He did a quick count. Only ten kids this time. Okay. Maybe that wouldn't take too long.

"We'll want to load things in the jeep before it rains."

"Thanks for stating the obvious," Lexi said. She finished poking a needle in the third child and disposed of it in a red, sharps container. A single drop of rain hit his arm. At least he was pretty sure it was rain. Chad shifted his weight and cleared his throat.

"I felt a drop. Just sayin'."

"Don't worry. A light drizzle won't be a problem."

Kid number six. She was efficient. He had to give her that. She had this down to an art form.

"Those clouds mean business. I assure you, this won't be a drizzle. A major storm is about to hit."

And possibly one that wasn't about the weather. But he'd seen no other signs of the poacher since he'd spotted the print.

"All done." Lexi, holding the edge of the small folding table they'd brought, tried to stand but immediately plopped back onto the stool.

Chad took her hand and helped her the second time. He didn't let go until he was sure she had her balance. "You okay?"

"I'm totally fine. Just a pinch in my lower back when I tried to get up. I was sitting funny, I guess. Being front-loaded kind of puts a strain on your spine."

"Take it easy. I'll get this stuff."

She ignored him and began closing the containers and putting them in a lidded box. Chad braced the table on his hip so he could fold the legs, but Lexi's teen observer was at his side helping in a flash.

"When will the baby come?" she asked Lexi.

"Oh, not for at least another week or two. I'm almost thirty-eight weeks," Lexi said.

"Children are a gift. I'm happy for you. Thank you again for letting me watch."

"Of course. Thank *you*. Keep studying. Maybe someday we'll work side-by-side." That earned Lexi a huge grin.

Chad lifted the table under his left arm. He wanted to carry the box, too but couldn't. If he took two trips to the jeep, which was outside the fenced area, he'd have to leave Lexi here. He didn't want her to be alone out at the jeep, either. God, he hated asking for help. Lexi started to pick the box up.

"Don't lift that."

"It's not heavy at all."

"You just said your back hurt. Would you mind helping us take this to our vehicle?" he asked the girl.

"Of course not."

Another drop of rain hit him, this time on the cheek. They loaded up and he secured the jeep's top. He thanked the girl and waved goodbye.

He needed to get Lexi back home ASAP. *Home.* Since when was the clinic home? He brushed away the thought. Her home maybe. Not his. He'd meant *her* home.

The marine in him wanted to stay and investigate the print, but a deep rumble of thunder had him stepping on the gas.

The usual symphony of wildlife quieted as a shadow fell across the relentless Serengeti sun. Even the animals knew to take cover. He sped up, conscious of every rut in the road because of Lexi.

She hadn't argued about him driving. Usually she insisted on being behind the wheel on account of getting more nauseous if she wasn't. He glanced over. She was gripping the edge of her seat.

"Sorry. I just want to make good time.

Lex, I saw something back there. A footprint. Something isn't right."

"Is that why you were acting so strange?" she asked, raising her voice over the engine noise. She winced.

Was his driving that scary? Driving an automatic with one hand wasn't a big deal, at least not to him…anymore.

"If you call keeping an eye out for danger strange, then yes. I didn't want to say anything in front of everyone. Someone there could be working with a group of poachers. I'll report what I noticed as soon as we get to the clinic." What if there really was a criminal back there? What if he'd been hiding in one of the huts, waiting for Lexi and Chad to leave?

He stepped on the gas.

For a moment he was back in Afghanistan. The attack. The blood. The deafening sound of explosives.

With a loud snap, a lightning bolt cracked the sky. He jolted to the present and swerved around a granite rock lying in the middle of the dirt road. Rain began pelting the windshield, picking up tempo by the second.

He had no choice but to slow his speed. He couldn't see five feet in front of him.

"Chad!"

"Don't worry. I've driven through worse."

"I'm wet!"

"Shut your window!" He looked over. It was already shut.

"No. *I'm* wet. I think my water just broke. Ohhh...oh, oh, oooooh." Her face contorted and she panted then released her breath. "Are you freaking kidding me? If that was a contraction and that's just the beginning of the pain, I'm not doing this!"

Chad felt all his blood get sucked down to his feet like a riptide in action. This wasn't happening. Danger he could do. Pulling a gun on the enemy? All in a day's work. Lexi going into labor in the middle of nowhere in torrential rains? At least six curse words poured out of him.

"Have you been in labor this whole time? Why didn't you speak up?" He tightened his grip on the steering wheel. "Just...just don't let yourself have another contraction yet. Hold it in or something. We're at least thirty minutes from the clinic." The tire hit a rut in the road filled with water and mud splattered the windshield. He ran the wipers and slowed even more.

"Hold it in? *You* hold it in! You think I can control this? Are all you men—"

Whoa. And he thought *he* could curse.

"What am I supposed to do?" he asked.

Her face started to twist out of shape again and his gut churned as if it was following her lead. She howled and groaned like a hyena then started to do those panting breaths women in labor were taught.

Get in control. Suck it up, man. Show her she can count on you.

"Lexi, talk to me. Tell me how to help you."

"Chad, I can't do this alone. The contractions are already too close." She flopped her head back against the seat. "Of all the times a long labor would have been nice. Oh…oh, oh. I think another is coming on. Chad, hold my hand."

Dammit. He couldn't. Not while driving. Maybe they'd make it to the clinic. On second thought, the road was turning into a mud bath. Up ahead there was a dip in the road where it ran around a small hill. That dip was probably already filled with water.

Lexi all-out screamed this time and his throat closed up.

"Okay. Okay. It's going to be okay, Lex. I'm going to pull over near that outcropping."

If he parked under the rocks, they'd be protected from the rain and he could radio the clinic and hope they'd be able to hear him. That meant this was really happening. Lexi was in labor. She was about to have Tony's child. Reality smacked him in the face. God help them both.

They were stuck in the middle of nowhere and she was having a baby.

LEXI HAD NEVER felt anything remotely close to this level of pain. She often asked patients to rate their pain on a scale of one to ten, with ten being the worst possible pain on the face of the earth. That last contraction was a fifty.

Chad pulled to a stop and immediately reached over and held her hand.

"I'm honestly afraid you'll take this the wrong way and slap me, but you can do this, Lex. And if slapping or punching or cussing at me helps the pain, do it. I can take it," he said.

"You'd let me hit you?" That had come

out as a whimper. What was wrong with her voice?

Chad's face softened and he looked right in her eyes and nodded.

"Anything for you, Lex."

Oh my God, she was in love. He was so sweet.

"You're too nice. I don't want to hit you. Ahhhhyyye!"

The pain crashed down on her. Everything blurred. She totally wanted to hit him. But wait, this wasn't his fault. She couldn't think straight. She tried breathing. It was too hard to breathe.

Breathe. You have to. You know how this works. You read up on it. You've seen others do it.

She moaned and tried not to push. It didn't work. Those books didn't pop humans out when their pages were opened. Men didn't pop humans out, either. She tried to catch her breath. Chad looked terrible and so good all at once. He was so handsome. She really was losing it.

"We need to push the seat back or something so I can get into a better position. I don't think I can get into the rear seat without going outside first. Maybe I can turn sideways a little."

"I'll try the seat."

He reached his body over hers so that he could get to the lever. She put her hand on his waist as he lowered the seat just slightly. His face was so close. She was so confused. He wasn't Tony, but she needed him. She wanted to feel Chad holding her. She wanted to kiss him. He turned his face to hers…and kissed her forehead. Her sweaty, likely stinky forehead.

"You can do this. See if you can shift to your left and maybe hold on to the back of the seat. Wait." He reached over and locked the door as a precaution. She tried not to picture herself falling out.

She started to move and the next contraction came full-force. She grabbed his hand and held on tight. She caught her breath as the contraction subsided.

Chad reached into the back and opened one of the clinic storage boxes, grabbing a general emergency pack. He unfolded a plastic tarp and nudged it underneath her, covering the seat and gears, then pulled out several of the blue disposable drapes she usually used for putting under surgical supplies for minor procedures like stitches. He then grabbed disinfectant gel and rubbed some on his hand.

"These blue things are the closest thing to clean towels we have," he said.

"It'll work," she panted.

"I'm not cutting anything."

Did he mean the cord?

"You don't have to. It's actually healthier for the baby, and safer considering where we are, to leave the umbilical cord attached."

He looked relieved but only momentarily.

"Maybe you can reach down and catch the baby when it's coming out. I'll help guide you," he said.

"No, I push. You catch." She was feeling seriously irritated. Pain did that to a person. She knew this was a first for him, but it was a first for her, too, and she was the one doing the pushing, for crying out loud.

Chad looked pale.

"Lexi, I'm here to do what's needed, but I don't want to drop the baby. What if I can't hold him and I injure him somehow? Newborns are supposed to be as slippery as fish."

"Chad, look at me. You've played football, right?"

"With two hands and no slime!"

She squeezed her eyes and tried to sift through the pain for an ounce of patience and encouragement.

Could she have done this on her own? Maybe. She'd read plenty of stories about women squatting and giving birth by themselves…in the woods…in history books. But it was safer with help, with someone who could see what was happening down there. She took a deep breath. She didn't want to do this alone. She needed Chad to be there for her. Tony should have been the one to see her through this, but right now, the only person she wanted with her was Chad. She released her breath slowly and reached to cover his hand with hers.

"I trust you more than anyone. You can do this. *We* can do this. I'll try to help if I can, but no guarantees. And if I yell at you, ignore me and do whatever you have to do to make this okay. And don't get shocked when I pass the placenta after the baby." It was best to warn him. She'd seen the bravest, biggest men pass out from the tiniest things in hospitals. The elephant-mouse syndrome.

He nodded but a bead of sweat trickled down his temple.

"Okay. Okay," he said again with resolve. He tilted his head and wiped his temple on his shoulder. "But we've got to, um, uncover you, so the baby can get out. I'm assuming you're okay with that?"

Heaven help her. Had she been subconsciously avoiding that part? She wanted to cry.

"Do what you have to do," she said as the next wave of pain wiped out any sense of modesty or embarrassment. Oh God, this hurt.

He was quick. Professional. He'd been trained for all sorts of emergencies, no doubt, but clearly not this.

Damn. Another contraction was building already. What in the name of— Forget Pain Level Fifty. This was at least a seventy. Someone was swearing. She wasn't sure if it was Chad or her. She didn't care.

"Oh my God, I see the head. Lexi, I see the head. We're having a baby!"

"Just get it out of me!"

"Push again!"

Push! We... We're having...

She strained. Panic set in. What if the umbilical cord was knotted or looped around the neck? What if it was a shoulder dystocia delivery? What if—

Just breathe. Remember your training. Chances are you wouldn't be progressing so fast if there was a problem. Push again.

She hugged the back of her seat tighter and pushed. Her abdomen suddenly lost pressure, like air swooshing out of a balloon.

"I got him! Quick, lean back so I can lay him on your chest," Chad said.

Lexi slumped against the door and reached out to help Chad as he brought the baby to her chest. *Him*. A boy.

"He's not crying," Chad said.

She wiped her fingers down the baby's nose to clear the fluid and they both rubbed at his tiny body. The best, sweetest, wail filled the jeep.

Tears brimmed in her eyes. She could see Chad's Adam's apple rise and fall as he sniffed and cleared his throat.

"It's a boy. A little Tony," he said.

"Little Tony," she whispered. Her chin quivered and she bit her lip. "He's going to be named Reth, after his grandfather. Tony would want that. And Tony can be his middle name. Reth Tony Galen."

"Reth. I think that's Swahili for king or ruler." Chad held a tiny foot between his fingers. "Just incredible. Now I understand why they call it a miracle."

"He's pretty amazing and beautiful, if I say so myself."

"He is." The corner of Chad's mouth lifted as he turned his attention to her. "You're amazing and beautiful, too."

For a moment Chad wasn't sure if he'd said too much or if he'd gone too far. This was supposed to be his best friend's moment. Fatherhood.

But Chad couldn't seem to hold back the emotions that had taken hold of him any more than Lexi could have stopped her contractions from happening. Nothing mattered anymore. Nothing but Lexi and the baby. They were suddenly his world, even if he didn't have a right to them.

He'd never understood exactly what Tony had been feeling when he'd said he'd fallen in love, but right now, this very second, Chad couldn't help but wonder if this was it. If the swelling in his chest and the buzzing energy that seemed to race through every cell in his body and rewire his brain…was love. All he knew was that the rain and thunder seemed to disappear when he looked at her. All he could feel was an overwhelming, desperate need to hold them both.

Lexi didn't say anything. She simply wove her fingers through his and didn't let go. Something undefinable swirled in his chest. He wanted to protect them. Not because of a promise, but because of a visceral longing to do so. He had to make sure they'd be safe.

He just hoped he could. With the roads washed out and the rains coming down too hard for anyone to come and get them by air—and his gut telling him that whoever was working with the poachers was out there—right now, they were sitting ducks.

IT RAINED NONSTOP for almost two hours—more than the parched ground could drink up all at once. The road ahead turned out to be a dry creek bed. It wasn't so dry anymore. All they could do was sit tight until the help Chad had radioed for arrived.

Lexi knew there'd be more rain, even if it had finally stopped fifteen minutes ago. Afternoon storms would be the norm for the next couple of months. She'd heard about how long and persistent the rainy season was once it finally started, but it was a good omen. She'd heard that, too. All life here counted on rain returning to the lands. Rain brought fertility and hope from the Masai Mara and Kenya's Serengeti region to Amboseli and Tsavo in the south. It also brought death, of course. Life was about balance, not extremes.

Maybe her baby was meant to bring balance back into her life. Not in a way that would burden him. Just in terms of having someone to give all the love she'd been holding in since Tony's death. She gave through her work, yes, but it wasn't the same deep-seated, aching love she was experiencing right now. The connection between a mother and child. A connection she'd never had, at least not at an age where she'd have remembered it.

She kissed the top of her baby's head as he nursed. Chad rubbed the pad of his thumb against the back of her hand. She looked at him and something stirred in her. *Love.* Was she falling in love with Chad? Was he also meant to bring balance into her life? Or perhaps they were meant to bring it into each other's lives. Or was she simply overwhelmed with emotion at the moment?

It had to be her imagination and hormones. Chad was being caring. He understood pain. He understood being vulnerable and had just been there for her in the most vulnerable moment of her life, next to the day she'd learned of Tony's death. That didn't mean that Chad felt any more for her than she felt for him. She considered him a friend. He was looking out for his best friend's family. That's all.

Family. Tony had been the first real family she'd had, and they'd barely had the chance to live and experience marriage like the average person because he'd been in Afghanistan. She'd met his parents a couple of times—they'd each moved to a different city since their divorce when he was a teen—and they were good, loving people. But she hadn't spent enough time around either of them to form a bond or to *feel* like she was part of something.

That's why coming here had been so important to her. She and Tony were going to build a legacy that was more important than either of them. He had roots here and, through him and through their child, she would have roots, too. Even without Tony, she felt at home here. Being on the Masai Mara mattered on so many levels.

But what she hadn't expected was to be drawn into the love and open arms of Chad's family. His parents, his siblings, cousins and extended family and friends had all treated her as one of their own. She'd been welcomed into their circle, and she wanted to be a part of it, even if she wasn't sure she had a right to be.

She heard the sound of a helicopter approaching and Chad slipped his hand away from hers.

"Finally," he said, opening his door and sloshing through the mud to make his way around to her door.

He sounded relieved this was over. And here, she'd been cherishing the moment. Could she blame him? Most guys got pretty grossed out by childbirth. There was nothing attractive about her at the moment.

She pressed her lips to Baby Reth's head again and let his calming baby scent envelope her. Everything would turn out the way it was meant to. All that mattered was this tiny, fragile infant and his future. Her baby. She'd give her life for him.

"They're circling. Probably trying to spot a place they can land," he said. "Stay seated until my mom gets here and makes sure you're okay."

"I'm fine. Thank you. For everything." She hated the way her tone made it sound like an ending. Like something had escaped and would never be captured again.

But that was the cycle of life. All endings brought new life…new beginnings. And all things eventually came to an end.

CHAPTER ELEVEN

HOPE CRADLED Baby Reth against her shoulder and rubbed gentle circles on his back. Chad hadn't seen that look of bliss on her face since his youngest brother, Philip, had been born. He'd been too young to notice that sort of thing when Hope had first come to America to help his dad with Maddie, him and Ryan, who'd been a newborn at the time. Hope and Ben didn't have Philip until after they'd all settled down as a family in Nairobi. And Chad hadn't been around when Maddie and Haki had their first baby.

A burp came out of Reth and he immediately fell asleep against Hope's shoulder. Lexi was getting a little rest of her own in her room, under doctor's orders. Chad was beginning to think his mom was happy to give those orders so that she could have some baby time to herself.

He carried a bowl of stew over to the

wooden table where Taj and Jacey were already eating. Mac had left as soon as he'd delivered them to the clinic. He didn't want to get grounded in another downpour, though he said he'd return tomorrow, weather permitting.

In the meantime, everything had been moved indoors. It was pretty cramped inside the bungalow, and Chad found himself imagining building a small cottage like the one his sister and Haki had erected adjacent to the vet clinic. Only, there hadn't been recent reports of poaching activity down where they lived.

He'd told Mac about the print, which was undoubtedly washed away by now, and he'd called his dad about it, too. According to Ben, he'd checked in with his contacts at KWS and a small group of poachers had just been caught when their vehicle got trapped in mud during the storm. They were pretty sure that group and the print were related, given their proximity. They'd had some men check out the village but found no evidence of ivory or a weapons stash. The track might have been left by a poacher stalking the area at night, when the Masai were within the fenced area.

That meant the clinic was safe for now. Or at least as safe as any of the places his family lived, from his sister and Haki's lodge to Busara to the cottage home Pippa and her family lived in close to the rural school she'd established. Even Camp Jamba-Walker, where Mac's family lived, was as deep into Kenya's wilderness as possible. Yet they'd all lived in these remote places for years without incident. If this group of poachers had been caught, that meant this clinic was safe, didn't it? He set down his spoon. Worry had a way of stealing one's appetite.

"Honestly, is there anything better than babies? I know I'm not really his grandmother, but I feel like I was just blessed with another grandchild," Hope said, nuzzling the crook of his neck. "If only they could bottle baby scent."

"Did you not smell what came out of him thirty minutes ago?" Chad asked.

"Ditto what he just pointed out," Jacey added. "It's unreal that it came out of a cute thing his size. Kind of mind-blowing."

"Keep your voices down. You'll wake him and Lexi up," Hope said.

"You were all babies once," Taj pointed out.

"I still remember the first diaper I ever changed. It was your brother Ryan's, and a complete disaster. Pee sprayed everywhere and your father had to step in and rescue the situation," Hope said. A laugh escaped her and she covered her mouth when the baby almost woke.

"See. This is why I don't understand anyone wanting kids. They have a way of making grown-up conversations go downhill," Jacey said.

"Every bit worth it," Taj said. "Besides, in medical school, even single, childless grown-ups talk about things you'd never imagine, usually concerning bodily functions. Baby poop is nothing compared to that."

"I'm a realist, and the reality is that cuteness has a price. Like boiling diapers. This girl is never going to do that. Not to mention the cost of having a child. And being tied down. Me? I like being able to move when I want to. Explore the world," Jacey said.

"You guys will feel differently when you have your own kids," Hope said.

Chad knew she wasn't referring to him specifically, but for a second he'd almost pointed out that she was holding his kid. The one he'd helped birth. The one he had a primal urge to protect. He cranked his neck to the side and swallowed back his words. He wasn't a father. Not even close.

Jacey excused herself, grabbed her crutches and went outside. Hope's brow furrowed as she watched her leave.

"I think that might have been insensitive. Chad, can you hold the baby so I can go check on her?" Hope asked.

"I'll go," Taj said. He walked out before anyone could argue.

"Then here, you hold Reth, Chad. I'll clear the table," Hope said, glancing out the window. She held the baby out with one hand, supporting his head and neck, and placed him in the crook of Chad's arm.

Chad didn't object. He curved his arm in and cradled the baby safely against his chest. He was so light. So limp.

Hope smiled. "He looks good on you," she said, stepping away to clear the dishes.

"What did I miss?"

Chad glanced over his shoulder to find Lexi watching from the bedroom doorway, rosy-cheeked and groggy and just plain beautiful. She bit her lower lip.

"Taj went after Jacey," Chad offered, trying to deflect any attention from him holding the baby.

"I said something about having kids and she walked out," Hope explained.

"Oh, no. I'll be right back," Lexi said, glancing at Chad and the baby sound asleep in his arm before opening the screen door and closing it quietly behind her so it wouldn't slam shut.

Hope splayed both hands and shook her head. "Clearly there's something going on here that I didn't know about," she said.

"I have no idea what you mean. I'm holding the baby, that's all. I mean, I'm like his uncle and I helped bring him into the world and all, but Lexi and I are… I don't know. Friends? I think. We're not together. At least not in that way." He was babbling. He needed to shut up.

Hope cocked her head and grinned. She

sat on the stool next to him and leaned her elbow on the table.

"I wasn't referring to you and Lexi. But I'm all ears now."

LEXI STEPPED OUTSIDE, careful not to slip in the puddle of mud outside the door. Soon they'd have to build wooden paths between the clinic buildings, just above ground, to avoid the mud. The air was thick with humidity and the scent of wet grasses and overripe fruit ready to fall from the trees. Lions roared and monkeys chattered as the rest of the wildlife chimed in. They were celebrating the end of the drought.

She listened for Taj and Jacey. Voices carried from behind the clinic tent, where Jacey often went to be alone. A few months ago, Taj had found a small boulder perfectly shaped for sitting and dragged it under the mango tree back there. He had to have strained quite a few muscles moving it. Lexi had suspected he'd done it because he cared for Jacey, even that far back in time. Probably longer.

"I don't understand. What do you mean you're leaving? Where are you going?" Taj said.

"I think I'll check out India next," Jacey said.

Lexi didn't want to eavesdrop but she could hear them before she reached the clearing. Since when did Jacey plan on leaving? She couldn't leave now. Not when she was needed even more, since Lexi had a baby to raise. This hadn't been planned. This was Jacey running away. She rounded the tent.

"Jacey." That's all Lexi said. She couldn't say more without revealing her friend's secret. She was sure Jacey would understand. She looked at her pleadingly, willing her to tell Taj the truth.

"What's going on, Lexi? Is there something you know? Why's she leaving?"

"I'm sitting right here," Jacey said.

Taj looked at her and braced his hands on his hips.

"Then talk to me. Just like that, you want to leave? Don't we matter to you? Didn't any of the last eight months matter?"

He'd said "we" but Lexi knew he meant himself.

Jacey's face flushed and she ground the end of her crutches into the mud.

Man, these two were stubborn.

"I'm about to step right into the middle of what's none of my business. It's probably wrong, but I'm going to do it anyway. Blame it on my feeling hormonal and sentimental."

"Don't say it, Lexi," Jacey warned.

"That part I leave to you. But enough, you two. You both like each other and have for a long time. Why can't you just admit it? Jacey, that rock you've enjoyed for months on end, lounging on it with a book…do you really think Taj killed himself rolling it here for him? Or me?"

Jacey looked off into a grove of pepper trees, but Lexi could see she was trying to remain stoic.

"And what about you, Taj? Are you blind? I've noticed the way you both look at each other and how you choose to work together even when I'm available and you don't have to. And Jacey hates cooking, but she always makes your favorite dish on the weekends when you come out here. Did you really believe it was because she couldn't cook anything else?

"I'm going to say it now since neither of you is brave enough and I don't want to see two people I care about miss out on something that's so rare. You more than care for each other. I've been watching this romance unfold but it has been like a soap opera with no end. Why can't you just admit your feelings and work it out?"

"Because it *can't* work out." Jacey wiped a tear off her face, stood and positioned her crutches.

Taj's face softened and he sucked in a breath.

"Then she's right? What's between us hasn't been my imagination?" he asked.

Jacey stared at the ground.

Taj scratched the back of his head and stepped closer to her.

"Talk to me, Jace. If it hasn't been all in my head, then why are you running off? Did I do something wrong? Tell me what I did. I'll make it right. Jace… I've… I've never felt about anyone the way I feel about you."

"You can't make it right," she blurted. "I… I can't have children, Taj. Lexi only found out recently. I can't have kids and all you've ever spoken about was how big a family you want. I'm not that girl. I can't give you that, and I won't take it away from you."

Taj froze for a second before glancing back at Lexi, as if he needed confirmation that what he was hearing was true.

"Jace, I'm sorry," he said.

"Don't be. See? I was trying to spare you getting put on the spot."

"You think I'm being put on the spot? You think whether you can have children or not matters to me?"

"Of course it does."

"Don't speak for me, Jace. If you believe I'm so closed-minded and selfish that I'd insist my kids had to come from me—or you—then you don't know and respect me as well as I thought you did.

"Look at Mac. Didn't you hear that he and Tessa adopted Tai just over a year ago? I thought you met them at the baby shower. Does it look to you like Hope loves Chad, Maddie or Ryan any less than Philip? Open your eyes, Jacey. I've been trying to show you I care every way I know how, but I held back because I felt something was wrong. That you weren't ready for a relationship, or that maybe you weren't interested. But if this is what it's about, then give me—give us—a chance."

Jacey, who Lexi had never seen so much as shed a tear, covered her face and tried to muffle a sob. Taj closed the gap between them and put his arms around her. Lexi wiped her own face and turned to leave. She'd done her part. They needed privacy now. She couldn't keep herself from looking back one more time, though, just as Taj pressed a kiss to the top of Jacey's head. Then, finally, Jacey wrapped her arms around his waist and let herself be held.

CHAPTER TWELVE

CHAD FLIPPED THE eggs in the pan and switched off the burner. It had only taken one flick of his wrist to get it right this time and no egg had ended up on the floor. Mac had picked up Hope and Taj that morning to fly them to Nairobi, and Jacey had gone with them. She and Taj wanted to spend time together in Nairobi. He wanted Jacey to see where he spent his days when he wasn't at the clinic camp and maybe take her on a real date.

That resulted in Chad being left alone with Lexi and the baby. But it wasn't like it was a date day for them or anything. Definitely not. At least he didn't think so. Lexi had simply refused to return to Nairobi, insisting that the helicopter noise wouldn't be good for Reth, and with the rainstorms as unpredictable as they were, traveling into the city by car wasn't going to happen, either. She'd said she felt safer here, and all her baby supplies were here, too, including the crib he'd put together for her. He obviously couldn't have let her stay alone, so he'd chose to stay, as well. And so what if he was cooking for her? She had to eat.

But this really wasn't a date.

"Hey, you're making food?" Lexi said, cracking the door behind her so she could listen for the baby. She flicked on the monitor she'd gotten from Maddie at the shower, but she didn't trust it yet. He'd seen her peeking in the room every few minutes all morning.

"It's not much. Just eggs." He put a plate on the table for her and filled another for himself.

"It's perfect. Thanks." She took a bite and nodded her approval. "Very good."

"I read that you need more calories when you're nursing, and I noticed you barely ate breakfast when everyone else did. Too busy feeding the little man."

"Calling him a man already, huh." She chuckled and took another bite before looking up at him from under her lashes. "You've been reading my baby books?"

He felt heat rise up the back of his neck. He shrugged.

"I couldn't sleep after about four in the morning, so I read the part about those first months after birth." He couldn't read her expression. She kept eating quietly. "More eggs?"

"No, I'm good. This was plenty. And nutritious. I appreciate it."

He practically jumped out of his seat and to the window when he heard the sound of voices approaching. He relaxed when he spotted two women from one of the nearby tribes making their way up the path.

"You do realize bad guys don't usually announce their presence?" Lexi teased after she looked past him and through the window screen.

"Of course, I know that," he scoffed. "I was just preparing myself in case there was an emergency."

"Do me a favor and stay here in case Reth wakes up. I secured the screen around his crib, but I don't want him left alone."

He completely agreed on that point. Everyone, even Anna and Niara, who'd raised Pippa and Haki in a tent, had warned Lexi about snakes, curious monkeys and other critters. He didn't understand why they'd seemed so matter-of-fact about it, but they'd all blasted him with the dangers of raising kids in the city. Danger was everywhere. You couldn't let it keep you from living life the way you saw fit, though.

Now where had he heard that before?

He listened for the baby, but kept his eyes on Lexi as she met with the women outside. One of the women handed her something then they waved and left. Apparently, they hadn't come for the clinic. Lexi came back inside, beaming.

"That was so kind of them. Look at this. They heard that I had my baby and wanted to bring a gift."

She showed him the colorful cloth with geometric designs in blue and orange.

"It's how they carry their babies while they work. Like a sling. This will be so useful," she said.

He knew what it was. He'd grown up in Kenya and had seen it being used often, but he didn't point that out. She was happy and happy looked good on her. So did the gift.

"But you're not carrying him in that sling while seeing patients. He could get exposed to stuff."

"I won't. I do have a brain and common sense, Chad. But when I'm just walking or washing clothes or taking inventory, I can keep him against me and have my hands free."

It hit him that, apart from the fact that he'd look ridiculous in it, the sling would free up his hand while he carried the baby, too. Maybe, just maybe, he'd try it if he mustered up the courage to look silly.

"My mom said that Dalila, the woman who helped raise her and then me and my siblings, is willing to come out here to help until you find someone more permanent. And don't argue that point—you *do* need help and a second set of eyes, especially for when the rains end and you start doing more off-site clinics. And then when the little guy starts walking. If he's anything like I was as a toddler—"

He stopped his sentence short, not because he couldn't compare all little boys to the handful he'd been, but because it seemed to emphasize the fact that Reth was more likely to be a mellow kid like his father had been than a rambunctious, hyperactive one like Chad had been.

"That's so nice of her. I can't stop saying

thank you, but the fact of the matter is, I underestimated how much is involved in having a baby. I thought I could do all of this—living out here—alone, but now I understand why they say 'it takes a village.' Your family is so special, Chad. You're lucky to have them. I'm so grateful for how nice they've all been to me."

"We are a close family and a very, *very* big, extended family, too. You've yet to meet everyone. We tend to consider 'friends' and 'family' to be synonyms. Everyone is an aunt or uncle, blood-related or not," he said.

"Someone always has your back."

"Yeah, I guess so." Chad nodded.

They were standing so close. He wanted to hold her. He brushed her hair from her forehead and tucked it behind her ear. She tipped her chin up, just as rain began splattering against the roof and the baby started crying. Lexi put her head against his chest and sighed.

"I swear it seems like I just fed him and changed him."

"You did. I'll burp him for you when you're done."

"First you make me eggs, then you volunteer for burp duty? What would I do without you?"

The rain picked up tempo as he watched her disappear into the room. What would she do if he returned to Nairobi and or even to the marines? What if she found out about the appointments he'd begun to schedule for next month, in the hopes of speeding his recovery and qualifying to reenlist? He had already spent more weeks out here than he'd originally planned. But searching for the poacher and finding that footstep had made him feel like he had a reason to live.

He'd also let himself fall for her, though, something he'd sworn he wouldn't do. There was no future for him out here. He wasn't a family man. He was a military man. Always had been, always would be.

Sure, he'd started off thinking he had no future in military service, but that wasn't the case anymore. He wasn't as incapable as he'd once thought, but that also meant he needed to do more. He didn't want to be a burden to his parents. He needed to figure out his future and to contribute to society the way everyone in his family did, whether in saving children or saving elephants and other wildlife. *Once a marine, always a marine.* He came from a family of healers and warriors. A family of doers. The possibility that the marines might take him back made him feel like he'd regained a tiny part of himself.

But another part of him wanted Lexi in his life. And yet, if he stayed, was he even truly capable of keeping everyone safe? Or was he going to fall into the role of stay-at-home-dad at the clinic?

Dad? Tony had to be looking down on him right now, furious as the thunder that kept growling and snapping at the sky. Chad needed to step back before he fell any further for Lexi and Reth. He couldn't make her move, now that the immediate threat had passed and the fence was almost built. He now understood how critical it was for so many men, women and children to have access to this clinic.

And if she was safe, what need was there for him to be there? Why was he lingering? Once Taj and Jacey returned and Dalila arrived to help out, there'd really be no reason for him to stay. And if he did, how long would it take for him to get restless?

HAVING DALILA AROUND was beyond amazing. Lexi felt like she had a grandmother on top of being practically adopted into Chad's family circle.

In just two days, they'd settled into a routine. The number-one priority was making sure Baby Reth was watched like a hawk and never left alone. They traded duties. If Dalila was tending to him, Lexi either boiled cloth diapers or tended to anyone who made it out in the rain to the clinic. If Lexi was nursing or spending time with him, Dalila usually cooked up foods worthy of a five-star restaurant. Savory potato and pea stew, *chapati* done on an open fire, and everyone's favorite, *mandazi*, the best doughnuts she'd ever had.

Chad seemed a little out of sorts and quiet lately. She hoped it was nothing more than the effect of the long, rainy days. He, Taj and Jacey, when not helping with patients, worked on adding a much needed second bathroom to the bungalow. It really did feel like home now. She didn't think of it as simply the clinic anymore. It was their bungalow. Their home.

Taj was in Nairobi today. Jacey kept busy but if the way she kept checking the weather and chopper clearing was any indication, she couldn't wait for him to return.

Chad was in his room trying to thread a sewing needle that he'd stuck partway into a potato. Lexi had suggested it as a way to improve his fine motor skills. It would help with his handwriting, too. The last time she'd walked past his door, though, he'd abandoned the needle and was doing curl-ups with a hand-held weight. It was great to see how motivated he finally was in terms of physical recovery.

She finished nursing and burping Reth, then lay him down to change his diaper. Dalila came in with freshly folded towels and receiving blankets.

"Would you mind watching him for a minute? I ran out of alcohol wipes in here and need some for his umbilical cord stump. I'll get some from the exam tent. I won't be long."

"Of course. I would watch this little one to the moon and back," Dalila said, scooping him up and kissing his miniature toes. His little wrinkled foot in her wise and caring wrinkled hand. Life was beautiful indeed.

"Thanks."

Lexi passed through the kitchen and stole a *mandazi* on her way out. Not the healthiest treat, but one more wouldn't hurt, would it? She was taking advantage and enjoying them while Dalila was here. Her food alone would be incentive to visit the Corallis' home in Nairobi after Dalila went back. Then it really would be only a treat.

She could smell the rain in the midday air. The clouds were building again...getting ready for another release so that a rainbow could grace the plains. There was so much that people could learn from nature. The sky billowed like a gray canopy and a vervet monkey scampered up a tree with a mango in his hand and swung his way to an afternoon shelter among the leaves. Lexi smiled as she shook out her mud boots—no one put shoes on out here without shaking them first...just in case a snake or some other critter was inside—then slipped them on and trudged out to the medical tent.

She thought she heard a rustle inside, but when she paused, she spotted a russet bird shaking the branches of a nearby tree. It flew off and Lexi let out the breath she'd been holding. She reached for the tarp that covered the entrance of the tent just as something clattered, like metal against metal or a glass vial hitting a surgical tray. Jacey had to be taking inventory or something.

"Jacey, everything okay?" she said as she stepped inside. Her blood rushed to her feet as a musty hand covered her mouth. A knife held to her throat served as a warning not to scream. It worked. He wasn't much taller than she was, judging from the height of the arm that held her against his chest. He was wearing a *shuka*. And designer sneakers caked in dirt.

He spun her around and pushed her to the end of the tent, keeping the knife only inches away. He was a boy. A mere boy. He couldn't have been more than sixteen. His hand shook ever so slightly and he was breathing rapidly, but there was fiery determination in his eyes.

"I need antibiotics and the needle for it. Or pills for swallowing," he said. Many boys his age were off at an *emanyatta*, unless his height made him seem older than he was and he'd not yet been initiated into a warriors camp. But what if this had to do with a traditional teenaged *emuratta* gone wrong. Circumcisions could get infected. Then again, what if that injured poacher had actually survived this long because this boy had been aiding him? She held up her palms.

"I need to know more if I'm to help you. Who is sick? What exactly is wrong with them? And you can put down the knife. I'm a nurse. I'm willing to help."

He gripped the knife even tighter and brought it an inch closer to her face. Her mind raced. How could she warn everyone? She had to keep Reth safe.

"No. Just give me the medicine. Put it in this now." He tossed a leather pouch at her.

"Okay. Okay. I'm going to open this cabinet for the supplies." She inched toward the metal cabinet and began turning the combination lock that kept it secure. The other cabinet and shelf weren't locked. She recalled the way some of their supplies had seemed to run out too quickly over the past few weeks. "Is it for a cough? A fever? Or a skin wound? Because if I give you the wrong medicine, it could kill the patient." Unlikely, unless they were allergic to penicillin, which she had no way of knowing. But she wanted to scare him. Then again, if this was about the poacher, at this point, he'd need major

IV antibiotics…if that could even save him. The man was lucky he'd survived this long. Most of what she had was broad spectrum, but the threat of death had a way of drawing out the truth sometimes. She glanced at the boy quickly and opened the cabinet. He'd hesitated, flinching when she'd said "could kill the patient." Sweat beaded on his face.

"It's for the skin. And fever."

Septicemia.

"For you?"

"No. You ask too many questions. Just give me what I need. And don't make a sound or I'll use this. I'm not afraid to use it."

The knife.

She picked out a few vials of penicillin and searched for a weapon of her own. She glanced at the bin where they kept sterilized equipment for minor emergency procedures. A scalpel wouldn't cut as deep as his dagger, but it was something. The women's defense class she'd taken years ago in college had taught her to go for where it counted.

Could she do it? Could she injure him? Blind him? He was a desperate kid—another woman's son—and her gut told her someone, if not the poacher, was putting him up to this.

But she had a right to defend herself, too. To keep her home safe. To keep her own child safe.

She fumbled with a few packs of syringes so he wouldn't get suspicious as she checked the bin. It was empty. Where was the surgical equipment? Her chest sank. Jacey must have taken it all to the autoclave. She took a breath and placed the requested supplies in the dingy pouch.

"Bandages, too."

She nodded. She needed to think straight. Why wouldn't he just bring the patient here, like all the villagers in the area did? The rain? The roads? What had driven him to attack her with a knife?

"Do you want me to call our doctor to go with you to treat the patient?" she hedged.

"No." He shook his head and grabbed the pouch from her. "The bandages."

Only criminals don't come in person for treatment.

Her pulse skittered. But the KWS had said they believed the man to be dead or safe across the border. Why was he still in the vicinity? How had he convinced this boy to help him? His wounds had to have prevented him from traveling far or fast enough not to get caught. Shattered leg? Bullet to bone would definitely do that.

She closed the cabinet and pretended to struggle with the latch on the plastic bin where the bandages were kept. She was trying to buy time. If she stayed out here long enough, Dalila would wonder what was taking her so long. *Please, please don't come outside with the baby looking for me. Tell Chad to go look for me. Tell Chad.* She willed the other woman to hear her thoughts. She prayed for Chad to sense something was wrong. For him to feel it in his gut.

He had been right all along. She wished he had never stopped trusting and believing in himself. *Trust your instincts, Chad.*

She opened the box and pulled out a roll of bandages.

How many people scoffed at gut feelings and chalked them up to fear and paranoia? Was she also guilty of dismissing Chad for being overprotective because of the trauma he'd suffered? Yes, she was. And she was guilty of wanting him in her life and loving him, too. Was this karma? Some sort of punishment for betraying Tony by loving Chad?

Tony, if you're looking down on us right now, forgive me. Help me. Somehow, get through to Chad. Please. I love you, but I love him, too, and I need him. I have to survive this for the sake of our son.

She tried to stay strong. She had to come up with a way to keep the boy from leaving. He needed to be caught. If he left with the medication, they might never see him again…or he could keep returning for more. A constant threat that would shut this place down. But if he was caught, he might reveal information that could lead to the poacher or poachers he was collaborating with. She swallowed hard and tipped her chin up as she handed over the roll of gauze.

"Is someone threatening you? Or your family? You don't have to do this. We can help."

He moved swiftly, grasping her arm and spinning her around.

Then she felt the tip of his blade on the back of her neck.

CHAD AIMED FOR the eye of the needle and focused. His arm was tired after all the arm curls, but if he could do this when his muscles were fatigued, it would be a breeze when he was rested. It was something his sergeant used to say back when he was a new recruit. Until you've pushed yourself beyond your limits, you haven't seen your baseline and you'll never know what you're really capable of.

Bullseye. The thread hung loosely through the eye of the needle. Oh, the satisfaction.

He scooted his chair back and bumped into the leg of the table, causing the weight he'd been pumping to fall off and land on the floor with a thud, with half of it landing on his foot. He cursed and kicked it out of the way, then rubbed at the pain, only something wasn't right. The thud and sound of his own voice made him hyperaware of how quiet it was. No cooking sounds. No voices outside or the usual noises of people puttering around the clinic grounds. The baby was probably asleep, but the rest gnawed at him. Where was everyone?

He stepped out of his room and tapped quietly at the door of Lexi and the baby's room before opening it. Dalila was zipping up the mosquito netting around the crib.

"Chad," she whispered, "I was just about

to come ask you to go see what happened to Lexi. She went for alcohol swabs, but that was ten minutes ago."

Alarms went off in his head. There was no reason for her to be gone that long. Maybe a patient had showed up and she was helping them. It sounded reasonable in his head, but everything else in him screamed that something was off.

"No problem. I'll go tell her to hurry it up," he said, hoping his voice didn't sound concerned.

He glanced out the window on his way to the door and adrenaline flooded through him. Lexi appeared at the entrance to the medic tent. But her body was too rigid and she moved awkwardly. Then he glimpsed the man still partially covered by the tarp behind her and the glint of metal.

"No!" He rushed into his room for his gun. "Dalila, stay inside the bedroom. Don't come out unless I tell you to." He didn't have time to explain. He knew she'd pick up from his tone to listen to his instructions.

He stepped outside slowly, measuring every move and pointing the gun at the ground behind his thigh. Having it was a precaution but he knew better than to take aim. A loaded gun was never aimed at a target unless the intention was to shoot. That was ingrained in him. And he couldn't shoot, not with Lexi being used as a shield.

"Hey, Lex. What's up?" he asked as casually as he could.

She kept her neck still but tried signaling behind her with her eyes. He gave an almost imperceptible nod and she flattened her lips in understanding. She knew he could see what was happening.

"Um, nothing. Just a *kid* I was treating."

Kid. She'd stressed the word just enough for him to notice. She was being protective of her captor? He took a few more steps in her direction.

"I've *armed* him with the medicine he needs, so he's all done and he's leaving now. Right?" she said, looking over her shoulder. She was gutsy. She was trying to get the kid's guard down. The blade disappeared from behind her neck and the guy emerged from the tent, still too close for comfort.

His shoes. They were running shoes. His mind zipped to the he footprint at the Masai homestead. The facts started to cluster like iron shavings to a magnet. The kid must have gotten them as a bribe. He needed meds from the clinic for someone else. A drop of rain hit his cheek, then another.

In his peripheral vision, he saw Jacey in the shadows along the side of the tent. He avoided eye contact, keeping his gaze on Lexi.

"Right," the boy said, deciding to take the out Lexi had offered him. "I should go before it rains harder."

Chad tucked his gun behind his back and picked up his pace a bit. He waved the boy off and kept his hand held out for Lexi.

"You should hurry before the road floods," he told the kid. He wanted him to listen, to separate himself from Lexi.

He did.

In a matter of seconds Chad grabbed Lexi and pulled her away as Jacey tackled the kid to the ground. She pinned him down and twisted his arm behind his back, applying just enough pressure that he dropped the knife involuntarily.

"Don't hurt him," Lexi pleaded as Chad left her side to help Jacey.

"No one's getting hurt, if he cooperates,"

Chad said, keeping a hold on the boy as Jacey pulled him up from the ground. "Are you okay, Lexi?"

"I'm fine."

He shook his head at Jacey. "Remind me to stay on your good side."

Jacey grinned. "Did this little army girl just get complimented by a marine?"

"I plead the fifth," he said, as Jacey tied up the thief's hands.

"I'll allow that for now but don't expect me to let it go," she said. "Where do we take him?" The rain had become a downpour; they couldn't stay outside for much longer. But he didn't want the kid near Reth or Dalila.

"Bring him to the kitchen. I mean it," Lexi said when Chad started to protest. She had fire in her eyes.

"Remind me to stay on your good side, too," Chad said, as he pulled the kid into the bungalow.

LEXI STOLE A few minutes to check on the baby and change into a dry shirt. It took another few minutes to assure Dalila that they were all okay and that things were under control, though she instructed her to stay in the bedroom. Chad radioed through to both Ben and KWS, but they couldn't get out to the clinic until after the rain ended.

Lexi closed the bedroom door and padded back into the kitchen area. Chad had moved the table so that their prisoner was cornered in his chair, then he sat on a chair near the door, which Jacey stood guard at.

"No name?" Chad asked. He took a *mandazi* from a plate near him, popped the triangle doughnut in his mouth and brushed the powdered sugar off his fingertips against his jeans. The kid's eyes tracked his every move. "Okay, then. Guess I'll have to pick one for you. How about I call you *Mwoga*?"

"I'm no coward!"

Lexi had to hand it to Chad. He did know how to push people's buttons. At least he was putting that gift to good use now.

"Only cowards steal and can't stand up to bad people who do evil things. The brave always find a way to do what's right. A brave man should be proud to stand behind the name their mother gave them. Only cowards hide." Chad ate another *mandazi* and even hummed appreciatively as he chewed and swallowed. He turned to Lexi as if the kid wasn't really consuming his attention. "These are so good. I might fill up on them before the lamb and potato stew is done. Then again, I'm hungry enough to eat it all."

Lexi rolled her eyes at him. "Can I speak to you for a second?" she said.

"Me? Sure. You got this, Jacey?"

"Oh, yeah," she said, raising one brow at the kid and folding her arms. Man, Lexi had never seen this side of her. It was like Jacey was channeling her inner Amazon woman. She admired it.

Chad followed Lexi into his room and changed his tone the second she closed the door. "What? I'm in the middle of something."

"Are you seriously going to eat in front of him like that, just to get to him? He's just a teenager caught in a mess, Chad."

"Exactly. What teenage boy do you know that won't give his life for food? Trust me on that. I'm a guy. I *know*."

"Give him some credit. It took guts to come out here like he did. Yes, it was wrong, but clearly, he didn't do it for himself. All I'm saying is treat him the way you'd want a stranger treating our s—Reth—if he ever found himself in a bad situation. Teens make bad decisions and succumb easily to outside pressure and threats because their frontal lobes aren't fully connected yet. Trust me on that. I'm a nurse. I *know*."

"He had a knife to your throat," Chad hissed.

"I remember, and I'm not being stupid. It's just that there's more going on here."

"You're not stupid, just a bit reckless and more of a risk-taker than I'd thought. Not sure I like that."

"You're one to talk."

"Lexi. Don't worry. I'm not going to torture him…except maybe with food…just a little longer."

She shook her head and started out.

He put his hand on the door. "I'm trying to get him to work with us before the big guns arrive. KWS won't be so nice if he's not cooperating. And, by the way, Lex, you were great out there. Smart. Sharp. Quick thinking. Pretty amazing." He stole a kiss from her lips and left.

It took a second for her to register what he'd just said…and done. Why did he have this uncanny ability to throw her off balance?

She straightened her shirt and joined them in the kitchen.

"So, *Mwoga*, who sent you here for the drugs?" Chad asked.

"I said my name is not *Mwoga*. Don't call me that. I am protecting my family."

"Protecting? Who threatened them? Because you can't trust him, whoever he is. He's just using you, and as soon as he gets what he wants, you'll be in the way, if you understand what I mean. And then who will protect your family?"

The boy fidgeted with the blue beads strung around his wrist.

"I have KWS on the way, as well as others who have the kind of power to make whoever is threatening you afraid of his own shadow. We can keep you and your family safe. And if you help us find this man and his group, you'd be saving more than just your family."

Lexi had a feeling Chad wasn't only referring to the elephants that would be saved with every poacher caught and imprisoned. He also meant his family…his mother, Dalila, Lexi and the baby.

"He said if I told anyone where he was, he'd shoot my family. He can see my mother and sister when they go to gather wood. He said if I warned them and they stayed away, he'd know that I told on him and he'd kill me and my father's herd. But that if I help him, he will pay me. Our crops were not good this year."

"Where's your father?"

"He went to the city to sell wood carvings at the market."

"And the others in the *enkang*?"

"I won't put them all in danger. He said he would have his men come."

"Don't you think that he's beginning to wonder where you are right now? Why his medicine hasn't arrived? You need to tell us where he is so we can protect your family and the village."

"What if you are wrong and you fail?"

She noticed Chad flinch at the word "fail." His hesitation made her heart ache for him and what he must have experienced that day in Afghanistan.

"I won't fail. I know things. I know that the sneakers you're wearing were a bribe. I know that the guy is hiding very close to your village homestead and that you take the goats to the north side, up the hill to the left of the gate so that you can smuggle him food or whatever he needs without anyone suspecting.

"I know he's a poacher who was injured and that he's bluffing you. He has no men who'll come back to hurt you. They've abandoned him. That's the kind of people they are. If they knew he was still alive and on the verge of being caught, they'd kill him themselves to keep him from talking. I also know his wound is infected, badly, probably putrid and smelly, and he has a fever and he's lying there with his hand on a gun that he pretends he can shoot but he probably doesn't have the energy to. He probably would have died already if he hadn't convinced you to help steal medical supplies for him."

The kid's eyes widened. He looked at Jacey and Lexi then back at Chad. "Are you a *laibon*?"

Lexi hid her smile. Not a *laibon*. A marine like no other.

"I'm not a seer or a medicine man any more than you are *mwoga*. Listen. You can put an end to this. If we get to this guy before he dies, he can tell us things that will help KWS stop the other poachers out there.

The amount of good you'd be doing would be like that of an entire army. Something tells me you're brave enough to do that."

There was a moment of silence. Lexi held her breath and exchanged looks with Jacey.

"I did not want to hurt you," the boy said to Lexi. "I said I would, but I do not think I could have. I'm sorry for what I did."

"I know you are. Just, please, take this chance to do what's right," Lexi said.

"You promise you will keep my mother and sister safe?"

"I promise. We will help keep each other's families safe," Chad said.

He slid the plate of *mandazi* to the center of the table.

"Eat. You'll need your energy, *Warrior*."

The kid took a doughnut but paused before taking a bite. The corner of his mouth quirked up and his worry was replaced with a more typical, cocky, teen-boy grin.

"My name is Leboo. But *Warrior* is good, too."

THREE DAYS LATER and it was over.

Lexi couldn't believe how fast it all happened.

Everything Chad had suspected about the

injured poacher had been true. His team had betrayed and abandoned him. But, according to Ben, that had made it easier to milk him for information, which in turn had led them to the ring leader.

She was relieved that everything could get back to normal…this time, for real. She picked a fig and added it to the small, wicker basket. She'd already managed to fill one with mangoes and wanted to pick as much as she could before it rained again.

Reth was nursing well and Dalila had insisted on burping him for her. Lexi was supposed to be taking advantage of that time to rest, but she really needed fresh air more than anything. She wanted to think after all that had happened.

Since the poacher had been caught, Chad had been pulling back. He'd gone from relaxing with her and the baby to spending more and more time talking to KWS and his dad about the ring leader and going out target shooting.

Was he planning to leave her and Reth? Or did he want to pursue whatever was between them? The way he looked at her and at the baby made Lexi feel confident and wonderful inside.

She found herself imagining them living in the bungalow here at the clinic, helping people, raising Reth…maybe even having more children. She'd be part of a family at last—not just the three of them, but the extended Corallis clan. Coming out here had been good for Chad, but more importantly, it had brought them together. And now she couldn't imagine being apart. Being together felt so right. She wanted to be with him for the rest of their lives. But did Chad even want that? Did he even love her that way? Did she have the courage to ask?

Did she dare?

She stopped picking fruit and stared beyond the clinic grounds and across the savannah grasses that were already shedding their golden sheaths in favor of shades of promising, opulent greens. Transformation. Change. Life depended on it. How willing would Chad be to change his life forever? To change hers?

Ask him.

She bit her lower lip. She couldn't ask. She was moving too fast. Expecting too much.

But you want this so badly. You love him. Take the risk.

"Daydreaming?"

She jolted and dropped the basket then slapped her hands to her chest.

"You scared the living daylight out of me!"

"I'm sorry. I didn't mean to." Chad pulled her in close, then picked up the basket and the few figs left in it. The rest were better left where they'd rolled. Critters would enjoy them.

"I'm okay. You just took me by surprise."

He narrowed his eyes. "This is because of what happened—Leboo taking you at knife-point in the tent."

Maybe it was a mild case of PTSD, but very mild. It wasn't like she had nightmares about it, probably because everything had ended well.

"My mind was elsewhere. That's all." She scanned the camp. "Is he going to be okay? Leboo, I mean."

"He will be. I asked my dad and Maddie to look out for him when he testifies and to get him back home safely. He can be a harsh guy, my dad, but I reminded him of some of the trouble I got myself into at that age."

"You're not going to share, are you?"

"Got that right," he said, scratching his jaw. "Let's just say my dad smiled, shook his head and told me not to worry about the kid."

She had to laugh. "You'd make a great father yourself, you know. I can see it. Your patience, understanding...the experience you have to draw from so the kid can't blindside you with his antics."

He didn't smile. Instead he tucked his hand in his pocket and looked down the wet road.

Tell him. You pushed Jacey and Taj to face their feelings and open up to each other. Practice what you preach. Ask him.

She swallowed back the lump in her throat and wiped her hands against her shirt.

"You'd make a great husband, too."

He frowned and looked at his boots before meeting her gaze.

"What are you doing, Lexi?"

"I'm... I'm asking you to marry me. To be a family and raise our kids here. I'm in love with you, Chad. I can't help it. I tried to fight it because of Tony, but I can't anymore. I don't think he'd want me or our baby to suffer forever because he's gone. And being without you would be the worst kind of suffering. I'm sure you must feel at least a little of what I do. I'm hoping you do."

His face fell and she immediately knew the answer. Her chest tightened and squeezed against her throat. Why had she said anything? Why?

"I can't do this, Lex. I can't live out here, knowing you'll always be a step away from danger. It took teamwork to keep you safe this time. I'm not sure I could have pulled it off alone. If it's not more poachers and evil men, then it'll be a lion or snake or something else with jaws.

"I can't stand by and watch as you put yourself in danger. I made a promise to Tony and I've done what I can to make sure you're okay. But I can't force you to leave. I realize that now. The fence should be done soon and my mom hired several of the Masai teens who were helping with the fence to work here, one as a guard and the other who's interested in studying medicine someday. Ben also told me he had a new recruit and he was going to station him here as a permanent guard." The guy was about Chad's age. What if he was single and he fell for Lexi?

He hated feeling jealous. He had no right to. "I have to go Lex."

"No. You know I'm needed out here. I can't leave. But you don't have anything tying you down right now. You could move. Be here with us. With me."

He pressed his finger and thumb against his eyes then rested his hand on his belt.

"I do have something. I'm planning to re-enlist."

"Reenlist? With your level of injuries?"

"I might not be able to participate in special ops, but at least I could be doing something that would make a difference. Combat isn't the only way to find the bad guys and root out evil. I was born to do that. I can understand why this clinic is important to you and I'll admit, it's needed out here, but I can't live each day worrying about what's going to happen and if next time I won't be so lucky. The guys my parents hired can protect and help you and the baby better than I can. And I believe I can make the world safer by reenlisting."

The baby. He was keeping it impersonal. He hadn't even said that he loved her, too.

"This is your calling, to be out here, Lexi,

but it isn't mine. I'm not a doctor or a nurse. I can't be what Tony was for you. I need to reclaim my life and get back to doing the only thing I ever did well."

She was such a fool. What was all this then? The holding, kisses and tugging energy between them that she knew she hadn't imagined...was he bored out here and using her for entertainment?

"Lexi, please understand. Being a marine is my calling in life. I can't turn down a chance to go back. You helped me get to this place. You helped me heal beyond my injuries. I owe you for that. No words could express how grateful I am for it. You made me realize I'm more than my scars and capable of doing more. That's the greatest gift anyone has ever given me."

She bit her lower lip and scratched her chin to stop it from quivering, but she could tell by the pain on his face that he'd noticed.

"I don't want to hurt you, Lexi. And I don't want to leave you. But I have to. It's my duty to serve. By leaving, I'll be making the world safer for you and Reth."

"No, this isn't some noble pursuit. You're a coward," she said. "And you're running away."

"You're wrong. I'm headed toward something that—" He scrubbed his mouth with his hand. "I do love you, Lexi. I love you both. But my leaving is best for everyone. How long would I last here doing nothing? What kind of example would that set for a child?"

"Your father gave up his career for you."

"That was different. Our mother died. And he'd had a chance to serve for years. This is different. I've always idolized my dad, and I wanted to be just like him. But I realize now we're not the same. I have to follow my own path, and that means reenlisting. That's the best way I can help you and Reth."

"Don't you dare pretend you're doing this for us. You're doing this for yourself. You're protecting yourself. Chad, just because your father lost his first wife doesn't mean that will happen to you. Have you forgotten that I know what it's like to lose parents? You were old enough to remember Zoe, and her death must have had an impact on you, but you can't use your career as an avoidance tactic."

"Don't accuse a marine of being a coward. Just don't even go there. I'm not avoiding anything. I think I've proved that I face things head-on. I walk around with that proof every day. And finally…finally…I've come to realize that there had to be a reason I survived that explosion. I'm still alive because I'm meant to go back."

"Right. Your reason for being alive couldn't possibly be right in front of your eyes. That would be too simple. Your reason to live has to be some grandiose, medal-earning, risk-taking, adrenaline-laden martyrdom."

"I won't be serving in the same way, but at least I'd be serving my dream the way you've insisted on pursuing yours here. You're not being fair."

"I don't care if I am or if I'm not. I'm done. Go. Just go. I was fine before you came into my life and I'll be fine—if not better—when you leave. I may not have given an arm but I'm a strong person, too. My life out here matters. If it's not all good enough for you, that's your loss. You're throwing away more than you'll ever know, because if it ever came to it, I would have given more than my right arm for you. I'd have given my life for you, Chad. But if you can't understand that, then you don't deserve me."

He had no response to that.

"Well, I'm going to save what's left of my

pride and go back to the house to check on *my* baby. And you're not going to follow me or call after me or anything. Understood?"

"Lexi—" He started to reach out but she shrugged him off.

"I mean it. Don't ever look at me like I mean something to you. Just don't."

A single sob escaped with her last word, but she kept her back straight and marched away.

She should never have let her guard down. She should have kept her focus on helping others…not indulging what she wanted for herself. She should have never let him into her heart.

She would never make that mistake again.

CHAPTER THIRTEEN

"It's just going to be you and me, little guy. That's just how it was meant to be. You and me. We don't need anyone else."

Lexi had learned early on in life, through all her foster care years, that she could survive on her own. She didn't have to count on anyone. She was a survivor...everyone else's caretaker and more comfortable with giving than taking. She didn't need anyone looking after her. That only set a person up for disappointment.

First all the families that didn't want her. Then Tony's death. Now Chad leaving. Both men were so different, yet each had worked their way into her heart without her realizing it. Each had been driven to save the world in a different way. They were givers, like she was...like their families clearly were, too.

She pressed her lips to her baby's soft, sweet forehead and closed her eyes against the burn of tears. Family.

Heaven help her, she missed Tony, but the pain of losing Chad was the rawest right now. She loved him. Really loved him. She'd let him in. She'd let his family embrace her. It had felt good to be part of something…part of a family…a tribe.

Her work here made her a part of something big and fulfilling, and the people from all the surrounding villages meant so much to her. They were her community. But Chad and his family had made her feel like a part of their inner circle…their family unit. They had been her tribe.

And now it was all gone.

"We don't need anyone," she whispered again to Reth. She dried a tear that had fallen on her baby's cheek. It felt like a lie.

She longed for Chad to be a part of their lives. She wanted him around because…because she enjoyed seeing him every morning or watching him cradle Baby Reth. She missed the way he looked at her. He'd enveloped her in a sacred kind of love. He'd made her feel cared for…like she mattered. And being able to lean on someone she trusted the way she trusted Chad with her life, made her feel like she had finally surfaced and filled her lungs after years of holding her breath, as though trapped in deep waters. With Chad, she wasn't just surviving. She was able to live life and take it all in, openhearted.

How would she breathe without him?

A sob escaped her and Reth opened his eyes and shoved his fist in his mouth.

"It's okay. I'll be here for you. Always."

Promises. She needed to be careful with them. Tony had made that promise. One he couldn't keep. And now Chad wanted to head back out to a war zone. She couldn't put herself through that again. The waiting, not knowing, or worse…getting soul-crushing news. Going through that again would destroy her.

She gritted her teeth and swallowed hard. Weren't she and Baby Reth enough? Weren't they enough for Chad…enough for his heart, mind and soul to choose staying here with them over his urge to chase the bad guys or to be a hero?

Would she ever be enough for someone?

Why couldn't he be her hero?

The baby's gurgling and fussing turned to crying. She shifted in the chair, adjusted her shirt and began nursing.

"You're a lucky kid. You almost had two dads—the one who made you and the one who brought you into the world. Even without them around, you'll be surrounded by love from friends and from me. That's one thing you can count on. You'll always be loved."

THE PAIN WAS BACK.

Chad only now realized that he hadn't felt the phantom pain where his right arm had been since the first couple of days at the clinic, when he'd managed to keep the attacks from taking full hold. This wasn't as bad as when he'd first returned to Kenya, but it was still enough to come out of nowhere and sweep through him mercilessly.

Why now, when he hadn't felt it back at the clinic in several weeks? Was it stress induced? Or because he'd returned to his parents' home? Maybe being around Lexi had given him something else to focus on. Maybe his days with her, working on the fence, relaxing with her in the evenings and living in a way that hadn't been defined—a way of life his brain had to adjust to—had helped his brain accept his injury. It was as if being with Lexi had rewired him. Not in a bad way. She'd just made him see life differently.

He took a drink of water and dragged himself downstairs. Roosevelt met him at the bottom step, sitting patiently, yet wagging his tail hard enough to polish the floor behind him.

"What's up?" Chad scratched behind Roosevelt's ear and kept walking to the patio door. Roosevelt kept to his side and even sat next to him on the top step overlooking the yard. He gazed at Chad and made an odd guttural sound.

"If I didn't know any better, I'd swear you just asked me what's wrong." That earned a paw on his knee. "You are one intuitive dog."

Chad gave him another ear scratch. "Where's your ball? Go get your ball. Play fetch."

Roosevelt didn't hesitate. He ran straight for the bushes—actually, one specific bush—and came back with the ball. Did that dog know where each of his dozen toys was hidden in the fenced garden? Of all the toys he had stashed, he'd found the ball.

Chad looked him in the eyes the way he used to look at Aries during training.

"Get me your red bone. Fetch the red bone, Roosevelt."

It was worth a shot. A little entertainment, if anything. Something to distract him from the tingling on his right side. It already seemed to be fading. Lexi hadn't faded from his mind, though. Nor had the little, wrinkly but admittedly cute face of Baby Reth. But she'd asked for more than he could give. She'd wanted him to be a father and husband. How could he do that if he didn't even know where his life was going?

Roosevelt returned with the red bone. Amazing.

"Good boy. Fetch." He aimed the blue ball for the tree at the back of the yard. "Think I can do it?" The dog barked. Chad threw the ball. It hit the trunk then zigzagged around the yard, bouncing off the fence on one side and rolling to the other. It was like a perfect shot in a game of pool.

Roosevelt followed the ball and nabbed it, then suddenly his ears perked. He dropped the toy, ran to the fence gate and barked.

Intruder alert. Chad hurried to the gate and looked out to the driveway. His dad was there. He was back from getting his cast taken off and probably starving for lunch, though it would be leftovers, seeing that Dalila and Hope had stayed with Lexi.

Taj was at the clinic, too, with Jacey, as were their new helpers and the new guard. So Chad had worried less about leaving the women and Reth alone. Besides, things seemed to have gotten back to normal there. Without him in the way.

He sat on the steps again. No doubt his dad had a talk in mind. No doubt his mom had told Ben all about her suspicions that Chad had a thing for Lexi. Suspicions he'd denied. He threw the bone this time and it landed in the middle of the yard. Pretty much where he'd aimed.

"Fetch is pretty meditative. Especially since Roosevelt never tires and will hypnotize you with his running back and forth," Ben said, closing the screen door behind him and sitting.

"He's pretty sharp. Did you train him?" Chad said.

"It didn't take much. He's got good stuff between his ears. A good nose, too. Not sharp enough to be a tracker, but still good."

Chad tore a mint leaf off the potted plant

next to him and ate it. It was better than gum. Fresher.

"Did the KWS team that first scoped the area and the surrounding homesteads not have sniffer dogs? If they did, you'd think the hounds would have picked up on that gangrenous wound and hiding place. Just a suggestion, since I've heard a lot of KWS teams are using dogs to track down poachers now," Chad said.

"That particular unit didn't have a canine sniffer. And yes, you're right, they are useful to track poachers. But it's a relatively new program and more properly trained dogs are needed than we have in the field. It's a work in progress. So," Ben added, "it's just you and me at the house for a couple of days. Even Jamal took time off to visit his kids. I think he feared eating my cooking. Can't blame him. It's pretty awful compared to Dalila's masterpieces."

"Just us guys. We could drink beer and play fetch all night. No women to complain about it."

"Sounds good on paper. Doesn't it? But I hate it when Hope's not here. Drives me nuts," Ben said.

"You two are good together. Always have been."

"I don't just miss her when she's gone on one of her rural clinic trips. I worry about her."

"Then why don't you tag along? Or convince her not to go if it's dangerous?"

"Because I trust her. She's smart and cautious. She never goes without her crew, and I picked her driver...someone *trained*, if you know what I mean. And I taught her how to defend herself if necessary. Plus, I finally came to realize that I was going to worry no matter where she was. She has her regular pediatric clinic just blocks away, here in the city, and I even worry when she goes there. Accidents and bad things can happen anywhere at any time. You and I know that firsthand. As marines. And you must understand, after the random, out-of-nowhere way your mama Zoe was killed, how hard it was for me not to think of the worst-case scenario every time Hope left for work."

He did understand. He remembered how agitated Ben would get while Chad and his siblings were eating breakfast, until Hope called to say she was at the office. She'd been so patient with him. So patient with all of them.

"Did Hope tell you to sit me down today?"

"No idea what you're talking about."

Yeah, right.

"I get what you're saying, Dad. You trained your mind. But if you're referring to Lexi, it's different. You were already a father."

"I didn't know how to be one. I had to learn that, too."

"You also had your own career after the marines. You didn't have the same kind of injuries I have."

"I struggled to find my place, just as you are, and at first I had no clue what I was going to do with my life. At least not what I ended up doing. I figured it all out based on one crucial starting point. I knew whatever decision I made, it had to include my children and Hope or I'd die a miserable, lonely man full of regrets. And I told you once and I'll say it again, nothing can hold you back. Not even the loss of a limb. Just don't lose your heart and will. Keep the people you love in your life and the rest of the pieces will fall into place."

"It's different."

"We're a lot alike, you and I. Hope used to joke about how you'd imitate me as a kid and how we act the same sometimes."

"I don't see it."

"I don't, either." Ben chuckled. "But my point is, we do have some things in common. The marines for one. Falling in love with healers. Go figure. A doc and a nurse. Both strong women who want to save the world. I've got to wonder what that says about us."

"That *we* need healing?"

Roosevelt looked between the two of them as if he could understand the conversation.

"So you do love her, then?"

"What?"

"You didn't object when I said we both fell in love with healers."

He had him there. Chad threw the ball.

"Why are you here, Chad?" Ben pressed.

"I want to go back to the marines and serve in whatever capacity they'll let me."

"I'm going to ask you one more time. *Why* are you here?"

Chad paused. Ben was questioning him returning to the marines? Of all people, he thought his dad would be the one to say suck it up and get back out there. Didn't he see that Chad was defined by the elite pride that made him a Special Forces veteran? Or was Ben trying to tell him he was running away from something, just as Lexi had?

Was he being a coward?

"I'm not sure anymore. I don't know where to be or how to be. Besides, I can't go back to the clinic now. I broke it off with her. Told her I was going to try to reenlist."

"Now, why would you do that?"

"Because she wanted more than I could give, and my purpose has always been to serve in the military, to be more."

Ben hung his head and sighed.

"Son, Hope once begged me to ask her to stay with us, and I told her I couldn't. All I had to do was ask. She had been willing to give up life as she knew it because she loved us that much, but I had loved her too much to let her sacrifice everything she'd worked for. I couldn't live without her and you kids loved her, too, so we traveled to the other side of the world just to find her and be with her. Can you imagine what our lives would be like…what we would have missed out on had I let her go? And in the process, I learned that the hardest job I've ever taken on, and the one I'm proudest of, is being as good a father and husband as I can be."

Chad didn't answer. He took in a deep breath. Maybe he was the one who'd earned the name *Mwoga*. He was nothing but a coward. Afraid of change. Afraid of loss. Afraid to love.

"She told me never to speak to her again."

Ben laughed and Roosevelt's ears perked again.

"Boy, you really did a number on her. Beg. Roosevelt here can show you how. Honestly, though, ask yourself one question. Can you live day after day without ever seeing her or her baby again? Or knowing, in the future, that someone else might sweep in and steal her heart? Will you go to bed every night wondering if she's okay? Or how her day went? Or if there was something you could have done to make their lives better, or to make your relationship work?"

Chad hadn't slept since he'd left her. He had been wondering all of those things since returning to Nairobi. What if she met someone else? Like that new guard. Would he have any more right to be jealous than Tony had from his grave? Could he let her go?

Roosevelt licked the back of his hand then curled up at his feet.

Or maybe he'd licked his ring finger because he agreed with Ben.

Being away from Lexi really was jumbling his thoughts. He needed to convince her to hear him out. To forgive him.

But he could use a wing man. Or a fur man, in this case. The pieces were falling into place.

"I have an idea, Dad, but you won't like it. In fact, you'll probably kill it before it takes its first step."

LEXI DIDN'T SEEM happy to see Chad step out of the chopper. But that wasn't the only surprise he had for her.

"You brought your dog with you? Did you really think he'd make me forget what you said the last time you were here?" Lexi was cradling Reth in the sling she wore.

Man, it was good to see them again. Roosevelt sniffed her feet, but otherwise stayed close to Chad. Poor guy seemed a little nervous with the new surroundings. Chad couldn't blame him. He was nervous, too, though for other reasons.

"Roosevelt is technically my younger brother's dog. My sister got him as a puppy for Philip, but he couldn't take him to college, so he's been bonding with my dad instead. He's, um, good with kids. Clean. A good listener. Trainable. Loves hugs. Is loyal and a good protector."

Her brow furrowed and she cocked her head. "Are you giving me the dog's résumé or yours?"

He gave her a lopsided smile.

"Both?"

"No use in applying for a job if it's unavailable."

Ouch. He deserved that.

"Except that I wouldn't call living by your side a job. I'd call it a privilege."

For a second her chest stopped rising and falling and she seemed frozen to the spot.

"Don't mess with me, Chad. You walked away. Plain and simple."

"I messed up. Lexi, all I ask is that you hear me out. Give me two minutes and if you want me to leave and take this adorable, loving dog with me, I will."

"I'm not falling for the sweet dog trick, but nice try," she said.

Roosevelt let out a two-syllable whine and Chad was pretty sure he caught the flicker of a smile on Lexi's face.

"Lex, the fact is, I love you. You were right. There is something amazing between us. A once-in-a-lifetime kind of love. And it scared me because I didn't think I deserved it or that I could live up to it. And I was also afraid I would lose it if something happened to you or the baby."

"Chad—"

"Let me finish. When I was in Nairobi, I realized that I could recover from a lot of things, physically, but I'd never be able to recover from losing you. And it didn't matter if I was afraid of not being able to protect you, because if I walked away over something that *might* happen, I'd have already lost you for no good reason at all.

"I thought my purpose in life was to chase after the bad guy and fight hatred, but I realized that evil can be fought in more than one way. Maybe I was meant to fight evil by finding love and protecting and nurturing it.

"I can't live without you, Lex. I want you and Baby Reth in my life, forever. Walking away from you and what we have would be a mistake. I might as well give up all the rest of my limbs and stop my heart from beating because you're that much a part of me."

She bit her lip and tears brimmed in her eyes.

"But you said you'd never be happy here. That you needed to go after your own career. I can't abandon all the people who rely on this clinic…especially the children."

"I know. I don't want you to. That's why I brought Roosevelt."

"I don't get it."

"I've worked with dogs before. I had one in the marines—the best—his name was Aries. I trained him and other dogs and screened them for service duty. I want to do the same here—establishing canine units to serve with the KWS anti-poaching units and with Ben's teams. It hit me that many of the village homesteads not only have acacia fences, but dogs, too. Even Haki had a dog out at his place. There's no reason why we can't do the same around here. There's space to build kennels just out there, behind the bungalow. It would be far enough not to scare patients or violate any medical regulations. And I could help other veterans by bringing them on board. And Roosevelt here would help out, too, but he'd stay with us and guard the clinic and our kids, starting with this little guy. A family dog. A family, Lexi."

He took a step closer, keeping hold of the dog's leash, and was encouraged by the fact that she didn't step away.

"Say something," he said.

"I'm not sure what to say. It sounds…perfect. But I'm still not over the shock of you leaving and turning me down."

"I'm sorry, Lex. I didn't mean to hurt you or lose your trust. I'd like to live here and help you raise Reth…as an uncle, if that's all it can be. I don't ever expect you to ask me to marry you again."

"Good. Because I won't ever ask again. That was a one-time deal." Her voice shook.

"But I can ask you."

Her lips parted and a tear rolled down her cheek.

"Chad, don't feel pressured to take a risk like that."

"I'm a risk-taker by nature, but marrying you wouldn't be taking one. I've never been more certain of anything in my life. Marrying *me* on the other hand… I don't know.

You'd have to be pretty gutsy. I'm told I can be a lot to handle."

That earned a laugh and Roosevelt started wagging his tail.

"You? Difficult? Let's just say that your mom and Dalila have been entertaining me with stories," she said. "I wasn't sure if their intention was to help me get over you or to embarrass you by sharing. After all, they were pretty upset that you left."

"Did they scare you off ever letting me into your life again?"

"No. It made me love you even more."

He took another step closer.

"So, is that a yes?"

Roosevelt barked, Reth started crying and several drops of rain mottled the ground.

"Yes."

He brushed his lips against hers then pressed them into a kiss.

"I'll never stop loving you, Lexi. I'd gather every star in the Serengeti sky for you if that's what it takes to make you happy."

"You're all I need, Chad. You make me happy." She kissed him and rested her head against his. "Now, every time the rains come and clouds fill the sky and cover the stars,

I'm going to think it's because you've gone and gathered them for me."

And then, as if on cue, it rained. A good omen. A promise that their lives out here in Kenya's Serengeti would always be blessed with joy, all of their family and friends and an abundance of love. The promise that, no matter what challenges they faced on their adventure together, they'd always have each other…and as long as they cherished that love, at the end of each day for the rest of their lives, they'd always have a place to return to, a place called home.

EPILOGUE

BUSARA. THE HEARTBEAT of their family. A place that had started as a remote and very rustic veterinary research and elephant rescue camp—literally a few tents, a bucket shower and well water—had grown into a truly beautiful sanctuary over the years. Like the sprawling canopy of the Serengeti's acacia trees that sheltered all life within their reach, Busara embraced all its inhabitants, from baby elephants orphaned by poachers, to critters in need, to three generations of family and friends. It always had.

Chad leaned back in the wicker chair that sat on the front porch of what everyone referred to as Busara House, built after his Aunt Anna and Uncle Jack married, when his cousin Pippa was only four years older than Reth was now.

He gazed across the central, open courtyard area of Busara to the wooden elephant pens, the small vet clinic and the old, repurposed framed tents where Pippa and Haki had lived when they were born, much like Reth growing up at their clinic.

Chad cradled Reth against his shoulder, as Roosevelt lay by the chair. The dog had appointed himself loyal guardian to Reth. Even Mosi, Busara's resident vervet monkey and prankster, couldn't rouse more than an eyebrow wrinkle and ear twitching from him when Reth was near.

It was hard to believe Reth was turning a year-old today. Judging from the drool on Chad's shirt and the elephant trumpeting he'd slept through, the kid wasn't even close to waking up. He loved going on jeep rides, especially if he spotted giraffes, zebras and other wildlife along the way. That morning, he had worn himself out, laughing hysterically every time the jeep had bounced when they hit a stone or rut in the dirt road during their trip over from Camp Hope.

Camp Hope. It was the perfect name for their medical clinic and service dog training camp. His, Lexi and Reth's home. It was where they'd exchanged their vows seven months ago. Lexi…his wife…and Reth… his son. God, he loved the sound of that… the feel of it.

He loved them.

If only Tony could see them now and be reassured that they were all going to be okay. Or maybe he'd known that they'd end up together, when he'd asked Chad to look after Lexi if something happened to him.

The sound of her laugh carried through the symphony of wildlife chatter and distant roars as Lexi, Pippa and Dax's twins, Ivy and Fern, tried to bottle feed one of Busara's newest baby elephants, who seemed to have a sense of humor and streak of mischief.

Lexi glanced over at him, cocked her head and smiled. God, he loved her. She was glowing, beautiful. She gently rubbed the soft spot behind the elephant's ear as she rested one hand absentmindedly on her belly. His parents and Jacey and Taj, who were getting married in just a month, were the only ones who officially knew about Lexi being ten weeks along, but he suspected everyone else could tell. Lexi and Chad were planning to make the announcement today, on Reth's birthday.

Chad was happy so many of their friends and family had been able to make it today. Chad's uncles Jack and Kamau—Pippa and Haki's fathers—were sitting on old wooden stools at a small table near the old tents, deep in a chess match. His cousin Nick—Mac and Tessa's nephew, whom they'd raised after Nick lost his parents at the age of thirteen—watched on.

It was crazy seeing Nick again after so many years. His shoulder-length hair was the total opposite of the military cut Chad still preferred, but the guy had an adventurous spirit Chad liked. Mac and Tessa had been hoping Nick would finish his archaeological studies in Morocco and Algeria and move back to Kenya so that his new little brother, Tai, could get to know him. But Chad could tell the guy had fire behind him and was nowhere near ready to settle down. Then again, Chad never thought he would settle down and here he was, a husband and father, with one more on the way.

The screen door to the house creaked as

his aunt Niara stepped out with a pot of hot, aromatic *githeri* to add to the buffet being set up in front of the porch.

"Oh, I didn't realize he was still asleep," she said, trying to stop the screen from slamming shut with her foot.

"Don't worry about noise. He needs to wake up or he'll miss his party. By the way, thank you again. All of you coming to this party really means a lot to Lexi and me. I'm sorry that you've been cooking all day. This family is not a small crowd."

"Ah, but I enjoy it, and being part of a big family has its benefits," she said, taking the steps carefully and setting the pot down on the folding table. "With Tessa, Pippa, Hope, Anna and the boys helping in the kitchen, I feel like I haven't done much."

Chad knew that by "the boys" she meant Huru, Noah, Ryan and Philip, who had all taken a few days off from college to come home for the mini-reunion.

"Well, it's good to see everyone in one place," he said.

"That it is."

The screen door creaked again and Roosevelt sat a little taller, sniffing the air hopefully. Anna stepped out with a tray of *chapati*, Chad's favorite kind of bread since the day he'd first set foot in Kenya as a toddler.

"If I don't set this tray out here, the guys in there are going to eat it all before we're ready. I think they've been nibbling and tasting more food than they've prepared," Anna said with a chuckle.

She set the tray down and tucked a strand of graying hair that had escaped her clip behind her ear. "Where is everyone? We're almost ready but Pippa has a special gift for Reth and wants everyone to be here for the reveal."

"Maddie and Haki took Tai and Zoe, for a walk to the lookout. Tai wanted to climb it again," Chad said, standing and bouncing Reth gently to get him to wake up.

The lookout was a platform under an old acacia tree, which Anna had built, along with Kamau, back when she'd first established Busara with Kam's help.

"I think my dad, Mac, Dax, Mugi and Kesi and Jacey and Taj are all out back behind the house prepping a small bonfire for later,"

Chad added. "If anyone wants to take over holding this little guy, I can go round them up."

Dax was pretty much a cousin now, since he'd married Pippa.

Mugi and Kesi, an older couple who had founded Camp Jamba before Mac had joined their venture, had always been like family, too. Just like Mac, even though he wasn't blood related.

It didn't matter who was friend or family here. Everyone was considered to be an aunt or uncle or cousin because their bonds were that close…that unbreakable. In fact, knowing his aunts and uncles, no one would be allowed to start eating until Busara's keepers had secured the calves and joined the celebration, too. The only family who hadn't been able to make it today were Chuki and Simba—Hope's nickname for her brother, Dr. David Alwanga, who'd married her best friend many years back—and their kids.

"I would love to take over baby snuggling. It's a great-aunt's privilege," Anna said, scooping Reth off his shoulder. He frowned as his eyes blinked open. He squinted at everyone, then buried his face against Anna's neck and gripped her arm. "But the twins can go get everyone. We could use your help getting everything set up here. Hey, Ivy and Fern, can you go get your dad and the others?"

"Yeah, sure!" Fern and Ivy ran off and Lexi let the keeper lead the baby elephant away. She headed over to the porch.

"You trust them to stay out of trouble? I've heard the stories," Lexi said, walking up and wrapping her arms around Chad's waist. He held her close and pressed a kiss to the top of her head, lingering a moment to just breathe her in and feel her warmth.

"Well, the more unbelievable, the truer those stories are, but Pippa has had a remarkable impact on those girls," Niara said as she headed up the steps, too. "They're going to grow up and make a difference in this world, just as all of you children have."

Chad loved how his parents and aunts and uncles still referred to him and his cousins and siblings as children, even if they were all parents, too, now.

Lexi looked up at Chad, still holding on to him, and met his lips halfway.

"I better go nurse Reth before everyone is ready to eat." She slipped her arms from around Chad and took Reth from Anna.

"You know we'll all fight over who gets to carry him afterward," Anna said.

"So long as you all fight over who gets to change his diaper, too. We wouldn't want to deprive everyone of that joy," Chad said.

Lexi slapped his arm playfully and Niara laughed just as Dax and the twins appeared around the corner. Haki and Maddie with the two youngsters in tow appeared down the path that led through the brush and trees from the lookout.

Pippa appeared in the doorway with a bag and eased past Niara, who was headed in.

"Wait. Don't go in yet. Can Reth hang in there for a moment longer, Lexi? I'll hurry. But, if everyone goes in and out we'll never get started. I want to make this special announcement before we eat."

Dax came up behind her, wrapped his arms around her shoulders and planted a kiss on her cheek. She smiled up at him and Chad could see even in that split-second eye contact that those two loved each other the way he loved Lexi.

"Oh, my gosh. I think I figured out your surprise, Pippa," Lexi said. "You found out if you're having a boy or a girl. Is that it?"

Pippa held her stomach and grinned just as Dax looked over his shoulder at the twins, who were grabbing rounds of *chapati*.

"Hey, you two, no dipping into the food yet," Dax said.

"But we have to keep our mouths full or else we'll accidentally blurt out the surprise," Ivy said. Fern giggled and raised her brows at him like their reasoning was valid.

"Actually," Pippa said, as everyone else began to gather around. "We did find out, but that's only part of the surprise. We're having a—" she glanced up at Dax and waited for him to say it with her "—girl."

A chorus of congratulations rang out.

"Ivy and Fern have already chosen a name for their little sister," Dax said.

"Sienna," the twins said together.

"That's a beautiful name," Kesi said, as she stood next to Mugi, Mac and Tessa.

"Is there anything better than being grandparents?" Jack asked, taking Anna's hand in his and weaving his fingers through hers.

"Nothing better," Anna said. "I'm so blessed to have all of you as family."

"I second that," Hope said.

Ben put his arm around her. "Agreed, but don't forget great-grandkids, too," he said.

"Let's take this one generation at a time, Dad. We're working on it," Chad said. Everyone laughed.

"But wait, she said there was more to the surprise," Tessa reminded them.

"Yes! Is everyone here?" Pippa asked, hugging the bag she was holding against her chest.

Chad was beginning to catch on that Pippa was very nervous about something. She kept nibbling at her lip and trying repeatedly to push back her corkscrew-curly hair. Chad had a feeling he knew why she was so apprehensive.

The box had come.

He put his arm around Lexi and kissed her temple. A lump rose in his throat.

Pippa took a deep breath.

"Chad, Lexi. I know embracing family history has always been important to you, especially now as you raise Reth. Lexi, your desire to fulfill Tony's wish and make sure Reth experiences part of his heritage is what brought you to Kenya…to us. And we're so grateful that you're part of our family now."

A tear trailed down Lexi's cheek and Chad wiped it away for her with the pad of his thumb. She sniffed and held on to his hand.

"I wanted to give Reth a gift for his first birthday that he could cherish for life," Pippa continued. "A gift that would tie us all together…forever…and even for generations to come. I'll be sharing this with all of you, especially all of our children, but I wanted Reth to have the honor of getting the first copy."

There was a hush. Chad took in the anticipation on everyone's faces. Hope and Anna covered their mouths.

Pippa bit her lower lip then stepped closer and held out the gift.

Chad let go of Lexi's hand and took the bag. Lexi propped Reth on her hip and slipped her free hand into the bag then pulled out the gift of all gifts.

The book.

A gasp escaped Lexi as she tried to hold back the tears. And it wasn't because she was pregnant. Chad knew the emotions would have poured out regardless. He didn't have pregnancy hormones raging through him but the sight of the cover and title made his chest and throat tighten. Tears stung the rims of his eyes and one glance around told him he wasn't alone.

Even Ben, his father who never cried, was wiping his face. Jack and Anna, who had always been the patriarch and matriarch of this incredible, inspiring, loving tribe of theirs, were crying openly and unashamedly.

"This is it?" he asked.

Pippa nodded, her cheeks flushed and the tip of her nose turned pink.

"*'The Promise of Rain,'*" he read. "That's a beautiful title." It was. It held so much meaning. Reth had been born in the rain. The rains also brought life after death in the Serengeti, in the Masai Mara and all of Kenya's vast wilderness. Rain was a good omen, a giver of life and hope.

Lexi held the book against her heart.

"Thank you for this. I don't know what to say."

"Pip, there are no words. This is amazing. You did it," Chad said.

"No, all of you did it. I couldn't have written the story of us—all of us—without each of you. It starts from the time my mom first touched this very ground beneath our feet, here at Busara, and made it home, to when Uncle Ben brought you Chad, Maddie and Ryan out here to marry Auntie Hope, to Uncle Mac bringing Auntie Tessa and Nick into our lives. And even what I went through to find the loves of my life," Pippa said, looking at Dax and the twins. "Every one of you that's here is in this book. Uncle Kam and Niara, Haki, Mugi and Kesi, you, too. All of you. And I couldn't have written your stories without your belief and trust in me. You all shared things that I know were immensely personal and sometimes painful to relive, and I hope I did your stories justice. I tried my best to tell them with love."

Reth grabbed the corner of the book and tried to gnaw at it. Laughs broke through the tears of the crowd.

"We may need to keep this copy out of his reach until he stops teething and drooling," Lexi said. "I can't wait to read it. We'll treasure this forever."

"Pippa," Anna said. "You've been at Busara since the beginning, too, and yes, I may be biased, but I think everyone here would agree that you have such a genuine, limitless and giving heart that it would be impossible for all that love not to come through in this story. And I can't thank you enough for using the book to help raise funds for all of our causes, from Busara's elephant rescue to fighting poachers to humanitarian causes and your efforts to spread reading and education access out here."

Chad cleared his throat. "Bottom line is that we're all about to read up on each other's personal lives and, I'm hoping, some juicy secrets. And thanks to Reth, here, I'll have a head start with reading it," Chad said. That earned some chuckles and sly looks. "But seriously, ditto what Anna said, Pippa. We'll treasure this gift forever. I'm sure I can speak for all of us when I say we're proud of you, Pip."

Everyone swarmed in to give her hugs and to see the cover of the book.

The Promise of Rain by Pippa Harper-Calder.

The story of their lives.

Lexi touched her belly as Reth's tiny hand patted at her cheek. He hugged her close and she looked up at Chad. No words were needed. He could see it in her eyes and feel it in the way her heart beat against him. Breathtaking love. A love story that would last forever, in this life and beyond.

And it had all begun with the promise of rain.

* * * * *